Badlands

Writers and Readers Publishing, Inc.
P.O. Box 461, Village Station
New York, New York 10014

Copyright © 1996 by Melinda Camber Porter
Cover Art: Melinda Camber Porter
Cover and Book Design: Terrie Dunkelberger
Editor: Partricia A. Allen

ISBN 0-86316-149-9

0 9 8 7 6 5 4 3 2 1

Manufactured in the United States of America

Library of Congress Cataloging-in-Publication Data

Porter, Melinda Camber.
    Badlands / Melinda Camber Porter
        p.   cm.
    ISBN 0-86316-149-9
    I. Title.
    PR6066.0725B34   1996
    823' .914—dc20   96-4019
                                                              CIP

adlands

Melinda Camber Porter

Writers and Readers

for darling Joe, who showed me the Badlands, and for our darling sons Robert and James, with deepest love

ACKNOWLEDGMENTS

To Glenn Thompson, my publisher, I give thanks. His steadfast commitment to my poetry and fiction has become an integral part of my passion for writing. Few publishers can boast their commitment to new literary fiction, but Glenn can. I sing his praises.

My infinite gratitude is with Tracy Brown. His passionate and indefatigable belief in my writing is a constant source of pleasure and inspiration. I feel blessed to know him.

I also thank my husband, Joe, who always nurtures and supports my endeavors, and to our sons, Robert and James, all of whom inspire everything I create.

The desire of Man being Infinite,

the possession is Infinite &

himself Infinite.

William Blake

There is a wound in this country, a gaping wound, wide as the open sky that graces it, hidden deep in the earth and covered with the sentimental growth of wheat. It is Indian country. As in South Africa, the Homelands were reduced to dirt track roads and empty spaces, so, in this country, there is a bleeding wound, a sorrowful land stretching for miles that few tourists visit. The population, reduced to statistics, welfare dwellers, alcoholics, lives in an unending nightmare of a ghetto that has been excommunicated for good. The land bakes in the summer and in winter is cold and featureless. This is the place called God's Country. The big sky in which God lives lies heavy and sagging over the dust tracks, like an old half-dead cow, udders drooping, dead with the heat, smothering Indian country. For to see these people, one would be tempted to believe that God gave the good life to his fan club, a narcissistic guy who couldn't see beyond his own big toe. To see these people, one would be tempted to believe that the Good Lord had sick ideas about white and red and yellow and black skins, and that even when the Indians built their churches to him, even then He left them unrewarded with a dank plot of land and, worse still, with no will to make it blossom green with rare scents. To see these people one feels sad with oneself. For to have myth and magic in one's past, to be part of the childworld, believing in mountains becoming men, and such, seems to be the stuff of which failure is made.

So, night came over Pine Ridge, and the unlikely pair of us drove madcap through the flat plains. We had watched the clouds and the occasional entry of a police car, like a joke wandering with no audience, aimless across the brown fields. We stepped out to see a cemetery covered with weeds and wheat grass. It was protected with a barbed-wire fence that no longer held up, and it, too, was wooed to sleep by the unending growths from the earth. Soon, no one will know for no one will be left. They are the Incas of America. And now despair will kill them off. There is no need for guns. For the old guns are latched and open, ready to shoot the mind through and through. Just think how time has been on our side. If you subjugate a people enough, for enough time (I'm not sure how long you have to do it, the exact requirement of intensity and time), they end up doing it to themselves for you. It's strange, really. Is this something to do with the survival of the species? The strongest man wins? The rights of the strongest? I don't think so, for now the weak in mind and spirit seem to have gained ground. Conformity reigns here. How soothing it is to belong to the ruling class (the middle class here), to be a big fish in a small pond, to live in the little villages about which so much sentimental adorational, romantic drivel has been written. And it is said that these are still the pioneers, still the very last people to live on the frontier. But to live on the frontier of two hundred years ago is to live in the past. So, there is a madness to the pioneering spirit here, the "rugged" life, living off the land: they play at it. Food is probably cheaper bought in the local supermarket when you think of what it costs to hunt. The time taken, after all. Adam, you took me here to teach me something. Is it what I see today? The smug conformity in the faces of the old farmers and farm hands, those wrinkled faces, bitter with the play of wind and the mistrust of strangers written in their faces? I mused, or rather, at this point, I think I actually said something, sitting in the Blue Bar, in Interior, the first town that hinted of tourism, just a little, with its view of the Badlands buttes. I spoke, through their deep silence. "Shall we stop off here for the night?"

The bar restaurant in Interior is a home with a poorly stocked fridge. The owner, a fat, dishevelled, distracted, no-eyed matron, offered us a broken sandwich and asked us to leave when

Adam took it and rubbed it against my lips, muttering, "Sweetie, sweetie." He had done this in a desperate way, for it was quite unlike him to play with his food, and I wondered, "And if he has brought me here so he could kill himself?" It was such an unlikely thought, but fierce like a dream to a sleeper, and the fear of it grew as he drove into a dust cloud made by a huge truck that veered into our path and out again, sparing us. I was safe. The thought of Adam taking a knife to himself vanished, and I laughed aloud at it.

"So, shall we drive through the night?" I asked.

"You look so tired," he said, pulling over to the side of the road to take a swill of his Diet Pepsi.

"Why hurry?" I said. "There's nothing to see."

"You're tired," he said, again and sadly, as if tiredness were worthy of sympathy, a reason perhaps for him to feel pain.

"I'll survive."

So we drove through the night, taking turns to watch the empty plains and listen to the deathlike stillness that made me wish for Manhattan. The stillness was piercing, more distracting than the rumble and sudden rushes of noise, like water moving, like the stream of life that is always there in the city. But here, the stillness distracts my thoughts from love. Some other force has its dwelling in the sand, within the wrinkled skin of mountain, made of bone. These were not real mountains. They were caked mud, and they dipped and rose, wrinkled horribly, twisting and turning, a labyrinth without issue. We should not have come here.

"There is no eternity here," I said, as dawn struck, and like a chord that echoed, the sky filled with light, reverberating.

"Oh, there is, just look at it," he said, pointing at the rainbow light covering the buttes.

"Maya," I said. "Pure illusion."

"You can't leave a mark here," I said. "It's like living on quicksand. Too much death destroys history, takes away human time. There's nothing to see. No past."

"Oh, but there is. I'll show you the hideouts, Billy the Kid and Wounded Knee, and Custer's Last Stand. All around here. This is America," said Adam, suddenly ecstatic. The light was splintering across the sky. Pinks and blues and violets all so majestic, reigning in a vast sky. I had never seen a sky like this in Europe. Never even in the remotest parts of Scotland.

"This is America. The real America," said Adam. "On the East Coast, we think it's us. But the real story of America is here."

"Oh, come on," I said affectionately. "I don't see any history. I haven't seen one thing made by man. It's all restless nature. Skies, trees, and those mud-caked rocks, the Badland buttes."

"This is the spirit of America," said Adam, still ecstatic. "I wanted to show it to you, so you'd see something that's real."

"If this is real, give me what's fake," I said, and thought much darker thoughts, seeming to match the barrenness I sensed in the land. We had come here together, partly so as not to be apart, and although Adam's work should have been done without me, this particular piece of business he was set on was an emotional journey too. So, it was right, in our minds, for me to be there. He wanted it, anyway, wanting to induct me into and drive me through the spirit of America. From Manhattan to Nebraska, making our stopping-off point the Pine Ridge Reservation. But the Indians were his business, his wish to help, being one of the reasons I loved him deeply, had always struck me with such force, as had his likeness to his father first introduced us. Both defined him. The way Nature or God had stamped him with the very same features as his father. So, where in his father there were wrinkles, in Adam was smoothness, and where in his father there was greyness, Adam's hair was light brown, flaxen-tinged. But the doubly rolling nose, slanted like a Roman nose, was identical. Not one angle differed. And the eyes were identical, except where in his father was kindness and a gentle intensity, in Adam was fire and the staring madness of some unquenchable thirst.

"We seem to have gone in a circle," I said, noticing the same buttes we had seen in Interior, like mountains reversed, sandy white at the base, the peak capped with dark soil rivulets, rivers of decay. The wind fashioned all this and left behind no trees, so the plains are flat except for where man has built a windbreak, a line of luxuriant trees now glistening in the sun which had fully awoken.

"You can see the buttes from all over. They're probably forty miles away, even fifty. You never seem to leave them behind."

In Adam's voice was such weariness. The innocence that had marked the earlier outburst of enthusiasm and his naive belief in "a real America" contrasted so sharply with his sudden tone of despair. I knew he was also here to get away from something, and the buttes, ever present, were reminders of an archaic feeling, bone deep, dream deep, that he would never be able to leave behind his awareness, acute sensitivity and the pain that this intensity of character had somehow inflicted on him.

"Let's get some sleep," I said. "Poor darling, you look so tired and hot." I stroked his forehead, noticing, as I often did, the way the hair receded already a little, just like his father's. When fathers pass down stuff to their sons, like God to Jesus, why should the children suffer so?

Joseph lived in the somewhat untroubled world of cosmology, reaping fame without knowing quite how his ideas brought with them so much baggage, so much additional life to deal with, to dispense with, to forget. Joseph lived on another planet, truly. But Adam suffered so, being a son, watching as his father tried to squeeze the brilliance from his own mind, so the sap would flow from one to the other without obstacles, without love and hate.

"I want you to rest," I said softly. "I'll drive. I'll stop off when we see a motel. You can sleep in the back. I'm taking over, honey."

Adam did so, and in the motel room, I washed his hot brow with a cool motel towel, dripping wet, and let him lie between my breasts, drifting off to sleep to the sound of my heartbeat. His lips were open, pouting and thick, with the blood curling them so he was half smiling, as if in a dream of being completed, of his mouth meeting mine, of his hands in my hair. I thought of all this, of the two of us together, without obstacle, without Joseph's forehead covering Adam, without the imprint of his father stopping me.

"Love is you," I whispered, to take away the fear that held me back from him, made me cool and quip and act a little, just a little, as if I didn't care completely to be with him. These thoughts took on a pitch of such emergency that I longed to wake him. And when I woke the next morning they were still there, but had been softened, the edge of desperation being taken from them by a dream I now forget. We both woke slowly, and then were quickened to a sudden rush of panic with the dull thud of gunshots, rifle shots, heavy, like the footsteps of a giant reverberating through the land. Or was it thunder?

Adam opened the blinds. The sun was out over the neon sign of the ROSEBUD CAFE, glinting with the lights missing from the R and E. Little red roses were painted onto the wooden exterior, and a huge plastic Indian, at least eight feet or nine feet tall, in his plastic feathers and tribal gear, stared into space.

I went to the bathroom while Adam stood at the window, enraptured at the sight of this dowdy little town, with its gas station-cafe restaurant.

"It's always hunting season here," said Adam. "There's the real hunting season in the fall, but they do it all year round. You'll see. We'll go."

Some of the paint had been washed away from the chieftain's feathers to show his grey plastic body, deathly grey, so aptly grey. The Indian smiled. His mouth smiled while the eyes stared, his lips red, parted slightly, like an entertainer in some Las Vegas night club introducing another routine act.

"Don't you think it's in bad taste?" I asked, "considering that Indians *live* here."

Adam smiled.

"Everything's bad taste here. Except for Nature, it's all a wasteland of memorabilia, old myths, dump trucks full of what made America. This, for instance, your Sioux tribesman, chieftain. He's happy enough, wouldn't you say? Yes, he's happy. Give him a beer or two, and he'll smile like this. What's left for them but this? What kind of respect is this? Well, not much. But it's done in a kindly way. I'll show you the giant plastic cows, the other art works littering the plains. They don't mean harm with it."

"Who doesn't?" I asked.

"The Indians. Nor the whites. It's past that now. The myth's been told so many times, so differently, they don't care anymore. They just want the bare minimum."

I laughed, not being able to help it, but for the sadness of a whole nation, a wandering people whether good or bad, kind or hostile to whites, whatever they were, now here with nothing to be known for except that they escaped complete extinction. What a triumphant moment, to know you have not gone forever, but people can drive by (not that they want to) and watch you live, without feathers and war paint, but with those unmistakable cheekbones, almost Mexican, like Adam's cheekbones a bit, but the jaw much sturdier.

"I can understand your wanting to help," I said, "but it's not a place for a holiday."

"You can?" Adam snapped, with an angry irony that made his muscles flex in his arms and a tremble run through his body of cold sweat.

I nodded. "I haven't come here to mourn, to live a funeral."

"And Mexico last year, all those ruins, was that a funeral, and Greece, was that a funeral, seeing civilizations end? Is it just too sad to bear because this one's holding on? Not quite a museum yet, not quite dead?"

"No museum," I said.

"No, it's not art, when you're half-dying, half-living. But the Parthenon is and the Minoan ruins are, I suppose, because the culture's fully dead," said Adam, his face crushed with sadness. We argued full sail, but when the wind of first anger left us we always felt so alone, wanting not to have hurt each other, thoughtlessly, wildly even, at times.

"We'll have breakfast and talk it over," I suggested, mildly.

"Talk over the Indians?" he said with the irony rising again. "Why not piss over them?"

"Your anger," I said, "is what I can't stand," and my

temper flew out, like a bird set free.

"I don't have the right emotions, do I? I don't quite want what you want? Well, I don't. I want to lie on a beach. I want a holiday. Suntan lotion. Frisbee. The beach. That's American, isn't it? It's more American than *this*."

"I want, I want, I want ...," said Adam and then we grew quiet, both of us. The light had now risen well above the Rosebud Cafe, obliterating the neon sign in its huge planet radiance. The school bus of Wounded Knee Elementary had let out five or six Lakota children, no, there were more, two more stragglers: a little girl wearing leopard-skin tights and a shiny black swimming costume; a boy wearing a lasso around his waist and a leather jerkin with a sheriff's badge, reflecting the sun. It darted into our room, the long beam of crazy light, and then left us. The Indian boy, with huge, black-brown liquid eyes, limpid moist pools, unravelled his rope and whirled it in the air, screaming something unintelligible to the little girl with red hair (was it dyed? I wondered), to the other children who stood around the huge Sioux chieftain, smiling, it seemed, less sadly, now he had found his audience.

"Do you think this is some ritual?" I asked. "An Indian ritual?"

"I don't know," said Adam, perturbed.

We threw on our clothes, his jeans and T-shirt saying BADLANDS, and my black leggings and T-shirt saying BLACK HILLS. Down in the light we were rubbing our eyes from tiredness and that uncomfortable feeling of living in a hotel, of having one's cleaning routine disturbed, one's toothbrush and paraphernalia stranded in a little bag, not spread out regally in one's bathroom. And I thought about ritual, my own simple ones that comfort me and whose absence made me grumpy this morning (I told Adam this to apologize to him, as we walked downstairs to the Rosebud Cafe). And I thought about grand rituals, the religious ones, the ones that were mysterious to me, like these Sioux rituals, whose magic I both pitied and wanted to enter into. So, I was ready, like a worshipper, as if finding myself in a cathedral, suddenly, where this tacky Rosebud Cafe stood in the filthy road littered with beer cans, and the torn newspapers, and I was in awe, under the vaulted sky, the light falling, falling magnificently onto the now stained-glass windows of the Rosebud Cafe. My breath was caught in my throat, as it always was in cathedrals with the force of the music, and I hated it, being had, because I don't want to worship anything in a cathedral. I wanted this to be an artistic experience, not to fall into worship, not to fall for the music, not to join the crowd and become one with it. I wanted to be an individual, not a worshipper. But here, I have no fear of believing in this Indian God or that, and so I can let myself fall into a state of awe.

"I'm *so* pleased we came," I said to Adam, clutching his hand, as the children began dancing wildly round the plastic Sioux chieftain, making war cries (the kind I recognized from TV Westerns), and the little boy with the liquid black eyes took the little girl with her long, frizzy red hair and skinny bones showing through the leopard tights, and he put the lasso round her, fiercely, round her waist, round her thighs, round her knees, so she couldn't move. Two Indian cops came out of the Rosebud Cafe to watch. Everyone had begun chanting except us.

"I'm Clint Eastwood," said the little boy to the little girl.

"You're not," said the little girl, derisively. "I'm Madonna."

I went over to her and asked, "What's your real name, sweetie?"

"Minnehaha," whispered the little girl, smiling.

"Oh, from the Longfellow poem, *Hiawatha*, I remember that. I can't remember the lines, can you?"

"My name's Madonna," said the little girl decisively.

"Yeah, and I'm Mickey Mouse," said the little boy.

"I'm Frank Viola," said another little boy.

"I kill Injuns," said the little boy with liquid black eyes. "I shoot them down, bang-bang, with a rifle."

"I'm Madonna," said the little girl furiously to the little boy. "You don't believe me, do you?"

The policemen laughed, the children laughed.

"I do," said the little boy. "I'm Clint Eastwood."

A dam was behind me, his arms around my shoulder, comforting me. Afterwards, he told me that I had gone white and that he feared for me. I had placed myself in the center of this child's game, and the little boy was now asking me, fiercely:

"Who are you then, are you *no one?*"

I didn't answer, but I was caught in his stare, and though he was a little wisp and wimp of a boy, I was caught in his eyes that had such a derisive stare, such a disdain for me in them, that my old feeling of self-doubt was stabbed back into life, like a painful jolt backwards into some tunnel of childhood, leading to all those memories, perhaps at school, of cruel games, of being outside the group. I felt like a scapegoat standing there. I felt like a child.

Minnehaha smiled at me, in a conspiratorial way, as if to tell me that we could enjoy this. It was fun for her, so why not for me? She was beautiful. Her eyes were framed by lashes so long and curled that the sweep of her eyes was exaggerated to such moon-shaped, light-filled blue. Her mouth was thick and the underlip so sensual, like a woman's.

"Come on," said Adam. "It's breakfast time."

I believe that snakes do this with their prey. Just this. They stare in disdain at their prey, a little mouse, for instance, or a bird (I read it once, perhaps in "Rikki Tikki Tavi"), I told Adam afterwards in the Rosebud Cafe, over our eggs and bacon. They make you feel so small that you want to die, you deserve to die. And if you've ever felt it, felt that sense that you're no good, underneath it all, not worth much, well, if you have felt that once, but never let it get the better of you, then the snake senses it out, looks at you in that special knowing way, and you stare in disbelief. Your sense of shame paralyzes you, and then the snake pounces. "That little boy was a snake," I said. I kept talking. It made me calm to talk it over, and Adam listened sympathetically. He believed that talking things out and through was magical, in its own way.

"And it was like an accident," I said. "You remember when we were in Cuernavaca, and we'd had too much to drink, thinking of Lowry and his good reasons for despair, and we drove round the curve of the beautiful precipice with those mountain flowers, so red and orange and blue, and then suddenly we were on the precipice, almost over it, and everything went still. One second took a day to occur, and my life came back to me in a rush. It was like that."

"Funny how small things can have such an effect on you. I mean it was only a bunch of kids."

"Yeah," I said. I looked around and found I had an audience. I had been talking loudly, feverishly, excitedly, and perhaps it was my English accent, or the strident tone in my voice which Adam had often remarked on, the overbearing, unselfconscious way I sometimes had, which had caught the attention of the Rosebud folk.

The Rosebud Cafe was dark, a place for drinking all night and day, so night and day became indistinguishable. It smelt of tobacco, and beer, and burnt toast. The Indian policemen, a group of white construction workers daubed in paint, and some farmers were at the bar. They turned to stare at me but not to greet me. We were voyeurs of their despair. Was it picturesque? Clichéd enough for us? their eyes asked me. Did they illustrate so well the point that life had become too much for them? Here they rubbed shoulders with oblivion on the tin-topped bar before returning to the day bleary-eyed, to live another bout of life. Not yet seduced by oblivion. In this place you could innoculate yourself against death for it was everywhere, the smell of it, I told Adam.

He smiled. He liked me wild, liked it when I just came out with things.

"I sense it. It's in the air. Death's in the shadows," I said.

But then, all changed, miraculously, the sense of outcastness, the scent of death, all my fears went, for some Indian came and joined us, and I felt a friend at hand.

"You goin' to Mount Rushmore?" he asked.

"No," said Adam. "We're here for the lawsuit that Henry Blackfoot's filing against the Pennington farm. We're here for that. A round of beers on me?"

The Indian nodded and went over to the bar. "A round of beers," he said softly to the little bartender.

"I'll join you, if it's all right with you," said the Indian. "I'm Jim."

"Good to meet you," said Adam, shaking his hand. "I'm Adam."

"You the lawyer?"

"You got it."

"And I'm the tourist," I said.

"Not much to see," said Jim.

"You think so?"

"I know so," said Jim.

"It depends on what you like," I said. "I like looking at new things. This is new to me."

"I don't expect it is," said Jim with a malicious look in his eyes.

"Is the Pennington farm near here?" asked Adam, like a journalist, quite unable to make small talk, so desperate to get the information immediately, and so he will miss out on the feel of the event. He'll come back with what he wants to hear, a truth directed by his questions.

"About twenty miles."

"The farm's been in the family for two generations?"

"I dunno," said Jim listlessly.

"It has," said Adam. "You must have heard the story."

"Yeah, I heard it," said Jim. "Injun bones. The old folk coming back, that's all it is. Like you bein' haunted by your father or grandfather. That simple. Henry Blackfoot built fences at night around the bones so the tractors wouldn't keep getting those old folks to wake. Big groans rolling through his house. Not much in it excep' the bones. But the law don' see it Blackfoot's way."

"The law sees things many ways," said Adam. "I see it that Blackfoot has got every right to do that."

"He does it for the publicity. For the newspapers," he added, as if there was a difference between the two.

"That's the only way you get people to listen nowadays," said Adam.

"It worked, because on the East Coast it's become quite a little story. Do you want to see the clippings?" I asked. "We've got them in the car."

"Henry showed me the newspapers. I'm a friend o' Henry Blackfoot."

Some friend, I thought.

"And what do you do, I mean for a living?" asked Adam.

"Build the highways. A bridge now an' then. Seasonal work. An' then you take the long vacations in-between."

Jim paused to drink his beer slowly. His cheeks were like brick walls, rough and hard, and they came first in his face, leaving behind all his other features, except his mouth, which was quite agreeable. It was soft, not fleshy, telling of a kindly temperament.

"You like music?" he asked.

"Oh, *yes*," I said with exaggerated enthusiasm.

Jim took a quarter out of his pocket and asked me to make the choice on the jukebox. I felt a terrible sense of having too much. I felt I couldn't take from him. What, after all, could Jim be earning, dangling from the flying trapeze, with the waters waiting to engulf him, as he earned a pittance, risking his life on the bridges?

"What do *you* like?" I asked in a tone that was becoming embarrassing to me, but I could not change it. My pity for him came through in its ugly way, ruining my mild enjoyment of being with him.

Jim helped me out. He made his choice: Sting singing "Every move you make, every breath you take, I'll be watching you."

"I think he's lost it now," I said.

"Yeah, Sting lost it," said Jim in his listless tone.

"Do we depress you?" I asked, "being here?" I saw a flicker of amusement in his eyes.

"Everyone's got a right to a job, haven't they? In America," he added, "the land of opportunity. Right, man? So, Henry's got his ghost job and he's got a point. Lucky my ancestors aren't buried in Pennington's sheep farm." Jim laughed raucously.

I laughed with him.

Adam stared at me in wonderment and slight disgust. "Sweetie, this is serious. It's no joke."

"Same thing," said Jim. "If something's sacred, it's a joke."

And then a cloud fell over Jim, covering his face, making his eyes unfocused, so he saw nothing, not even his two new friends. He was mulling over his words, swilling them down with a whole glass of beer, celebrating the misery of his thoughts.

"A round on me?" he asked.

"Thanks, I will," said Adam, who never drank in the morning and rarely in the evening.

"You don't want one," I said.

The door opened, letting in light that hurt my eyes. The Death Spirits moved into the shadows. I heard them retreating as the door opened wide and children's laughter and screams filled the room. Minnehaha ran full speed to Jim and pulled at his leather studded belt.

"See-saw. See-saw. Hee-haw," she chanted.

"Little one," said Jim, and picked her up, whirled her round and round, and again.

"Little terror," said Jim as he let her down with a thud to the floor.

"Gimme a quarter," she ordered; he gave her one.

Minnehaha hauled herself up on the bar and danced. She danced to the end of Sting's undanceable song. She danced to Eric Clapton's "After Midnight." She danced in an ungainly way. Sweetly. Clapping her hands, throwing her arms up in the air, slightly out of time, at times, with the music. She was letting off steam, the little bundle of energy was tiring herself out. And when Madonna came on singing "Like a Virgin," Minnehaha started to cry.

"I'm Madonna," she said furiously.

She leapt from the bar into the shadows, onto the cigarette butts, in her leopard-skin tights and her shiny black swimsuit with her knobbly knees sticking through, ungainly.

"You're not," said the Snake Boy.

"I am," she said. "I'll show you."

And Minnehaha danced again, this time sexily. It wasn't really, but she tried so hard.

Jim had joined us smiling, good-naturedly.

"Where're her parents?" I asked.

"Back over by the Church at Wounded Knee. She's Blackfoot's daughter."

Adam looked as if he had been told a lie. "How old is she?"

"Nearly ten," said Jim.

"Who's going to take her home? We can drop her off. She looks so overtired and worn-out by these games," I said, wanting to pick her up in my arms and cuddle and comfort her.

"I'm takin' her home," said Jim, "if Blackfoot don't come over by noon."

"They're out of school early," Adam said.

"No school. School's seasonal work," said Jim. "They're partyin'. The good life."

Jim stood up.

"I can show you the way to Henry. Take you there, if you want, and drop her off at the same time. I can do it now if you want. No need to wait. The Blackfoot home never sleeps."

But Adam declined. He had an appointment with Blackfoot the following day and he said he didn't want to barge in on him, unannounced. Actually, Adam was worn out. The beers had soaked him with sleep, and he knew that his mind was too dream-filled to talk sense, so he stood up and led me into daylight. It was brutal, showing the dust of the road, toneless dust, no trees, the open sky running amok with clouds, so fast they moved in the wind, bent on some hellish purpose.

We drove through a few egg-yolk yellow fields cut by the harvester, like a sheep shorn. But many of the fields were bare and had never been harvested. They gave the worst land to the Indians, so I didn't need to ask which were the parched brownish fields on slightly rolling land, tobacco colored, exuding musty smells. Then, we were out of Indian land, back again into the surgically tended fields. Yes, these were precision hands, cutting and growing, changing God's work, changing the length of the stem, the size of the ear of corn, the very life force, the germ of the crops to fit the harvester, the climate, the soil. Somehow, it made me sick. I might have admired it, man's control of the soil. I might have despised the Indians for losing out, for ending up with the bad land and not having the wherewithal to tend the land quite like the whites. But I didn't.

Blue, such deep blue sky sailed triumphantly over the perfect wheat and barley and corn. We had been driving for about twenty minutes already over the Stonberg farm before we saw their dark red barn and next to it such a modest farm house and such perfect white fences, and in their back yard some children's bicycles, bright plastic red and blue, and the cleanliness of this kind of Nature made one marvel. Perhaps it was a sensuality, or perhaps it was merely character, but some essential part of life had been erased, and in its place was this neutered dwelling.

The children were in the fields with Daddy. But Marta, whose face I seemed to see through, was waiting for us. Her long brown hair and white face with little specks of green for eyes were see-through, and I saw her home, as if it were her mind. Whenever I looked at her, the presence of her nicely wallpapered living room seemed to dominate and overcome her. Adam tried to get her on the subject of Blackfoot's daughter, but she kept saying in a dutiful tone (one was perhaps meant to interpret as fidelity to Bobby) that we must wait for Bobby. "Blackfoot is Bobby's baby," she kept saying in a high-pitched tone, consciously, very carefully controlled and overlaid with a sort of gentleness. I noticed her computerized sewing machine, and then the paper cut-outs of Indians, lying casually on the sewing desk. These were the kind of Indians I saw in westerns with their feathers and plaits and war paint.

"Isn't it in bad taste?" I asked both of them, "these paper cut-outs?"

"Oh, no. It's part of the museum," she said. "It makes some money. Cut-outs are so popular with children. They're actually stickers. Take a look."

Marta worked in the Museum of the American Indian Culture on the reservation. It was a part-time job, she said. Before she had the children, it had been full-time. But now she needed time for them. Didn't I know that she had come out here to help?

"To help whom?" I asked naively.

"The Native Americans, of course," she said with a piercing accusatory stare. And then, without asking if we were interested, she told us about her life. She rambled on about leading an empty life in Manhattan, doing publicity for films. She worked on Fifth Avenue and Fifty-eighth Street and lived on East Seventy-second Street (I was meant to understand, I suppose, that there was something particularly empty about these addresses, for she spoke of them with such disdain). She spoke of the restaurants, the socializing, all the things that she and Bobby did that gave them no purpose. I'm not sure why she had to be so disdainful of Manhattan. Perhaps because she missed it, perhaps she longed to be back, away from the Indians and the herb garden and the odd mixture of "belongings," by that I mean her jumbled membership of so many faiths, for she had given herself body and soul to Manhattan life, then to Bobby, then to God, and God had led her to the Indians and she had then hated the church, the routine of it, and yet somehow, meanwhile, the Sioux had taught her that life was sacred. Even in their despair they had the answer, and in giving her a purpose now, a *raison d'etre*, she now had some knowledge about what mattered. But why did she disappear so? Was she pure spirit now, just an emanation of mind, scantily clothed in human form? That was what she said, more-or-less, that the material world was dead for her. So I said:

"It must get lonely round here."

"No," she said. The Indians had given her a purpose (part-time as it was nowadays), and though there wasn't much to do in these parts (except for Weight Watchers, and she was too thin for that, and churchgoing, and she had momentarily seen the light in Manhattan, but it had since gone out, gone dark, and left her in God's country), she was happy.

"I wonder why the final test for the believer is to lose faith," I said. "I saw a wonderful film about it, a French film, I've forgotten the title - but the young saint is abandoned by Jesus at the end and has to find her faith back through her black, blind disbelief in Him."

"But social religion, the kind you find out here, would turn anyone off," she said. The Indians had the answer. She loved the Indians, she said. And she crumpled herself up, a little exhausted by her outpouring. Adam, in an inept, embarrassed way, told us how good she was at publicity for the Indians, as if to cover up for her.

"Blackfoot taught me a lot," said Marta, fingering the Indian cut-out. She sounded sad, as if he had taught her how to look at life with cynicism. I thought I saw her eyes water but didn't have time to verify it, for the children arrived, muddy and wild-eyed, and ran up to Adam, embracing him like an uncle. I felt a little left out. He had known these people for years, longer than he had known me. The toddlers burst out and giggled, emitting light, fresh sounds, the glee of new sight. They loved Adam, crawled over him, rubbed mud on his lips, and he smiled and kicked his legs up in the air, pretending to be a bucking horse. The evening was spent around the kids. None of their mother's deep sadness had marred their brightness, their nimble thoughts. Before long they had made friends with me, so I no longer felt like a stranger. I could not yet decipher much of Bobby's temperament for he was so placid, so smiling in his silence and so unready to talk. He distanced me, as his wife had, for both of them projected a version of themselves, in chatter and silence, that whittled away idiosyncracy and gave a false permanence to one side of themselves. I was discussing this with Adam in the dark in the guest house, landlocked in the middle of unpeopled fields. The silence stung my ears. But sometimes, I could hear the clouds creaking so white outside the window. Adam said I just didn't understand America. He said, "I know so many Americans like Marta, touched by some terrible need to find meaning, life never being enough."

"She's hiding something," I said, rubbing myself to warm my thoughts against Adam.

He pulled away. "You're just being critical of my friends. You always have been," he said, turning away, so I was truly lonely. But I didn't fall into anger. I needed Adam, out in this empty land, bad land, dark night. But I didn't want to make love because I didn't want to let go. I imagined losing my body first into Adam and then going into the night, being splayed out in the darkness further and further and obliterated. But Adam was next to me, felt my body and entered me. I held back, feeling him just as some warmth rubbing against me. My thoughts were elsewhere so the rhythm of his moving backwards and forwards was like a whisper, muted. Funny, how making love can be like just lying there. Nothing more. That's what I asked for.

And then he was moving without thinking, just taking me in the whole time and wanting me more and more, moving without knowing it, just taken over by the movement, then I did too. I was carried up into his body, with him, and forgot it all, eating, eating, like one big mouth. Everything in me was licking Adam. But it was okay. Because he became part of me all of a sudden. I stopped being a mouth and became a mouth and a prick. And then, words like that don't mean much, because it was all of us really, a lock and key (I often think about how we often come together even when we start off so distracted, or even without the intention of making it a passionate matter). So we were stuck together, and then I was calm, my thoughts had stopped going in circles, and I was warm and not afraid. I didn't really mind if the holiday wouldn't be much fun (and staying with Marta and Bobby didn't look like fun to me), and Wounded Knee seemed so sad, its history and the dead old farms and bars for beer drinking didn't seem like a place for a holiday. But if we could make love at night I'd get through it, I told Adam and he smiled.

"The only reason you live in America is because of Manhattan. The moment I take you out of your hothouse you wilt."

"I don't see why *this* is more American than *that*."

"These places don't change much. There's no surface to them. No fashions to camouflage the unchanging essence of America."

"I'll find her sometime," I said, and fell into sleep.

The silence woke me out of a dream, the lack of fire trucks, police cars sirens that lullaby me to rest, the city's signs of life. But here there's no diversion from dreams. Christ was on the Mount of Olives, kneeling. His body white and gnarled, a Cranach-style painting. But the painting moved. Father, why hast Thou abandoned me, he kept saying, so slowly, like a music box repeating a single tune, and as the mechanism wound down it became slower and slower. F-a-t-h-e-r — F-a-t-h-e-r ... and there were brown acorns on the trees and olives dotted around the gnarled earth. But the sky was triumphant turquoise, Mediterranean, not like this true blue sky here that has no hues of the sea coloring it. No sea for miles. I felt cold and alone, wanting the harbor, the sea lapping against my ear, the life of the city, something of the city. But the painting kept talking and all was abandoned. The whole world went cold. I thought of making love again to stop the feeling, the reverberating aloneness of man coming to me. That we must die alone. I thought these kind of thoughts, that life ends and nothing replaces it. Well, I didn't know. For now, it seemed like it would be a perpetual abandonment, with none of the deities holding their hands out, to welcome me.

have come a long way, travelled really far from my birth, I said
to Adam as we walked along the path from the guest house back
to the farm house in the afterdawn light. Some white butterflies
went by, like a skirt upturned in the wind, little errant frills across
the cornfields. I could hear a harvester in the distance. Bobby had
told us that they come from Kansas, sweeping the farmland as they
go. It's seasonal work like all the work round here. For months
you just sit around, when it's wintertime, and drink to keep warm.
I was telling Adam about the sense of aloneness I have out here. I
felt it in my childhood, hiding, always hiding, finding a little nest
somewhere in my house to hide. Your parents can be alive and
seem to be dead so that you're mourning them every day. And
then, they can give you almost nothing, but it seems like enough. I
often ramble on like this with Adam. It seems to soothe him,
letting him know that I don't have much to hide, can let myself
think aloud with him.

Adam stopped in his tracks. "This place is making you real
upset. I know you're *upset*. Even making love last night, you felt
so distant, removed from it."

"Perhaps it's the land," I said, "but it could be you. *You*
seem upset. You know, when two people are together it's easy to
pick up the other's mood. It's quite frightening sometimes how
quickly it can happen. It's some kind of guilt because I can feel *that*
now. I can taste the guilt in you."

"The place makes me feel guilty. It makes me feel in
conflict about being American."

"Oh, come on, don't say it's political," I said.

But what I actually love about Adam surfaced. One of the many qualities that overlapped and intermingled and became so tangled up in his eyes and body that I enjoyed extricating a quality or two and saying this or that made me love him. It wasn't true that these qualities made me love him. It was his presence, and then when he wasn't there, the smell, the aftermath of his presence that I loved. It was actually all that he was all the time, with and without me. Anyhow, what I love about Adam came through: for he said, in his painfully honest tone, that he was guilty about Marta. He wasn't sure if he was here to help Marta or Blackfoot, and not knowing made him uncomfortable.

"I know her too well," said Adam. "I knew her too well."

"When did it end?"

"It ended quickly, like fireworks. It shone and exploded, and that was the end of it."

"I asked you when?"

"Long before I met you," said Adam, amused at my show of jealousy.

"Well, why did you tell me, now that we're on her doorstep?" I said.

"I don't think we'd get much out of discussing it, anyway," Adam said.

Marta was at the door, sad, with her long straggly hair that shone a little in the sun.

"Blackfoot's in the bathroom," she said to Adam.

"Damn," said Adam.

And so we met up, already angry for one reason or another at each other, morose and silent when Blackfoot came out of the bathroom, smirking with his green eyes and blondish hair, and in an instant I felt the shock of finding him handsome, his aquiline nose, his smiling, arrogant eyes, knowledgeable eyes, eyes that saw our ill temper and enjoyed it. He was above us, friendly to each in turn. But Marta flinched whenever he spoke as if his words were pummelling her.

He didn't talk much about the legal fight with the

Penningtons, mentioning casually that Adam and he had an appointment so he wouldn't spoil our breakfast with business. Adam seemed relieved; Blackfoot looked cold; Blackfoot switched to warmth, smiling, soft lips smiling; Blackfoot's face clouded over; he didn't camouflage the anger hardening, making a show of it when Marta said that she had to leave for the Museum of American Indian Culture. "They put the bones on show there. Bones that should be buried, stuck in a glass cage for the tourists to watch. You might ask yourself why it's called the Museum of American Indian Culture since it's not got any respect for what's sacred."

"People are," said Marta, almost in tears, and she gathered up her handbag and Peruvian cardigan with white ponies and an emerald green background, and left.

None of us went after her.

"She still goes there," he said. "No matter what I say."

"Whites don't seem to be able to put a foot right," said Adam, almost to himself.

Blackfoot nodded.

"When you go around thinking you know better what to do with our culture than we know, it's not gonna work. *We* know. Some of us," Blackfoot said, and then, swift as the wind, he changed his tone, making us breakfast as he spoke, offering us tours here and there, telling us jokes mostly directed against the Bureau of American Indian Affairs.

"There has to be a dialogue with whites," said Adam pompously. Blackfoot was impressed, agreed with Adam, rambled on about Marta doing good work on the publicity campaign as if she were his secretary, and said that since there was a lot of publicity there *would* be a dialogue with the public.

Blackfoot brightened up at the word "publicity." He also liked the word "event." He said that everything he did, from waking to sleeping, and even his dreams ("I had a dream" ... he said ... "we could use in our poster...") had the never-ending possibility of being used.

"Hunting season's here in a few weeks. We should hunt

like we used to, over our land. That'd cause a stir," said Blackfoot.

"That's trespassing. Real trespassing. You can't," said Adam.

"Okay. You know the law." How far could he go? Adam knew, and Blackfoot became momentarily docile, almost childlike. Then, he moved on quickly to a new topic, a new event for Adam to monitor.

Blackfoot was charismatic with the unselfconscious power of his body, the hunterlike readiness which fed into his mind, so there was a listening in his face, as though he heard sounds of the land, small sounds, whisperings of fish in streams, footprints of a deer echoed for him. He tracked down whites, finding ways to trick and cheat and hit back at them for all they did; it had become a sport.

"Listen here, man," said Adam (who never called people "man" or "brother"), "if you go walking over anyone's private property just to get attention, you won't get the right attention. You want people to be on your side, and they are, when it comes to your ancestors' burial ground. A lot of churchgoers understand that. But you can't start hunting over the farmers' lands just because it was your hunting grounds. You can't use all the land."

"That's it, man. Quick thinking. It'd be *all* the land," said Blackfoot. "Mass demonstrations across the country. It'd be big time."

"It's not going to help your cause," said Adam, showing signs of irritation. I wondered why he came here, to defend someone he seemed to feel little for.

"Your old man would understand," said Blackfoot. "He understands big time."

"That's the last thing my father understands. He's an academic, an intellectual. He has no interest in big time."

"Oh, no? Then why's he got all those prizes, Nobel Prize for science. Why's he on TV? D'you think he just dropped down from nowhere. No, that guy's got savvy," said Blackfoot.

I laughed, but Adam could not, tormented as he often was when Joseph was mentioned in public. No. Dad wasn't some cheap showman, whore, narcissistic bastard, said Adam. Blackfoot watched. He wasn't pleased he had riled his lawyer. He watched Adam intently, trying to work out how to calm him down, to make amends.

"Your old man'd understand, not the big time. No, he's not on TV because he wants to be there. He's jus' forced up there because of his ideas. I got that, man. Cool it, man. But your dad'd get the meaning of my culture, man, not like these kids what think it's hip to defend the Native Americans like you'd "Save the Whales". Same yuppies what came with guns and shot us down. Same exact people who did what was trendy two, three hundred years ago, killing Injuns," screamed Blackfoot furiously.

"You use us," Adam said. "A lot of us make it possible for you to hang out publicizing your cause. A lot of yuppies give their money to your cause."

"Damn shit, man," said Blackfoot. "No more than they pay for some cheap shit French meal in some fancy restaurant. Cheap shit. I use it, because I ain't got no other source. But don't you tell me I have to like 'em because they give me money. Don't tell me I have to grovel. No, they come an' grovel to me. Those mystic bitches."

Soon they'll be at each other's throats, but I wasn't afraid for I liked the absurd spectacle of Adam losing his temper with his client. I wanted to hug him. I wanted to make him laugh a little at himself. I can do it sometimes, mock him a little, mimic him, and then his grimness turns, so fast, into a smile or laugh. It's like pressing a button and I can do it to him because he knows I'm trying to get him out of the cloud mood that stops him from seeing out.

So I did. Blackfoot turned away. Adam laughed. The balance of power had shifted. Blackfoot looked disconsolate, lost without his sense of humor.

"My father's got nothing to do with this case," said Adam. "He won't help your cause."

And the sadness returned, the look of torment, of being faced with some idea that was merely a throbbing pain. It had no way of being calmed, it was just like being stung by a wasp or kicked by a horse, the idea of Joseph always being implicit in everything that Adam did. I know him well enough: I know that he realizes that his father's name, his sharing of features with the old man, all that goes with him, like a shadow where he goes. Like a shadow, Joseph walks in his footsteps, selfishly, reminding people of his presence, overshadowing Adam's being. Adam sometimes says it takes years for a community to change the connotation of a word, and his father's name is a household word, so he'll be associated with what his father stands for, no matter what he does.

"Your dad," said Blackfoot, "knows what it's like to be up against the wall. I saw that program on him on Public TV, how he came here from Germany. Nazis everywhere, and your dad escaped."

"He was helped. People in England and America helped him out, before it was too late."

"He was up against it, being a Jew in Germany's like bein' an Injun here. Same genocide."

"I won't get into this conversation with you," said Adam quietly.

"Do you have it a lot?" I asked.

"No," said Blackfoot, "I jus' saw the program six months ago. Ever since then, though, I bin' trying to use it for my own ends."

I stared at Adam and then at Blackfoot. Blackfoot and Adam were smiling at each other, knowingly. The look of relief on Adam's face became a man-to-man look, so they were like two men standing naked in a shower, Adam and Blackfoot were just then. Knowing the weakest part of Adam, his loss of face, his sense of losing his own person in his father's presence, all that Blackfoot sensed and told Adam he knew it. It was done with no graciousness or sensitivity. I will use it against you, said Blackfoot, and so loses his trump card. I think Adam likes it that way. He likes it when I tell him everything, even the thoughts that hurt him. So, I watched him with admiration as he dealt with Blackfoot man to man, not as some knowledgeable superior intellect, pruned and polished at Harvard, not as some Manhattan do-gooder coming to feel good over the bones of the Indians. Adam had somehow ditched all the facade. The thing that made him break was in view, but he held himself strong, knowing it was there.

"I'm gonna make the hunting season into *my* event, anyhows," said Blackfoot grimly.

Adam closed his eyes, put his hands over his face, and spoke to Blackfoot through this pose.

"You bastard," he said. "I can't take on every damn lawsuit under the sun for you. One after another, each one ruining the case I can make for the last <u>event</u>."

"I'm sick to my bones of this small-time, small-town stuff. I don't give fuck-all if it makes you sweat. You're scared shitless, man, about the big time. Getting into competition with the old man, so you'll stay in the shade. Well, I'm takin' you out there, man, in the limelight."

"Blackfoot," said Adam slowly, "you won't get the kind of attention you need for your cause."

"All publicity's good publicity," said Blackfoot.

He smiled. He was happy like a kid who has thrown all his toys out of the window and watches his mother throw up her hands in frustration. He was teasing Adam, he had Adam now, because the two of them were in it together now. Adam had to take all of his antics on, one after the other, like a mother and son.

That night, a dark, windy night, filled with small talk, sounding of the huge depths of sea that were so far away but had sent their winds to chill us, the dinner at Bobby Stonberg's farm was evanescent, almost like a mirage. Lamb was discussed, the price of wheat, the fish they caught, the hunting season which was soon to arrive. But the wind was all I could hear and all that made sense to me. Marta Stonberg spoke about the museum, the artifacts (and never mentioned Blackfoot's visit), the children were sent crying to bed, and then Marta excused herself. She felt tired, she said, though she looked feverishly awake. Bobby was left to us, in his cheerfulness and his inaccessible tranquillity. He began again on the fish, the ones he'd caught in the lake he'd just bought, on the edge of their property. It wasn't really a lake. It was partly man-made, but lakes were scarce, not like in Minnesota. He'd thought of getting a lake there and driving away at the weekends. But Marta didn't like the upheaval. Moves hurt her, said Bobby. She got attached to places, glued to them, you might say. They clung to her skin. That's how it seemed, because some weekends she'd cry before leaving the farm. She'd disappear for hours, drive through the property in any weather, just drive, and take it all in. Adam didn't seem to find it strange at all. He said that since he'd known Marta she attached herself to people, places, even objects.

"You're lucky," said Adam. "Some women would run from the isolation of this place."

"But she knows the Indians," said Bobby. "She's found a place in their world."

"I wish I could be like that," I said, thinking of my restlessness, my moving from one place to another, the fear that I would leave Adam sometime, find an excuse to leave him. Perhaps even this trip, I would find a reason to leave.

"With the Indians?" asked Bobby. "You know you wouldn't want to be mixed up with the Indians. There's no sense in it. They use you. Manipulative little bastards," said Bobby.

"You mean Blackfoot?" I asked.

"The lot of them. The whole lot of them. Exploitative bastards. You know they live off welfare. Work half the year when they feel like it. Drink themselves to death when they feel like it, have kids but don't send them to school...."

Bobby was red-faced with anger. It sickened me. I wanted to leave.

"But they have so much to deal with. So much despair." said Adam.

"We've all got our crosses to bear. I only put up with it because it gives her peace of mind. It keeps her happy, in a way. But I'd kill the bastard that trespassed on my land looking for ghosts and burial grounds. Blackfoot's kept quiet about it so far. I told him my mind. So he's keeping it under wraps. Partly because he's scared I'll kill the bastard. Partly because of Marta. She keeps him quiet in her own way."

"I didn't know there were sacred burial grounds on your farm," said Adam quietly.

"It's down by the lake. The new land I bought. There's some bluffs. And then the lake has a history. They say the lake's possessed with rain. So when the Rain God came to live in the lake, the fish came to feed him. You're not allowed to fish in that lake. And all around here are gravestones."

"Real ones, or underground ones?"

"Real ones," said Bobby, uncomfortably.

"So what did you do with them?"

"I leave them there. They're useful for picnicking or when you're hunting."

Bobby went to the fridge and poured himself another beer.

He forgot to offer us anything and we didn't ask.

He was red with beer.

"The whole damn land is filled with this stuff. You can't put a foot down on anything here that isn't sacred. Moon Gods. Sun Gods. Rain Gods. You name it, they've got it. The prairie's eaten over most of it now, thank God."

"Thank God? Thank which God?" asked Adam.

"It's easy to be liberal when they're not playing their tricks on your land."

"In a way," said Adam, "in a way, I'd get pretty angry if some guy told me I didn't have a right to my West Side apartment because two hundred years ago his dad had an Indian burial ground where the elevator now stands. You could look at it that way. But visually it doesn't work. It works, the idea of ownership out here. You can see it, imagine what it was like. It hasn't changed that much. The wind's the same. It's just so convincing to one's eyes — the beauty of Blackfoot's proposition is that you can see him when he gets on his horse, rides across the plains, you can see he owned it all. In his stance and those blue eyes. He isn't..."

"You find him pretty?" asked Bobby, threateningly.

"Yes," said Adam, "I find him pretty."

"Like a dumb blonde?" asked Bobby.

"No, like a man," said Adam. "He's pretty masculine, don't you think?"

"He's no dumb blonde. His mind is just an apparatus for manipulation. You should just watch him, with Marta, with you, just watch him next time."

Bobby went to the fridge for another beer, and Adam, sensing that the alcohol might unleash further venom from his friend, said that he would take his leave. It was late.

"He uses you," said Bobby, disregarding Adam's movement toward the door. "He uses his kids. He uses you. He's impervious to others. He couldn't care if we ended up dead in a ditch, frozen to death on some highway. He'd pass by in his truck and leave us dying. You watch him, next time," said Bobby.

Bobby felt violent. It came out so suddenly, bypassing the

tranquillity, cutting through the cheerfulness, like the wind over the plains. When it gathers force, it erases all characteristics from the land, flattens everything over time. So, Bobby was left in a strange emptiness by his anger.

"And what does that matter to you, Bobby?" asked Adam. "Why should you care what some Indian thinks about you? Or me? So what if he doesn't give a damn?"

Bobby, in his hugeness, his huge anger, was bereft, and sad. "You're right. I shouldn't care," he said, and tears came to his eyes. It wasn't the beer. It was something he wanted to release from himself. I could see the relief in his face. The lines around his mouth unwrinkled momentarily and he cried. He didn't actually make a sound, but the tears rolled down his face.

Adam's face hardened. He looked at Bobby, as at a spectacle of pain, as if he were hardening himself to his own self-pity. He'd often been moved to tears, by pain and other strong emotions. But lately, Adam had been trying to strengthen himself against his moods. I felt Bobby's tears roll warmly down my chest. They had reached me because of their abruptness and the feeling I still had that a man like Bobby could not cry.

"Do you want to take a walk?" asked Adam in a clipped tone.

"Not at night," said Bobby, and I detected a slight tremble in his lips, a twitch at the corner, of fear.

"We should get some sleep," said Adam.

"It's good of you to listen," said Bobby, ushering us to the porch. The night sky was punctuated by so many stars. Their light was chill, like icicles hanging coldly.

"You haven't really told me what's bugging you," said Adam.

Bobby nodded.

"Don't ask me to," said Bobby. "I don't need to go into the details."

I had the feeling that I wasn't wanted, for they walked back into the house and left the door to close in my face. I opened it and watched. They took a beer each and walked back onto the porch, down the steps into the grasslands, and I followed. Some unspoken message had passed between them. For there was a friendly air to them, a quiet padding to their steps, some sense that they were taking this walk together.

They said nothing, but the rhythm of walking seemed to talk for them. I could imagine them as students now, as friends. We had arrived at the lake, murky except where the clouds sailed across it, white on ink blue black. Indelible smudge, filled with the death of Indians. That's what Adam said later, that the lake smelt of death. So we walked away again, and said goodnight, and nothing had been explained, but Adam merely said later, when we were in bed, "He stole my girlfriend in our freshman year. He thinks I stole Marta to get even. But that's all the sense I can make of it. I still don't think that's his current humiliation. But it's something to do with sex."

"That's what I thought it'd be like. Underneath propriety, clean kitchens, insecticided fields, herb gardens and domestic scenes of happiness, I thought I'd find stories of cheap infidelities. I wouldn't even be surprised if Blackfoot's fucked her."

Adam tossed, turned off the bed light, and yawned.

"Look how she is with him, broken in two, weakened by need. Look how she stares when she's near him, with fear," I said.

Adam fell silent.

"See how she's hurt by him, just like a slave, the way she walked out, submissive."

"Blackfoot's not dumb enough to have an affair with her," said Adam.And then I cried. It comforted me to tears, the thought of desire surviving this neutered world, this life of church, rooted in neutered land, earth like a heavy snow covering us in a cold sleep. But desire comes out, limping, crucified, but alive, surviving the dead land.

Adam listened and stroked my lips. He hummed to me and rocked me to sleep.

Marta's moment to flaunt her sense of humiliation came the next morning. She was sitting, cross-legged, in some yogic position when Blackfoot walked in, without knocking, and said he needed Marta to come right away. Bobby walked towards her and called her a whore. Blackfoot said nothing. He just stared at Marta in a daze.

"You bitch," said Bobby and he walked to Blackfoot and put his hand on Blackfoot's shoulder. "Get out," he said grimly.

Marta began crying.

"Get out," said Bobby. "I'll kill you."

"Okay, man," said Blackfoot. "You got a point. It's not my scene anyhow. I got an appointment anyhow with my lawyer. Are you coming, Adam? I thought I'd get you initiated into the local scene. My scene. Not some goddamn fucked-up white-prick scene," said Blackfoot as he closed the door.

"They do it most nights," said Blackfoot. "She's going off it now. It's not my scene, them white racists like bein' beaten. I don' mean Marta. She's no racist. But that bastard is. Some Harvard dumbass. Pays Jim and the likes to run his farm and don't know the first thing about the land, don't know how to fuck his wife. Just knows how to give orders and buy up land. It's typical," said Blackfoot, ending his diatribe on a rather nonchalant tone. "Typical. It's all you can expect of them lot."

We found ourselves following Blackfoot. He led us, talking away, smiling to himself, occasionally letting out some curse against Bobby, but it was mild enough, nonchalant enough, his anger was soft at the edges. He had taken us through some fields (we followed the line of grasslands so as not to tread down the newly planted wheat whose tiny green stalks were just showing above the black clods).

"The earth's fertile. Always on the move. Toing and froing. Look at those goddamn grasshoppers — always moving like them clouds. The earth's fertile so why do these guys with no soul come out here and stifle her?"

Blackfoot had reached a clearing where the prairie grass was high and rough and swayed, wavelike, in the wind. When the wind went high and rough, the grass swirled endlessly, in infinite patterns. One's eye was never quick enough to see more than the swaying of such soft colors — grey green and soft blue of the sky, swirling too.

"You see 'em gravestones?"

We didn't.

Blackfoot pushed aside some weeds and grass. There was a gravestone which read:

EMMA BLUEGRASS HUSTON
In Memory.

We moved on, with Blackfoot kicking aside the grass and weeds.

HENRY FAST CLOUD BLACKFOOT
In Loving Memory

PETER BLACKFOOT
In Memory

"My father and brother and Mom," Blackfoot said.

A Michelob beer can and a packet of potato chips sat on Peter Blackfoot's grave.

"I used to bring flowers here. But it's private property. No trespassing. So I don't no more, excepts when Marta and me meets up. Out here. Late at night, in the morning. We look at the desecration together. She cries a bit. Reminds her of things of her own that were lost, and killed. She has a way of crying that makes me sad. So I cheer her up, and forget to think about myself. Just for a moment. Not for long," said Blackfoot in a menacing tone, as if to remind Adam that he would never forget his own best interests.

"I takes my kid here sometimes with Marta. So she can see. What it's come to. I want her to know what it's come to here."

"She's like a little girl," said Blackfoot, "Marta is. When I looks at her, she cries like a little girl."

"So why are we suing the Penningtons?" Adam asked. "Because Marta cries like a little girl? Because when we went to Pennington's farm I didn't see any sacred burial grounds, because this is your real burial ground, for your family, isn't it?" Adam said furiously. "You've lied to me," he added as an afterthought.

"This lot is recent," said Blackfoot. "But the other lot in the Penningtons' place is ancient. Been goin' there to bury their dead. I knows it. I'm not lying."

I felt the prairie sweep across the dead, covering them first with grass and then with earth. What Blackfoot said was true, and I told Adam not to be so logical, for the manifest gravestones, the ones that showed themselves to us, were no more homes for the dead than the great earth encircling us. Stone fell and sank, and in a few hundred years these gravestones would be covered too. It seemed natural. It seems that Nature was not cruel in reclaiming all for herself. It makes me wonder if Blackfoot is right, and the earth will take herself back, recoiling from man.

But what is left?

I asked Blackfoot a few times, but I didn't expect an answer from him, and the question just made me feel lonely. It made me think of leading a life that never touches anyone. The question lay in the prairies, in the body of unending wind that broke down all.

"So why aren't we suing the Stonberg farm?" asked Adam.

"Not for the moment," said Blackfoot. "Not yet, we don't."

It occurred to me that Blackfoot and Adam had shared the

same woman.

"I got to look after Marta," said Blackfoot. "I can't go causin' trouble for her. Can't you feel them? They've got powerful again, now I'm on their side. I make them live again. They're still around."

"I just feel nothingness," I said.

"That's how they make you feel. Never liked my dad much, made me feel small-time, always made me feel like a thief. He's doin' the same to you, making you feel small, that's his spirit, mean-spirited guy."

Blackfoot kicked the beer can off the gravestone, and then followed it down to the pond, kicking it as he went. He took off his shirt, his jeans, and waded into the water in his underpants. He tried to grab at the water with his hands, as if he was trying to catch fish.

"Why don't you two have a swim? You look so sad standing there in the grass."

We watched. Blackfoot frolicked, kicking his legs up, in the shallows. He dived into the water and came up with a tiny fish.

"That's trespassin', isn't it?" Blackfoot asked, mocking Adam.

"It don't matter," said Blackfoot, the sun glistening and goldening every drop of water that came from him. He put on his jeans and dried his chest with his shirt, and let it hang round his neck, dripping like some necklace.

"I want to marry her," Blackfoot said. "You can help me. You always help me," said Blackfoot. "After she's left him, we'll sue him, Bobby, that's when we'll move on this case. You saw the beer cans. The potato chips desecrating the grave. He uses those slabs for eating on. Marta told me. She'll be a witness. She told me the kids have picnics on them and Bobby tells them this is Injun graves. He teaches his kids to despise us. But the kids know better. She'll want the kids to live with us."

"She's said nothing to me," said Adam.

"You saw what he's like," said Blackfoot. "An' they ain't made love for months."

"That's no grounds for divorce."

"Oh, come on, Adam. You know a woman wants to make love."

For his ideological fight to be reduced to a matter of marriage and divorce depressed Adam. He had come out to help the Lakota people as he told Jim on their second round of beers and he admitted that he enjoyed bending the law to encompass Blackfoot's impossible ideals.

"But ain't you helping Blackfoot, personally?"

"Personally? As a friend? No. As a representative of the Lakota people, yes," said Adam. "I am helping the Native American people at large."

"Thanks," said Jim. "But now you won't help the Indian people because Blackfoot wants to marry Marta?"

"It's so petty," said Adam. "It's incredibly small-minded, small-town. Blackfoot's latest idea defied the world. His premise was simple, that all the land in America should be returned to the American Indians, not for them to own, but for all to roam on. Thank God it's impossible. I want my co-op on the West Side. I want to buy a place in the country. But Blackfoot's made us reassess our American roots. His events were games he played with consciousness, brilliant games, pulling the rug from under the feet of America. But this divorce stuff, it's soap opera time. Do you know how many divorces I handle in New York? And you know how much I charge people, just to listen to their problems?"

"But don't you help people?" asked Jim, perturbed.

"I *charge* people, but I don't charge concepts."

Adam was drunk. I felt embarrassed for him and begged him to leave. When Jim went for the third round of beers, I whispered to Adam to go back to the guest house and make love.

But Adam turned on me, accusing me of being like the rest of them, putting the personal above the general good.

"I'm sick of your sexual needs," he said.

"Marta will get herself killed if she don' get protection," said Jim, handing the beers round.

"I'm sorry," said Adam. He took my hand.

I'm sorry, he kept repeating.

"You gotta help Blackfoot," said Jim.

Then, Adam grew sober. A cloud came over him as Minnehaha walked in the bar, the Snake Boy in tow behind her. She waved a twig in the air, occasionally thrashing the Snake Boy.

"And what if I can't help Blackfoot?" asked Adam. "What if he'd be better off staying with his wife? He's got a kid hasn't he?"

"The kid's unhappy," said Jim, leaving the table, giving up on Adam.

"So you tell me why you're running away," I said, "now that it's no longer a game. Before it was like a videogame." (I used the metaphor because Adam likes playing them from time to time, when we're in bars.) "But now, Blackfoot's affair is with someone you went to bed with, and now you haven't got the archetypal German settlers, the damn Penningtons to blame. No, now *you're* involved and you're running and you've stopped wanting to make love. Now you're into this mud up to your neck."

"You think I bear a grudge against the Germans?" he asked sadly.

"After what they did? What with your father who had to leave and then cousins of yours who were killed?"

"So you think I'm really fighting my own vendetta against the Germans? You're crazy," said Adam.

"I know," I said. "But once the Penningtons aren't on the firing line, and once Blackfoot's antics aren't just games for the media, you want to run."

"I do," said Adam. "Let's go."

We got in the car, in the blazing sun. The seats of the rented Ford were stinking of plastic. Nature seemed to be bent on hounding us. Human nature too.

"It doesn't fit in any more, does it, Adam? It's sad, but it's getting completely out of hand. Aren't you compromised right from the start, representing Blackfoot, staying in the guest house of his mistress, taking walks to his real ancestral graves covered with popcorn?"

"Potato chips," said Adam, interrupting me with a smile.

"Potato chips," I repeated. "The surface of America, as usual littered with the garish debris of food containers, the political always revealed to be less important than individual needs. Perhaps that's what you came here to show me; perhaps this is really America. In the one place you'd expect to find a real political motivation, you find a soap opera. Instead of convictions, you find sex. Is that what you came here to show me? The likeable side of America?"

"Let's stop off," I said, as we drove past yet another cornfield. "Let's walk." We found ourselves knee deep in meadow daisies, yellow and white, nodding their heads at us, the ducks flying over the lake (as they do on those awful duck paintings, just skirting the surface of the lake), the yellow ears of corn sticky to the touch, and the blue sky softly daubed with smoke clouds and the hot sun pounding down on us and the fields binding us together in a sea of rustling heat, together. We walked until night fell. We made love near a Lutheran church, in the corn, excited at the thought of the pure white-washed building being near us, container of so much religiosity. It was empty, but never mind. We were defying it, adding to the confusion, poking at the surface of this place that wanted people to be simple-minded, hard-working, God-fearing. White. This part of the land leaves people with enough space so you can hide from color and other creeds. Except for the Indians, migrant workers, sometimes needed, always there, lying in wait, reminding us. If we made love, I told Adam, I could stand it, and I had promised him that. And within us warm, disheveled, moist, and dirty in the corn, I felt in love with him, said I would wait it out, this journey. If we are in it together, if we touch and love and break through this coldness between us, I'll stay. But I felt a woman separating us, a cold presence always between us, my mother or yours, who knows? Between our bodies, she's lying, I told Adam, as the night fell, more dazzling than other nights because the sun was a huge fruit, strawberry red, like a Bosch painting; it hung as a sign of delights, fruits of desire growing in the sky. It was lurid in its strawberry red, and then squashed by the oncoming darkness, it dripped wine, raspberry red all over the horizon, sucked in by the land. Like our lips, sucking each other, licking off sweat and dirt. Adam came quickly. He couldn't help it, and he left me behind, but I didn't care. I wasn't there for sex, that day. Not for the perfect moment, physical thrill or complete oneness. I just wanted to break through the coldness, and sometimes bodies can do it first and words will follow of love.

Adam said he was grateful to me for speaking my mind. It made him angry at first to hear things he didn't want to hear, but it made him quiet inside too. My words had calmed him, making it possible to think things over. The night was on us. The stars were covering us, making the sky seem flat, seem like a blanket that would cover our sleep, and Adam sensed a piece of land where we could rest, away from the road, past the signpost that read:

OREGON TRAIL

THE FIRST SETTLERS

CROSSED THIS WAGON TRAIL FROM GETTYSBURG TO

the rest was washed off and scratched in the wood was:

MURDERERS AND THIEVES

and underneath it read:

BUREAU OF AMERICAN INDIAN AFFAIRS

We climbed back over the barbed-wire fence, where the trail was marked by an indentation in the grass, hints of the wagon wheels that had continually passed over, or perhaps signs of another road that the prairie had washed away. The stars were bright enough to show us the way. We walked to a line of trees that would shield us from the so balmy wind, just caresses of cool air that became small gusts occasionally. We lay down under a large oak that swayed. The earth seemed to sway too, in an infinite dance with the winds. Small winds, large winds, eroding winds, God's air, and the demon of the dust winds, winds of locusts, that this earth we lay on had known. Now our bodies were tired, and the earth felt hard and unwelcoming.

The prairie began to shudder. It rustled, too, trying to disturb our bodies that were coming closer and closer. As we kissed hard and grabbed and clutched at each other, trying to eat in each other's flesh, his pulling ungraciously on my thighs, my hands on Adam's back, pushing him closer. And then we heard nothing. My ears were spinning with the sound of his breath. It sounded loud, like a death gasp. It sounded like horses' hooves pounding. It was like a thought, one that he couldn't control, like a dream coming to me. It was in him, and his passion for me.

It was not friendly. All this had nothing of companionship in it.

It was the sound of barking that killed it. I thought I was in a dream, that nothing could touch me. Though I was awake, with Adam, coming, it was so contained, and the closer we came the larger we seemed, and the world outside was gone, unimportant, like an ant crawling over us, too small to feel. It was the sound of dogs, and then voices, that seemed to come from within us. At first, I thought it was part of our lovemaking, part of our dream that we were hounded. But the torchlight was on us, and dogs were barking. Adam sat up, zipped up his jeans, and smiled.

"We were lost," he said, smiling.

"I'll be damned," said a fat man.

"It's her," said a young boy. It was the Snake Boy, Minnehaha's tormentor.

"Stand up," said the Snake Boy.

"You trespassing," said the fat man.

"We're lost," said Adam. "Whose farm do you work in?"

"None o' your business," said the Snake Boy.

"It is. Because you'll be in real trouble if we're coming as guests to your boss, and we got lost on the way. Just think of that. Do you want to be fired?" asked Adam, adopting a discordant, childish tone.

"Wait 'til I get the dogs on you," said the Snake Boy. "They'll eat you for breakfast."

"Shut up, Abe," said the fat man. "These soun' like folks from another place. Ain't from these parts. Perhaps they're guests."

"I'll get those dogs on you," said the Snake Boy. He jigged up and down in delight.

"Those dogs got sharp teeth. Gnaw, gnaw," said the Snake Boy, gnashing his teeth.

I laughed in fear.

"We got guns back there in the truck. Don't you laugh," said the Snake Boy.

"Oh, shut your mouth," said the fat man. "Perhaps these *are* guests."

"We got guns. We'll get these trespassin'. We'll get the guns. An' shoot 'em like they do on TV. Then we'll ride away an' the sheriff will come after us. He'll kill us in the end because we're bad folks but we'll have fun in-between. Watching the dogs eating them for breakfast."

"Don't listen to him," said the fat man. "He's a boy."

"I'll shoot you too. You shut up. I'll tell my dad you let them trespassin'. You didn't shoot 'em. I'll tell my dad."

"He's not your dad. Pennington's not your dad," said the fat man.

"Then we *are* on Pennington's farm," said Adam with actual relief. "Then we are his guests."

The fat man trembled. "I'm sorry," he said. "We don't mean harm."

"My dad'll shoot you. He'll eat you for breakfast," said the Snake Boy. "It don't hurt when you die. It just looks bad. You yell and scream a lot, but that's Jesus takin' you. An' if you're a sinner you don' wanna go. But Jesus forgives you. So you yell and scream a lot. On TV they don't tell you the full story. They don't tell you. Sometimes Steve McQueen does. Sometimes Clint Eastwood does. But usually they don't. My dad was a sinner," said the Snake Boy.

"Don' listen to him," said the fat man. "We'll drive you to the house."

"My dad yelled and screamed. He was a sinner. But Jesus wanted him. He kept yellin'. That's what they said. He wanted to stay here. But Jesus wanted him to live with him in a big farm with lots of dogs. This is Bonnie. She's my friend."

The dog began to lick the Snake Boy. It was a huge shiny labrador. The labrador sat, docile, at the Snake Boy's feet.

Jesus sits up with red hair in a bright gold throne. He's long and thin with nails stuck in his feet. When he moves, he cries because he has been so hurt. He just keeps dying. Every day, the nails dig into him, but he keeps living. It's so painful. It'd be better just to die and get it over with. But he's in pain because the world's a shit hole. He can't stand it. That's why he's in pain.

Some days he walks into heaven to see his kids. He plays with them. They are all the Good folks. And sometimes he goes to see the Sinners, and he smiles at them. He wants them to say Sorry Jesus.

The world's a shit hole. It's dark and cold, but Jesus takes you up away from it all. He sits you on his lap and plays with you, like a puppy. He has lots of pets. My dad is one of his pets. The Snake Boy said.

The fat man, Jake, told him to shut up.

One day, when dad, my new dad, took me to church, I heard angels. My mum ran away with Jesus, when I was little. Dad was jealous. I saw my mum standing in the church with wings. You don't believe me, but I did. She flew down with her golden wings and said she was in pain, with Jesus. She was dying. I asked her to stay with me, but she said no. When I told my dad that Jesus took my mum and dad, and I want to kill him, he put me in the kennel with the dogs.

The pickup truck took an eternity to reach the Pennington farm. Night smothered everything except for the Snake Boy. He was nurtured by the night, grew lustrous in its darkness. His voice went to my stomach and made me sick. Mrs. Pennington, thin with the face of a fat woman, such thick-jawed masculinity, was flustered and friendly. Her husband was asleep. She offered us a bed for the night and thanked the Lord for something. We were put in a room with a large wooden cross, a bed, and some plastic landscapes (the mountains of Switzerland indented, to make them look "real").

The Christ on the wall was looking sorry for himself. The Snake Boy clung to Mrs. Pennington's skirt and seemed suddenly to be in fear of us. He watched as she fussed around the room. And then, when she closed the door, all hell broke loose. Adam wept. He knelt on the bed, buried his head in the pillows, put his hands round his forehead (as if posing for some sculptor, some Rodin in the wings would have liked the completely expressive pose), and the Christ on the wall looked on, in exquisite pain.

I told Adam to sit up. Get a grip on himself.

He told me that he couldn't stand the sight of the boy. It made him despair. "The junk they've put in his mind. He's got nothing now. No mom. No dad. Just some junk ideas, not even myths, just some sick ideas they've drummed into his head. He doesn't even have his *own* mind," said Adam.

Adam turned round and lay on his back, staring at the Christ. He said that there was nothing left of the Snake Boy. He was a complete victim. He was ready for any junk that the society could sell him. He had no way of stopping the dirt from coming in. Steve McQueen and Jesus were one and the same. Deities, all of them. But none of them would save him from his lot, stuck in the kennels in some white man's farm.

Adam lamented, why, when they're poor and hungry, motherless and fatherless, orphans of the earth, why do these white folk try to own their minds? Give him love, hold his hand, don't give him those sadistic myths of Christ. Give them an education, don't give them lies.

"That's why I'm here, I suppose," said Adam, calming himself, holding back his emotions a little, getting a grip on himself.

"I came here because Blackfoot has something to offer. It's not just the land he wants to get back. That's a media game. He does it to gain attention. Stages events. That kind of thing. No. It's their culture he wants to get back, not that I understand half of it. Not even the beginning of it. But Blackfoot would want a kid like this one to be with the tribe. Learn the tribal ways, not be stuck in some house with Christs everywhere, and the kennel for punishment."

I told Adam that no particular kind of culture gives a kid love. Do the tribal ways guarantee the Snake Boy a mind?

The night was hostile. The wind had come up, as it does on the plains. Suddenly it whips up the land, each blade of grass beats against the next, like spears endlessly at war with each other. I imagined the yellow-black stalks doing this to each other all night. Adam's face remained strong when he wept, for sorrow was part of his beauty.

"I must tell Blackfoot about the kid," he said.

So he's staying on. The Snake boy will make him stay on. Now it seems that he just can't leave. He's tied to Blackfoot, will find any reason to hang around him. (I hate the Snake Boy, despite his sad lot. To me, he's not quite human.)

And in the morning, I looked out of the window and the dogs were there and the Snake Boy was there, waiting for me on the small lawn, waiting for me with those evil eyes, waiting to kill me, I saw it in him.

Down at the kitchen table, Mr. Pennington ate omelettes. Mrs. Pennington threw one after the other slimy omelette on his plate, and he wolfed them down, angrily. He told us that we were lucky to be on their farm (Thank the Lord) because we could have been caught trespassing (Wasn't Adam the lawyer for Blackfoot? He recognized his face). So, talking of trespassing, why not drop the case (Praise the Lord) and let there be peace? Mr. Pennington said that peace was a good thing. Sometimes you had to take up pick-axes and slay your enemy, but the Good Lord preferred it if you didn't. Go thou therefore in peace, said Pennington. Go thou amply peaceful. Mrs. Pennington smiled proudly. "Praise be to the Lord," she kept muttering, occasionally throwing more coffee into everyone's mug. The mugs had little mottos on them in italic print. *LOVE THY NEIGHBOR AS THYSELF* was mine. Adam's had *TO HIM THAT HATH IT SHALL BE GIVEN*. And on Mrs. Pennington's mug was *KNOCK, AND HE SHALL ENTER*.

"And so the Lord came into our house," said Mr. Pennington, "and took away Standing Bear."

"Who is Standing Bear?" asked Adam.

"A fine young man, loved by all, Abe's father. A nice Injun, you find them now and then. The boy's father was killed, taken up into the arms of heaven just like that, sudden like. We paid for the burial since Standing Bear had not one dollar to his name. Not even a dime to his name. And the boy had lost his mother at birth. So the Lord said, 'Take the boy unto yourself, and be to him as a father.' We were going to church on Sunday morning. Vividly in my mind I see it. The Good Lord came down into the pickup truck and said 'Let him be unto thee a son.' So we got out the adoption papers soon after and adopted the boy."

"Do you have any children of your own?" asked Adam, like a policeman.

"No. None of our own," said Mrs. Pennington.

"The boy's father was standing by a combine harvester, drunk, and the driver didn't see him. He was mowed down with the corn. Nothing was left of him. Like a head of corn, he was taken, just so casually. There was an investigation. But he was drunk, so they knew it was his fault. Who in their right mind stands by a harvester? Only kids have done it. A little girl was killed only last year by her father. He didn't know she went to surprise him, to say hello when he was harvesting. The Lord took her, pretty little thing," said Mrs. Pennington with tears in her eyes.

In between earth and heaven was death. Life was merely a moment in their eyes, a moment of transition to a better life, to golden mansions, white lambs, airport music. I didn't say that. Mrs. Pennington did. She told us that her father, a German from Köln, a baker whose father was a baker too, came back to her a few days ago and told her what it was like in heaven. He particularly liked the music, she said solemnly. They play music all the time. There are huge fields, like in Gettysburg, but no hail storms, just blue skies and pretty clouds.

"Not a magnificent place?" asked Adam with sarcasm. "He didn't say it was different? Turbulent meetings, dreamlike meetings in every time zone? Past and future? Something magnificent surely? Ideas bred between souls that had never met before from all centuries. Constant fertilization? That would be nice."

"No," said Mrs. Pennington. "It was a nice quiet place, just filled with the people you know. The good souls. There was room for everyone. But the bad ones were in hell. My father never saw them though. Bless his soul."

"So you adopted the boy — legally?" asked Adam, like a judge.

"Yes," said Mrs. Pennington firmly.

"Can we drive you to your car?" asked Mr. Pennington. "It's Sunday. We're late for church."

"And the case?" asked Mrs. Pennington. "Why pick on us. We don't want the publicity," she added sadly. She stood up, and her breastless body and thick ankles, huge feet and thin calves, made me pity her. Did her husband deny her his bed? What had made her so desiccated?

"It's a matter of principle," said Adam. He averted his eyes from the table.

"But the plains is filled with burial grounds. You can't even see them. For all we know it's one of their myths. One of their lies. Injun lies. Magic and such. Black magic. You never know. We're hard-working people. We don't drink. We don't go troubling others. We got their best interests at heart. We know what's best."

"Let's not take more of your time," said Adam, standing up.

"It's superstition," said Mrs. Pennington. "Believing the land's filled with ancestors. My grandparents came here and worked hard for every inch of land. Every acre. When they'd made enough from the bakery they bought themselves a small plot of land. They didn't just say, 'This land's mine, I'm gonna take it,' just like that."

Mrs. Pennington explained that the Indians thought that you got a good life by sitting around and drinking. No. They were wrong. If you worked hard, you made good. You paid for a nice big stone slab to put your ancestors in. And you owned it. You go there to pay your respects. You don't stick your ancestors where no one can tell they're there, and then complain because people bought land where your ancestors were. They don't know how to look after their own, said Mrs. Pennington. They don't know the right place for things either. Mrs. Pennington laughing coyly made a joke about a woman's place being in the kitchen and her husband listened to her intently, proudly. He didn't seem to care that Adam was fidgeting, wanting to leave. I sat there, silently, but noticing this time that I had become an observer. Even Adam seemed to be far away from me. But rather than making me feel lonely, this sense of being "out of reach," of not being on the line, made me feel drugged with some painkiller. I felt that nothing could touch me. I felt I had been forever in this place with the talk of death and heaven, the killing eyes of the Snake Boy, the endless cornfields etching a material infinity, the Indian ancestors crawling everywhere in an undefined graveyard. The Penningtons said they held sway over the earth and heavens and so did the Indians. Here in this land people looked out at the vast spaces and said they inherited all space and time. Here, in God's country, these people etched out a picture of existence and fought tooth and nail for it, with the help of a few words like heaven and hell, old words from so many centuries, misused words with a hundred thousand meanings, vague words, such damaged tools. I swam in this strange sea of faith with my double nature, wanting to know such faith, but delighting in the otherness of Adam's mind and my own, knowing we questioned, we did not take for granted the old words of the land.

Adam stood up, but Mrs. Pennington was oblivious to him. She kept talking. It was a sin to pick on innocent folk, and those that do it will be punished. "The wrath of the Lord," said Mr. Pennington, and then stopped suddenly. He had forgotten the rest of his sentence and just repeated "The wrath of God."

Adam contained his fury, shook Mrs. Pennington's hand, thanked her and said goodbye. And then he stood there, perturbed, and smiling, as if trying to work out some simple puzzle.

"I don't know where we are," he said slowly.

"I'd guess you're a good twenty-minutes drive from your car," said Mrs. Pennington, "if Abe's been tellin' the right road to us."

There was a silence during which Adam waited to have the strength to ask the Penningtons for a lift. He couldn't bring himself to ask for help, and they waited, basking in the conflict in his expression. Later, Adam told me that he was going to ask them for a map, so we would find our way home; but he asked for a lift, instead. "Those terrible conversations about God", he said, "remind me of being a child, with Dad trying to lay Judaism on us, without even believing a word of it himself. So all he taught was his skepticism. Such a brilliant guy didn't realize, you teach emotions, not just the facts, to a child. Perhaps there are no facts in childhood, except what one felt," said Adam when we were driving in our own car. "Perhaps it's the same in adulthood," I said, not making a statement, just wondering about the question. The fields were good to reflect on, so abstract were their shapes whizzing with edges torn by speed past the window.

Adam wanted something truly American, something solid and quiet and plastic, something you could find anywhere in America, a McDonald's preferably, but a Wendy's would do or a Kentucky Fried Chicken. He wanted no more bars and cornfields, nothing too particular, nothing with personality. When he was a kid growing up in Boston he would escape from the book-lined, mahogany-furnished living room, the sweet smell of his father's pipe, the polished smell of the wood, all shiny and filled with nature's veins and time. He'd get away from the intensity of conversations, the long intervals of silence after his father spoke, and they waited, all of them, trying to understand, hoping a moment of thought would let the thoughts sink in. Father spoke about God and politics. Wave-lengths and sonar beams and moons dancing. It tired him out. So he went to McDonald's. Now, in Manhattan, he'd drive out of the city, New Jersey was best, and sit for hours in the plastic chairs, eating a burger and ice cream.

He told me of the Snake Boy's loneliness and told me of his own. How the kindliness went sour, like old milk, from his father's face and made him cry with fear. How visitors would come to watch his father, dropping a casual look at him, like a cat found strolling around their living room. Adam said he knew how it felt to be filled with another's metaphysics, crammed full with world views till one's head spins. Whether it's Christ and heaven or Martin Buber, who cares? At a certain age, it leaves no room for thoughts, except the ones of rebellion, the pain of having to hide from what is given to one, in goodness, the sense that one's self is turning sour the kindness on one's father's face. It was his fault, fully. He was to blame, and then it was his father's fault; like a seesaw, blame fell, weighted with his full being from one to the other, never quite resting on either side.

But it happened, nonetheless, that his insides, like a stuffed turkey, were filled with his father's brilliance. He knew about Marx and Swift, Tennyson and Fourier, Hegel and Sartre by his adolescence. He was alone in that, too, in school. He was the only one who swam like a fish, brilliant and dumb, able to feel "Le silence de ces grands espaces infinis." He alone was able to look at the Pascalian emptiness in the sky. Man without God, Man without Soul was nothing, worse than a fly crawling on a carcass. For without a soul, the world *was* a carcass, dead to one's touch. He saw the emptiness, like a visionary, etched in the night sky, out of his window looking on the Boston Harbor. Time was nothing. He was in the present and the past, an old man and a boy at the same time. But his little thoughts felt too small. "My thoughts about chewing gum and blowing it up in bubbles, my thoughts about pulling my trousers tight so they left a ring round my waist like a scar from war." He was a pirate. But that was too childish, it seemed, shameful not to think his father's grand thoughts.

McDonald's would be an antidote to all that. We drove for half an hour and found a Perkins. It would do.

"America is miraculous," I said, to change the topic away from his father. "One minute you're an outsider. A few seconds later, be you black or white, English or Arab, you walk into a Perkins, order a burger and fries, and Diet Pepsi, and you're like everyone else, indulging in a sensual democracy."

"America absorbs everyone and everything," said Adam, "even father. Not that anyone ever understands a word he says. But because he's a genius, they listen with servile bated breath."

"So, shall we leave now? Drive to a ranch? Go riding through Wyoming?"

"I've been wanting to talk to you about dad. Our dad," said Adam. "Your surrogate dad, at least you'll admit that?"

I said nothing, but Adam was almost right. I was grateful

to his father for all sorts of actions, all the ways he'd helped me tirelessly, endlessly, sensibly in my career, but it was his love for me that made my arrival in Boston like the beginning of a new era.

"I want to talk about us," I said feebly. "Don't we count? Don't we come first? Why is the Snake Boy or Blackfoot always first on the list, and not us. Why is it someone who could get any old lawyer who comes first, and not me who loves you?"

"I take after dad," said Adam coldly. "Always giving to those I don't know. Always helping a colleague but never my own son."

"He loves you," I said.

"He loves *you*," said Adam feverishly. "He chose to love you. Not me. He ended up with me. He made do with me. I'm not quite what he wanted. I'm not a stuffed turkey now, stuffed with his ethics and ideas. I'm not brilliant, like him, more mediocre, a mind that's good for law. But I care. I can really put myself out for people. Not just a bit of help here and there. What he did for you was easy, getting your green card, getting your paper published, getting you a teaching job. It took a few hours of his time. Not much for someone you love. Not what I do for Blackfoot, or what I'll do for Abe. No. I give myself to people. I really feel about the American Indians. I'm not just locked up in some ivory tower helping people who live in my ivory tower."

"You are like Joe," I said. "Always putting yourself out, always trying to help the underdog, be it Blackfoot or Abe."

But I saw the underdog, not as a victim but as a devourer. I saw the Snake Boy's eyes trying to kill me, wanting to wish away with those eyes Adam's love for me. I felt possessed by him. He had entwined himself round our love, to kill it, a weed taking the water and soil from us. I felt he held death in his hands, casually. For the Snake Boy, death was a worm in a glass jar, a moth caught fluttering in his trap.

I'm frightened of having a child like that. It was a crazy idea, but I thought it and tried to hide it simultaneously. The image was more frightening to me than the idea of my own death. Perhaps it had been brought on by Adam comparing the Snake Boy's loneliness to his own. So which bits of people get passed on?

Which unknown self rises in a new baby? The lonely self? The selves that pass untouched by thought, but flow like dreams into another's being?

I thought all this as we made love, back in the Stonberg's guest house, weary and almost pleased to be coming home, back to the site of all our worries, to sleep on it together. I thought how small the gestures are that make a child, how sometimes it could pass for just a thrill, over so fast, the act of making love. How bodies touch, sometimes, resisting sensation, as they did then. Too much to take now that Adam's father and my past lovers walk so free now as we made love, filling my mind with thoughts other than Adam. For in Adam's mouth I saw his father's, and in his desperation as he held me, sweating, I saw the Snake Boy, and in his lovemaking I saw our child, and wondered if it would be Joseph's child, hold his features, smell of him, and have his mind. And though I was making love with Adam's body, his father's presence was there, in the conflict between them, the torment that appeared in Adam's face was a sign of them talking, talking away as we made love. So sensation went. Our love for each other went too, exiled by my thoughts. Adam didn't notice, it seemed. He smiled, kissed my forehead, and said he loved me.

He said softly and a little sadly that, if I wanted to, I should go home, but he would stay on to help Blackfoot and the Snake Boy. He said it wasn't really anything to do with me (and I disagreed), it was his cross to bear. His intuition, his guts, his mind told him he had to help. "You are given special moments in life, where life is offered to you for you to act on. A lot of the time, it's as if nothing happens. You chug along happily or unhappily with no opportunity to see yourself differently. But sometimes you can mold yourself through an event. It was partly selfish," Adam continued, "but it didn't matter. These American Indians were the victims on whom America was built. Their souls are still there, with the same culture, be it clever or foolish, instructive or hermetically sealed to the outsiders. It didn't matter. This is a problem in my backyard. I'm a little nationalistic," said Adam. "Not much. But this is my American problem, not yours. You have other problems in England."

"This is where all the sentimentality comes from. All that sickness of feeling, all those lies we tell ourselves about ourselves. This is the root of our sentimentality. Because we've forgotten we killed, almost killed a whole people. In these great farmlands, American farmlands, God's country, in our stupid belief in our own pure-souled goodness, our self-righteousness matched with our guilt, in all that whitewashing of our past lies our sickness. No one comes here. You saw the roads around Wounded Knee. Dust tracks," he said, "made of old bones and the dust storms of the thirties. People don't want to come here. What is there? Just a memory of our roots. Just a dirt track reminder."

He paused, exhausted. "The breast of America is here. I wanted you to see it. This is where our food comes from, but it's not sensual. There's nothing pleasurable about the arrangement of towns, the colors of buildings. It's Puritan through and through. Completely Germanic. Nordes of some sort built it. Vikings," he said, and laughed.

"The Penningtons want to own the soul of America. If you let them have their way, their illogical, crazy way, their Heaven with supermarkets, their Hell with Red Indians, if you let them try to turn the Snake Boy white, you're letting the soul of America die."

You're just like Joe, I thought, but didn't say it, for he felt that by helping the Blackfoots and Snake Boys he was distinguishing himself from his father and improving on him. That was fine and necessary. Catching myself feeling like a mother towards him, knowing better than him and keeping it quiet, made me uncomfortable. Would I spur on his growth by being silent?

So, it came out. How he was merely repeating his father, and that we should leave and be together. But Adam's eloquence had made him strong, fired up with pride. His sense of purpose had returned, and he said that I couldn't really sway him. By helping the Indians against the whites he would eventually end up helping the whites. Adam had seen Heaven in a grain of sand. Everything fell into place, and he slept calmly and late into the morning.

CHAPTER

For the next few days, Adam went his own way. He left for long walks with Marta and Blackfoot, drove over to the Tribal Council meeting, alone, and went hunting with Bobby. He did it quietly, with a sense of purpose, and only gave me snippets of information about the meetings. He was building a case, he said, but I had no idea whom it was against and whom it was for. It was a case, anyhow, something legal that required time. He reminded me of a small boy playing at Cowboys and Indians. He would stride around, a bit swaggering, a bit comically, and I watched but kept my distance. I didn't want to leave him here, alone, fearing he would lose his head, commit himself forever to some crazy scheme, to spite me and his father. I was convinced that Adam was trying to hurt himself, trying to make himself ridiculous, a figure of fun. For that would pain him most, to be laughed at. But I didn't mock him. I waited, driving in Marta's Land Rover through the fields, not knowing where one farm ended and the next began. It was all the same to me, endless colors and shapes, shaped by the movement of the Land Rover.

There was nothing drab about all these earth tones when the sun was out. Light breathed life, shadow and depth, wild endlessness of movement that took my breath away. Sheer beauty kept me company. The earth seemed sad, but good, gracious and perfect in its beauty, sad in its emptiness, as if man would have added greatness to this place. But here, man's things were merely stark: tools and machines, bright red and green, the odd tiny airplanes left dotted on the land, the grain silos, and an odd church here and there, and those cold blood red barns next to the ranch-style houses.

Cold too were the perfect straight lines of trees that had been made by settlers to halt the wild progress of the winds across their fields. For the wind could tear out crops, send dust into the roots, push the grasshoppers into the ear of the corn to die. It would soon be autumn, and some of the fields were thick black loam, planted with seedlings of winter wheat that was barely green, just a whisper of green above the soil. I loved the thick blackness with its heavy furrows like the brush of a Van Gogh, heavy with fertile soil. The earth was shiny there, glorious in its dirt, but dirt was full of new life. These deep black spaces offered a respite from the cleanliness of the rest. One early evening I saw stars chalked so palely against the denim blue sky. I was lost, too, needing to find some signs in the land to comfort me, and I did. I saw so simply imprinted in the black fields the tunnel of blindness that Adam had fallen into, and the green shoots as invisible signs that new life would grow from it.

When I thought of Adam, driving and driving in circles around and around the area he had chosen to play out his madnesses, I thought of a young man who now seemed to be in my past. Although we were still together, still talking and still making love, it seemed that Adam was merely a memory, a shadow of himself, for the rest of him was now owned by Blackfoot and Marta and Abe and the others. The drama had molded him into a person without doubts. He had made up his mind. His certainty was frightening to me, for he held it at the expense of his sensitivity and intelligence. He had begun to talk in slogans, like a politician.

I knew, in some way, that his certainty came as a weapon to fight me off, as a warning to me, not to dissuade him. There was nothing to discuss anymore, just certainty to show off, commitment to flaunt, and a singlemindedness to pursue, intently. Joe was like this, with his ideas. But his ideas were based on doubt, not a demagoguery. Adam would talk about "making big inroads today on the case," or would say, "No doubt about it, we'll show 'em, we'll win hands down." Everything had become "great." The coldness of the fields was "great." The stern greyness of the clouds was "great." The evil wrinkles of the Badlands were "great." My loneliness was "great" too. But the word was used really to shut me up. It meant: "Don't go into details, don't tell me how things actually feel, just keep life on the surface. That's how it'll work well between us, if you don't delve."

But my look was one that Adam knew. I couldn't help it. My eyes saw into him. They are big and penetrating and those little inflexions of feeling came out in the slight questioning in my eyes, my feeling for him that made me look sad from time to time. I didn't need to say much because my eyes told Adam what I knew, and he wanted to hide from me. He turned away as if burnt by my stare.

So, when I looked at Adam, in the morning, as he stood in the rays of cool, pale sunlight, in the whitewashed bedroom with just a bed in it and a lamp on the floor, in this pure landscape, in the softness of early rising, he was already on show. He whistled as he shaved. He smiled at me. (Adam wasn't one to be cheerful on rising.) Our easiness together, the way we'd at times lie around, saying nothing, feeling each other's presence, dreaming in the unspoken close space that we were making together, all that natural ease had gone. Adam made love as if trying to burrow a hole into me. Exhausted, he'd kiss me good night, worn out by the effort, as if I had not opened myself to him, as if he had no space inside me.

It was not all bad. I exaggerate. He drove me down to Wounded Knee one day, and he asked the guardian to open up the loftlike space inside one of the two churches, with its sparse wood frame and a few metal chairs. And we sat, in silence, smelling the warm wood and the smell of worship. The sunlight smashed violent color into the stained-glass windows depicting Christmas. There was the baby in the manger. The Three Wise Men. The Christmas tree. We smiled at each other. A natural smile of pure delight. Both of us marveled (and we both saw the wonder in each other) at the naivety of the images. The guardian left us in peace, thinking perhaps that we were praying and perhaps, in our way, we were. For delight, mutual delight, seemed to have fallen upon us, despite ourselves. It was as if the world had taken us up in her hands and shocked us out of our shells. The light had smashed through the glass, but was soft now, with little confetti daubs of blue and red reflected on the shiny pine floor. Afterwards, we walked out to the graveyard on the hill at Wounded Knee, enclosed by pale grey barbed-wire fences. I told Adam how I felt.

"It would be nice to belong like that," he said. "So easily. To belong in the world without making a place for oneself. Just to have it like Blackfoot wants. Just to be in it, easily, with others."

Then he walked away to examine the names on the gravestones, letting me know that he wasn't to be disturbed. He bent down on his hands and knees in the undergrowth, examining a chipped tombstone. The slab was surrounded by bricks that acted as a frame, and tiny red and white roses (that must have been put there that day, for they were like buds, unopened and strong-petalled with young sap) were placed under the wooden cross that had been planted at the top of the tombstone, a recent addition. It was as if someone had decided to mark the tomb as a Christian grave, as an afterthought. Adam's shadow fell over the grave so I couldn't see clearly the name until I was right over him. It read:

MATHILDA BLACKFOOT STANDING BEAR
1949 — 1982

Two Indian women were sitting on the wall surrounding the graveyard, humming. The clouds were large and moved quietly, pushed by the wind. I could hear a lament in the sounds of the grass rustling in the transience of the clouds moving and changing shape, and in the gravestones, those paltry dumb reminders of a person's presence.

I bent down to kiss Adam. "If you stay too long in these wide places, you go mad," I said. "There's too much sky, reminders of dying, the sadness of it all." I told Adam that we place death in the wrong place, here in the earth, the body, strait-jacketed by the heavy earth, silenced by the heavy door of a stone slab that never opens. We shouldn't come here to look for the living once the body has gone and served its purpose and been given back to all living things for them to feed off. That is the smallest way that the soul gives back to us, feeding the corn seeds.

"It's all wrong," I told him, "coming here, like a vulture to feed off the smell of death. It's no way to learn from the dead." I wanted to tear him away from here, from his easiness amongst the gravestones, for his lack of fear scared me. But he gave me his cheery smile, like a newscaster recounting murders with that strange, excited tone they have.

"I've got what I came for," he said. "Standing Bear, Abe's father, was mowed down four years after his father died. His wife was Mathilda, died in 1982 from drunk driving (so they say). But you can see from the grave that she was related to Blackfoot — Blackfoot's sister to be precise. So Standing Bear died in 1988, mowed down casually like an ear of corn, leaving Abe, the Snake Boy, Blackfoot's nephew."

Adam paused. "You get the point, don't you?"

"No," I said.

"That Blackfoot has a great case," said Adam. "A great case. He doesn't know how good his case is. It's watertight. Perfect. So *neat*."

"Because Abe is Blackfoot's nephew?"

"Because the boy was never adopted. I checked the records. The Penningtons kept him on without asking the law. Like they said, God came down into their pickup truck, and that was enough for them. But they lied to us, those God-fearing souls."

Adam smiled at me. "I can't say much more," he said. "I've got to keep quiet, but it's coming together, it's making sense. The case will be watertight, no holes in it, just shaped perfectly, like a Greek vase or something."

"Adam, you're crazy," I said.

"The deeper you get into it, the more sane you become. You see how the law's twisted in these parts. The migrant workers, Indians mainly, got no rights. If I were killed like that, in some accident, mowed down by a harvester, there'd be an inquiry. Do you think my kid, if I had one, would live on under the roof of the people who killed me? The wealthy get their rights, and the poor don't in this country."

"The Penningtons didn't kill Abe's father. It was an accident."

"Perhaps," said Adam, "but who knows? Did anyone ever ask? Were there witnesses?"

"And what does Blackfoot think?" I asked, surprised to find myself calling on Blackfoot as an ally in my fight with Adam.

"He kept it all from me. Perhaps through fear, who knows? Perhaps the Penningtons threatened him. Perhaps he brought it up at some Tribal Council, and they didn't want to pursue the matter. Who knows? Perhaps it never occurred to him that the Penningtons might have murdered Standing Bear so as to get his kid. Who knows? Perhaps he knew," said Adam, rubbing his eyes as if waking from a dream.

"I've gone too far," said Adam, "to leave it now. You know, some people distort the truth to save themselves from too much pain. Thus Blackfoot told himself the Penningtons desecrated his ancestors' graves. Something nice and abstract, but almost right, almost on the mark. What if the Penningtons had desecrated, that's to say, destroyed the life of his recent family? He said — don't you see — those Penningtons had been trying to kill the *souls* of his *ancestors* when in fact they killed the *soul* of his *brother-in-law* only a year ago. People think we live out what's in our past, Freud did anyhow. Didn't he? But look at this! Blackfoot's mind had pushed the present into the past, so as not to deal with the pain."

Adam was almost back to his old self. The anguish was there, the desperate wish to make himself understood. But something had changed. It was his certainty. He knew, without a doubt, that he was right. He was not interested in questioning his own motives. All that had gone, the self-searchingness I loved.

When a part of someone goes, where does it go to?

Who took it?

Did the black loam take it? Did the church take it back when we were sitting there, in awe? Did the inanimate want something human for itself? Would the light in the church mellow and smell sad because of Adam's doubt?

Where had it gone? Back into himself, was the doubt gnawing him, stuck under a stone slab as if dead and silenced?

"You remind me of the Penningtons," I said. "It's that certainty of yours that's chilling me."

Adam laughed. "You've just never seen me close up when I'm at work," he said. "This is how I am."

CHAPTER

13

But Adam was not himself. He seemed to be giving himself out, and losing himself as he gave. Every action of his wore him out instead of replenishing him. The Badlands were taking his soul into themselves, back into the wrinkled grey matter of their mud-caked, wrinkled hills, dipping and rising so precipitously that there was no room to walk, here on the prize piece of Badlands where the tourists came. It was as if the skull of the earth had been crushed open and the brain cells left on view. For the earth had a mind, and we were seeing it now. The tourist buses let out only a few straggling tourists, some Japanese, and a few Americans, kids, families, video cameras and bicycles. Adam had wanted to drive here, stopping off at the bar in Interior, and this time we had no problem, for Adam did not kiss me, feed me, or show any sensuality in his moves towards me. He just talked about Abe, and went backwards and forward over the "evidence."

And now he had taken me back to the evil mud of earth's mind. This land was once sand, wind-blown. And then, when the rain came, it grew thick, and new winds came to etch out lines into the mud. That was how the story went. But it looked as if it had always been there. It looked older than man, part of a dream that gave birth to reptiles. Then man followed, much later, out of the sea, far from the life-giving depths of water, where creatures drank new shapes and became all sorts of embryos dancing from womb to womb. But this earth was an evil creature, stifling life, for in the sand only a cactus here and there can grow. There is nothing for man to eat here, and nowhere to take shelter, for this place dates back to a time when there was no need of man, when his doings were not felt on the earth and no one missed him. The birds weren't around either. There are places on earth that make one feel less than unwanted. And we see them with fear, for these histories witnessed our complete annihilation, they witnessed a time before we were born, some would say a time before God.

And I imagined living then, in a place that was so strange to man, with no signs of his own making, no homes, no tamed animals, and no tools. Just the cold elements and the hot elements, wind and fire, love and hatred, blasting through one, hunger and satisfaction, and the terrible dreams of the Badlands, places worse than the wide plains, these fearful places of a hostile mind. It was easy to imagine it here, arriving, first man and woman on this earth.

"What are you thinking?" asked Adam suspiciously. And I told him, almost word for word, my thoughts, as we walked through the special path that had been made through the miniature mounds of Badlands territory. It was off at the side of the huge mountains that dipped, cut in two, like the waves parting in the Red Sea, frozen now in time forever, and so grey. We picked our way, carefully, and where there was no natural path, they had added stone slabs and small pointers to show the way. Now we were in it, surrounded on all sides by the dipping of these sand hillocks. Some were edged and crenelated, like a dinosaur's back, others were peaked with waves, and some were like canine teeth— sharp pointed, ready to bite.

Adam looked disdainful.

"Just as I thought," he said. "You'd find something that sounds good, something unreal. Don't you realize that here is where the dead souls walk? Where Abe's Dad and Mom walk? And the Lakota say the dead souls from Wounded Knee congregate here. Almost a whole people killed. That's why it feels like a concentration camp. You just sense the dead, the genocide. The cruelty of the place. Can't you feel man's inhumanity to man?"

"Don't talk in slogans," I said, "like a politician."

"Can't you feel it here? Not even here? Can't you feel the

American Indian tragedy? Here where their dead souls walk and their buffalo?"

"It's devouring *you*," I said.

"They rounded them up," said Adam, pointing to the parted mountains that had been frozen in time, but it seemed as he spoke he unleashed the force of their movement, for the mountains seemed to move for a split second like tidal waves, towards us.

"They were helpless. Women and children. How could they put up a fight, with no guns and not even a stone? Can women and children fight?"

Adam's voice was crying now, broken with held tears. "Can't you hear them, sometimes in the night?" asked Adam. "I can. I can hear them in my sleep. Like the lost souls on the edge of the underworld, wandering without rest. They want my voice," said Adam.

He stared at me in fear. "Sometimes it's suffocating," he said, and he laughed, brushing aside his fear.

I said nothing. I waited. And Adam was laughing now, about something else. The tourist bus. Something I couldn't hear. It made no sense.

"What do you mean, your voice?" I asked him. "Why should they have your voice?"

Adam sat down on the sand and smiled at me, beckoned with his eyes for me to join him. He fiddled with the sand, digging his nails into it, scratching at it like a cat clawing. He yawned. He seemed to be curiously detached from his confession, miles away from the statements of fear he had made. He was a little boy day-dreaming in the sand.

"There's nothing quite like a perfect case. It's like a theorem. It fits so well, like a woman's body. Like your body, when I see you sometimes at night sleeping, softly touched by the light of these South Dakotan stars. They're icy and make your body look polished, like a statue I'm meant to worship."

Adam said that when things fit, like a jigsaw puzzle, like our bodies placed in each other, like the lost souls congregating in the grey matter of the earth, when this happens, we love each other.

The world, in its rushing frenzy or slothful emptiness, doesn't count. It fades away, dips down to the side of the earth you can't see, and you can forget about it. The dregs of experience settle at the bottom of the wine glass, and one can see one's life with joy. Even if the foundation is waste and destruction.

"That's what it's like, when you'd come home and make me dinner," said Adam. "We'd sit in that alcove window, at the gnarled table we got in an auction in Maine for ten dollars, and we'd eat together, saying nothing." He described our happiness as if it had fallen into the past and was now unreachable. "For now," said Adam, sadly, "you don't fit in. You just confuse me. You hate me for the reasons you loved me. You want me in a jealous way I've never seen in you before. Everything you do is selfish. You don't care about the Indians. You just want me, but a castrated me. A me without my mind. A me without my balls. Just some guy to make love to you. Just someone to keep you company on a mindless vacation.

"You've always found sex so important. Always needed it every night, like a drug or something. Sure, I know. I know how it feels sometimes, but now I'm slowing down, thinking about other things, not just that body of yours, not just those needs of yours to be fucked and...."

Adam looked at me angrily, but the anger creased his face in pain, like a crumpled newspaper that's had its day. His dark eyes sank into his crinkled face in a daze.

"Like you need not me but something I've got to give. Not me, in a pure state of being, but what I can get for you. Do you think that's a way to love me? Hating me when I don't give you what you want? Hating me when I'm working on this case?"

And I said, "Your case is a cheap way of giving love. It's the cheapest way to do it, giving to people you do things *to*, not *with*. It's no strain on the soul, giving so as not to love."

We said a lot of other things, dried, desiccated words of loathing. They went back and forth, the words of hatred. Blame circled like a vulture over our bodies, not knowing where to land, but I knew that blame could eat us up, destroy us, leave us with nothing, not right nor wrong. But we stopped. Something in us, perhaps a look of love in each other that flickered, perhaps exhaustion with anger, but something came to us from within us.

Adam said he was sorry. I said I was sorry. He said the Penningtons were really to blame. It wasn't my fault, or Adam's fault, the fact that we were in such a state of ill temper. "Those Penningtons set me off. Don't you remember how we found Abe? I saw a kid, stuck with the animals, treated like a dog, coming from a generation of losers. One more won't count, that's what they think. No one will notice, evil will not really be there if you can shut your eyes to it, like I do, when we're together. But you're not to blame. The Penningtons are, reminding me of evil, setting my mind to rage. But I've got the perfect case. The evidence is there, and I'll kill them with it. I'll make an example of them, show the community that Indians count, that the Indians got rights, even if some crazy white guy has to help them."

"And what if there is no case?" I asked, standing up.

Adam laughed, dismissing my comment in a friendly way.

"There might not be a case. What if no one's guilty? What if you're the one who's just looking for someone to blame?"

Adam stood up and smirked. "You don't understand the law. You never have. I'm not guilty. The prosecution is never guilty. Do you think I'm going to get in trouble for taking the Penningtons to court? Of course not. I've got a right to prosecute them, even if they're innocent."

I told Adam I wasn't just talking about the law. I was talking about his sanity. Since we'd come here, something had come unhinged. Some door in his mind had closed and another one opened. Some balance was missing, so his moods seesawed from rage to sweetness, quickly, from lovingness to vituperous despair. It was different. Before we came here, he'd stay up late working on cases. Sometimes he'd have a headache, trying to work things out. But this case had become a magnet for all meaning in life. It had become his obsession, an easy way of apportioning blame, with Adam firmly on the right side in the war between good and evil. It was easy until I was around, for I clouded the picture that Adam was making of his new world, of black and white. For one, I didn't like it, the way he was wild with certainty. But I wanted more from him. I wanted love. I wanted touch. My world was loveless like the land we stood on. Loveless and dried out and gave no food, filled with dead souls from the past, like the Indians said the Badlands were, filled with demons and lost souls. It might be magnificent in ways— smashed through with rainbow colors like the sunset was just then, making the Badlands shudder with life, but it wasn't with flower. The colors were maya, illusion, hiding for a moment the dead land. "If I choose to be with you, Adam, when you're like this, I'm choosing to live in these Badlands," I said. "Imagine it now, battering out a word here and there of soft sounds, of warmth. Tell me you love me now."

You do.

We fell down on the light-splattered rock, as if in a faint.

Our tongues were wet over our cheeks, the only moisture in this dead land.

When we awoke it was night, and we found ourselves under the stars in this small ravine, nestled in each other's cold arms, for the rocks gave off a chill that our blood and our touch kept almost at bay. But in it we'd touched on hope. We were bent in prayer in each other, placing ourselves in waiting for each other, in silence, so as to harbor each other's thoughts.

Adam told me that he had reached the end of the world, where man's cruelty had eaten away the land, like an acid biting into flesh. If I hadn't been there to warm him, he could have circled and circled in his mind, in despair, wanting to end it all, just lying alone in misery, hating mankind. "But that's only out of the corner of my eye now. Just a small teaspoon of despair, nothing more. I've got you, which reminds me of all the other things in life that are good."

We tried to find our way back to the entrance to the Badlands, and the stars were bright enough to show us the way. The sky was ink blue like the poison from a snake's tongue, the ink from a squid. Little candles of light showed us the dried-out soil, windbitten, the wrinkles of some dead mind that was used to emptiness, the mind of a world that didn't care about man. The force of the hurricane, the ice of the hail storm came from this mind. It was something in the way of the world, not man's fault, just in the downward tilt of the world that I saw in the night. For Adam, mankind was cruel. Here was an emblem of the concentration camp, of man's genocidal tendencies, of the annihilation of the American Indian, but not for me. There is earth and stone that defies man, but he still builds on the edge of his own annihilation. There is death that happens, naturally, not the bloody murder of wars. Here was the ice-cold indifference of the earth's mind. This I had felt in waking, even though Adam was there. I told him. And he did not mock me this time. He was quiet, trying to take in my words, as we walked back to the car.

We were late for Blackfoot, who was waiting for us in the Rosebud Cafe with Minnehaha. We had slept till midday, and still half asleep, had driven recklessly fast across the plains to meet our appointment with him. Our tiredness was made warm by a new carefulness with each other. We were not yet at ease but no matter, for at least we took each other as forces to be reckoned with, difficult as we were, different as we now seemed from each other. Our conversation of the night had divided us, not in hatred as before, but with an instantaneous sense that we were with a stranger. There was something refreshing in this, knowing that we were new to each other, to be discovered, not laden with the old motives that made us know and despise each other, distort each other, in misunderstanding.

Blackfoot had rushed to greet us with a copy of the *Antelope Valley News* and the *Argus Leader* showing the same photo of Blackfoot, standing by a grave. The headline read "BLACKFOOT'S TRAGIC GRAVE." Minnehaha sat sweetly and docile, looking at her father in adoration. Her long red hair was pulled up in a pony-tail, and she swayed her head from side to side, swishing her hair like a young filly. Father and daughter were like husband and wife, gentle with each other, from time to time kissing each other on the cheek or holding hands, demonstrating some bond they were both proud of. It made me uneasy, watching the two of them with their tongues on each other's cheeks, their hands on each other's hands, backwards and forwards, displaying this bond, almost of sex.

I sat, watching, not hearing the sense of the words that passed between Blackfoot and Adam, struck immobile on those little hands fitting so neatly into the large palms of her father, making me shudder with something like fear, and a kind of intoxication that had come over me, despite myself.

Minnehaha's eyes sank into sadness. She clutched at Blackfoot. She said no. I looked up, woken from my concentration solely on those little hands. No, said Minnehaha again, he won't. Blackfoot patted her on the head, like a filly.

"You go home," said Blackfoot. "This isn't no place for a little girl."

But she stared at him, through him, with sad, burning eyes, filled with a hostility that was meant to burn out his pupils, hurt him forever for hurting her so.

"So you knew about Abe?" asked Adam menacingly. "You knew they'd taken him illegally?"

"Your law," said Blackfoot softly. "I couldn't go causing Minnehaha pain. She hates him. She'd tear his eyes out. It weren't safe for him or her. Together under the same roof. I've seen them fighting, whipping each other. That's small play. When he came into the house to stay she was up all night moaning. I couldn't have him stay. He'd murder her."

Adam laughed. Minnehaha smiled at Adam. You see, said her eyes, I win.

Adam told Blackfoot that he had a responsibility to his nephew. How could he stand that the boy be brought up like a white man, stuck in the kennels for punishment each time he said no. And what about the American Indian traditions? Didn't he care that the boy would be brought up white, never know his heritage? Was all this stuff about Indian rights a hoax? Adam held the photo of Blackfoot up the light. Is this all it is? A chance to have your picture in the papers?

"Don't think I'll let it go. Just like that, pretend you have a case. Your case mattered to me. But don't think I'll just be used for your ego."

Blackfoot stood up. He was very calm, sure of himself.

"I can't talk straight in front of her. You're crazy to ask me to talk now. You don't know her."

Minnehaha smiled again, proudly. She wins again, I thought. "Then send her home," said Adam, "now."

Blackfoot stood up.

"I'll do things in my own time. Adam, don't get forceful with me. It's no way to behave."

I was impressed with Blackfoot. He made Adam look small, bullying, even though Adam was fully right to have it out, but he needn't talk down, command the man to move to his whims.

"I'm sitting down now," said Blackfoot regally. "A round on me." The beers went round, and we all sat in silence, too many thoughts going around to feel self-conscious. It was like a family dinner, where people know each other so well you can see them daydreaming as they eat, almost mouthing their thoughts. So it was as we sat in our own worlds, not even wanting to talk to each other, except for Adam, who eyed Blackfoot with expectation.

"I tried to take the boy back," said Blackfoot after a while. He explained that Abe had a violent nature, liked killing for fun pets, plants, anything he could lay his hands on. So the house would be filled with dead mice, a snake, moths pinned to his bedroom wall, and then there was Minnehaha. He wanted to have her, rape her or something. Blackfoot wasn't quite sure what it really was. But she was scared. So he sent him back to the Penningtons. No one else wanted the boy, but the Penningtons thought they could help, through loving Jesus he'd change. And he has. He's a little nicer now. Not much. Blackfoot thought it was probably the dogs, good souls. Looked after the boy, the two dogs, nothing to do with Jesus and such. Probably the dogs who licked him to sleep, ran with him, carried his dead birds and snakes and all back to him, sat at his feet. "It was the dogs. I can't let him leave those dogs. He said he'd kill me if I did."

"I can believe that," I said. "That's what he did to us," and I told Blackfoot the story of our arrival at Pennington's farm.

"Adam's got style," said Blackfoot, "making love on the Penningtons' farm. Not that I mind they're white. Don't get me wrong, misquote me. I don't think there's nothing wrong with whites long as they don't go tellin' me where I'm at."

"Calling your bluff?" asked Adam sullenly.

He looked betrayed, angry with himself more than with Blackfoot, as if he had just discovered his own hypocrisy, his own lack of values, not Blackfoot's games. Some bond carried these two men into each other's madness. Something makes them fly off the handle at each other with so much passion. Just a moment after they seem like friends, the pain wells up, spills over like boiling oil. And then the way they can inflame each other's imagination, feed off each other's minds, helping each other—- Adam to feel in the right, to have a purpose and Blackfoot to keep one foot in sanity, in the mainstream. Perhaps I'm unfair to Adam, thinking he merely wants to be in the right. He does, but that's not what draws him into Blackfoot's web. He's immersed anyhow. I am too.

Minnehaha sat docile again, curled up by her father's side, possessive of him. The night came over me, a small blackout, like a thought washed away by another thought that obscured what I was really thinking at first. The second thought had no features and no shape, it was merely black, like a bat growing larger and larger, taking my breath. Then it went, fast as a sneeze, and I could see the Rosebud Cafe warming up with chatter and noise, and I thought of Manhattan, of the coffee shop round the corner, and compared to this, I didn't miss it.

Minnehaha smiled at Adam triumphantly. "Abe made a big mistake," she said, "getting me out of bed on the wrong foot." We didn't know what to say, so we waited for something to explain Minnehaha's comment. It was an offering, like a present she had made for us. She repeated it.

"Men make mistakes," she said, like a woman, probably mimicking her mother. She sounded serious and wise. Her expression altered in a split second, and she laughed at us.

"Abe had to go once he got on my wrong side," she said. "No two ways about it. He just had all his dead things packed up in a suitcase with him. And he went with it, with his case of bones."

"Bones?"

"Yeah, bones. He collected them. Chicken bones, really. He said he dug up his dad's bones to keep them with him. Dog bones. They weren't real people's bones. They were stuff from dinner. Like a leg of lamb, you know," said Minnehaha.

Minnehaha said that he liked skeletons. She called it "sketelons," but we knew what she meant. Things like the veins of leaves, like blood vessels, anything like a branch that fanned out and had more and more rivulets growing from it. She didn't say it quite like that, but she showed us her hand and tried to explain the shapes he liked. He wanted to put the bones together into the shape of a dinosaur, or into the shape of his dad, to put it back together again. So he killed things, took the skin (especially fish bones were good), she remembered that, and he'd catch them by hand in the lake by Marta's place and skin them alive. Then he'd dry the bones and wait for a while till they were white.

"I didn't mind that," said Minnehaha, "till he tried it on me. It made me scared when he said he'd skin me alive."

"There's always some justification for evil," said Adam.

"For killing? For the Snake Boy's killing?" I asked.

"No, for packing him off to the white man's farm," said Adam. "Always a good excuse to pass the buck, let the poor get poorer and the bereft be abandoned. Abandonment breeds abandonment. So the boy can hurt a fly. He can kill a newt, strip a fish. His killing, as you choose to call it, is perhaps just a little excessive, brought on by excessive grief, the loss of both parents, death all around him; his culture too, which could help him like a symbol of self, all that gone, and to boot, his uncle, like Hamlet's uncle, off in bed with some bitch unable to think of him, abandoning him to those ... Penningtons. Blackfoot, I'm ashamed of you. I'm dropping the whole thing. Except for Abe. I'm going back to Manhattan after I've helped the boy, even at your expense."

Blackfoot scowled at Minnehaha.

"I told you all this, didn't I? Almost in the same words as Adam, not as eloquent. But you didn't listen, did you?"

Minnehaha gasped, trying to catch her breath. She looked as if she might retch, for she went white, hid her head in her knees and rocked herself back and forth moaning.

"She gets like this when I criticize her," said Blackfoot.

Adam was looking on in guilty disbelief.

"I didn't mean to ... do this to her," said Adam.

"No, I don't neither. I don't want to hurt my baby," said Blackfoot, almost in tears.

Adam reached over and pressed Blackfoot's hand.

"So she gets like this — over Abe?"

"You can see it for yourself. Don't go asking me the obvious. *This* is obvious."

Blackfoot picked up Minnehaha and she straggled her knees around him. She clung to him, whimpering. She dug her nails into him. The shadows in the Rosebud Cafe covered her softly. It was almost beautiful, the way she fitted into her father, her little hands, her tininess made smaller by being near Blackfoot; and then all of a sudden she went limp and fell in a faint just as Blackfoot stood up, but he caught her in time, just as her limpness was complete.

There were tears in Blackfoot's eyes.

"Our family's got bad karma, man. None of us Blackfoots live together. But my baby's sick. I ain't got time to talk and explain."

Blackfoot went in a flash, with Minnehaha over his shoulder.

There was no issue in all of this for Adam. I saw him and understood him to be paralyzed by Minnehaha's show of temper. He wouldn't trespass on Blackfoot's love of her. It fell on him, like an executioner's hood, covering his eyes, making him feel that he had nowhere to go now. He couldn't risk her anger and her hysterical illness. That's what I called it, pure hysteria. I suffered from it myself in adolescence, knew that feeling of passing out, the dizzying coming of a thought that made one fall away from it, constantly skirting the full thought, day by day. But that thought was merely Minnehaha's love of her father, which became too strong when she thought she might lose him, so she hoped for love, imagined her love for him, larger than anything she had felt before. I told Adam all this as he drove in silence, partly to calm him down, for shame was on him and he wanted to hide from me in shame. I wasn't quite sure of my own words, but they put Minnehaha in her place and relieved Adam momentarily from the burden of his sense that he had caused her sickness. I wanted to give him me. I thought I could put myself in front of Blackfoot and the rest, obscuring them for a moment, so Adam could rest in me. I could be his world, like a mother and baby, if only he would rest his head on my breast and find it sufficient. I would be his world.

So I stroked his arm and felt a sense of disgrace, for I was unable to make myself felt. Adam just kept driving. We weren't going anywhere. He couldn't save Abe because it would be the death of Minnehaha, or so it seemed then, when we were fresh from her fit and Blackfoot's tears. Adam couldn't just take the boy away from the Penningtons without finding a good home for him. He kept repeating the same thought: of homelessness seeming worse than the life of an Indian kid in a fundamentalist's dog kennel.

"If his family won't take him and the Penningtons will, if the Penningtons want him ... " mused Adam, not talking to me but to himself, trying to work it out. "What does his culture matter? Just a bunch of myths that don't make sense anymore. Just a cliche I gobbled up, the one about needing your cultural roots to survive. Another of my lies to myself, unthought-out lies I believed. Did Dad really teach me this junk?" Adam turned to me and asked me the question again: "Did Dad ever teach me that junk?"

I said nothing. If I said no, Adam would think I was taking sides.

"He didn't, did he?" said Adam. "He lives in another world, where the context is larger than this. Planets, the earth as one sphere in thousands. He never got hot under the collar about being German or American or anything like that. So where did I get this junk from?"

I kept very quiet. Adam was not panicking. He was serious, grimly deep in thought. "I got it from myself," said Adam.

"From no one but me." He laughed. "I didn't get it from you, anyhow. You don't give a damn either, it seems, about your cultural roots." He spoke with cold irony now.

I remained silent, holding onto my temper, sick to death of Adam's inability to rest in my arms and trust me. I was so hurt by it then, quite suddenly, that the hurt came like a rough wind blowing me off course, lifting me up in its arms, taking hold of me. But I said nothing even as I swayed in its grip.

"Perhaps it doesn't matter at all, not one bit, these Indian rights. Blackfoot's rights to the land, Abe's right to his culture. Neither of them seem to give a damn about it anyway. I'm the only one who cares. The white man cares, like some belated guilt trip a few centuries too late, once the damage was done; but there's nothing to save really, and you can't do it for them, even if it is there to save, because it's like another kind of imposition on them. You can't pull a kid from his home and their land from some crazy religious folks. You can't just walk in and think you can change it all, like God, just change it all, not that I believe in God anyhow."

Adam rambled on like this as we drove, and I noticed that our driving now had a purpose, for I saw the buttes of Interior and realized we were leaving Pine Ridge and the Rosebud Cafe, perhaps for good. We drove on until we came to a small town. Adam stopped off outside a motel in one of the Victorian homes, splendidly white, with its own lush garden decked with orange and blue and yellow flowers so bright, with their sugary smell wafting to us.

I wanted to help Abe, I wanted to give a hand to the lonely and desperate, and the guys with imagination like Blackfoot who are stuck out here in some no man's land, like a ship sinking. I wanted to give what is best in me to them. So the world would be a better place, a small thing to do for the gift of life, just to give something back. But, you know, I wanted to feel good, to see it happening around me here and now, like a reward down from the sky from the Penningtons' God, that sort of hokey thing, so they'd all smile and Blackfoot would thank me, and Abe would have a home. But instead they all hate me. They want to use me, and then tell me just enough truth and just enough lies to suit themselves. And they hate me when I find out bits of the truth. They want me to fight for a partial truth, not caring if I end up ... reviled.

So, they revile me, find me worse than shit. My mind kills them, makes them hate me. Not that I love them, don't get me wrong, I don't love these people — Blackfoot perhaps, Marta perhaps, not Abe. But I could and I might, I might just love these people who hate me, need them in some way, need them, and love them like a family.

▲▲▲

Adam was walking in circles around the almost fluorescent intensity of the motel's garden. Flies were buzzing, a warm glow over the grass, little plastic ducks littered across the tiny pond, bobbing in the breeze, sweetest bird notes, all of it so sugary, like the smell in the air, sticky with the smell that calls the bees to mate.

In this honied place he was calmer. He kept talking, and I sat on the grass listening.

All that is good in me is reviled. Or perhaps it's not real salt-of-the-earth goodness that makes me come out here to help. I'd like to start again, be someone new, not me, who always ends up like this when I *feel*, said Adam, his voice a chorus, with so many tones in it, of self-indulgence and pain and a cloying pleasure. I'd like to start again somewhere else, try to do something good for the world, try to be more than some dumb ass living for just my own ends, some small-minded guy making money so I can buy a this or a that ... with no larger context, no view of the world further than my own back yard, uncaring.

Someone like Dad, said Adam, and he burst into tears.

I put my arms round him urgently.

"Someone like Dad," he repeated.

Adam said no more, but after he'd sobbed in my arms for a moment, we went upstairs to our floral room (pink flowers over everything, carpets and walls, and the bed, green flowers) and we slept.

It was dusk when we woke, and the room was softly grey, the pink flowers were almost greyish pink. A soft golden light sliced the room in half like a painting cut into a diptych, folded out like a window opening. That was how it seemed when I awoke, so I was not yet sure if we were still in a dream, and the feeling that had come over me seemed to be from my dream that I had forgotten. I wanted to touch Adam, but I couldn't. He had frozen me. I couldn't move. And then I awoke for real and saw Adam was looking over me, waiting for me.

I forgot you, said Adam. He stroked my forehead as he spoke, placing his lips on my cheeks.

You didn't lie to me, he said.

You .... He stopped in pain.

Why are you hanging around? I'm a jerk, not worth waiting for. Are you crazy to be with me?

And if I am? I asked. I was in tears because I loved him then, unquestioningly, just for that moment, and at others I didn't.

I thought I was crazy, or didn't think whether I loved or not, hadn't given what I was doing the apt word, and so wasn't doing it completely. Not until he asked me then, and I knew that I felt it with him, all those shifts of feeling, backwards, backwards in time as if he had shown me his childhood, taken me back into a world I had never lived in, unlocked the past. And I could see him playing on Joseph's knee, a young Joseph who looked like he does now, smelling of fame and the world, even in his own home, having that aura that women love, the unworldliness that survived the world.

I could see Adam trying to find a way into his father's mind, and failing, for father was somewhere else thinking, not quite giving himself to the boy, my boy.

Out of these two men I knew came Adam. The two of them had concocted this particular side of Adam at least, the torment I saw, the way that Adam would not leave himself alone to be simply what he was. Even in his goodness he hated himself and wondered if Joseph was really behind it all, being him, getting in on the act. This was my baby, Adam, my sweetheart to take care of, my honey to suckle, but it seemed that I'd had no part in his making, no say in this side of him, this hatred that racked him, and I suddenly hated Joseph for turning him so against himself. Whether he did it knowingly or not, and I knew that he didn't know what he did, in that delightful, abstracted way he'd walk over people's feelings, not knowing, for the planets loomed over him, like great gods to converse with, and sometimes us mortals were dull witted and unrewarding. Of course the two of them, now that Adam was no longer a baby, were responsible, but now that Adam was like a boy to me, lying nestled in my arms for me to watch over, I hated Joseph for the damage he had done, and wanted to be put back in time, so I could have been there when Adam was growing up, and give Joseph hell when he hid in his auras and clouds.

He lay there quietly, breathing softly, wrapped around me and into me, entwined, and all of me went to him in yearning, my heart and even my soul, that part of one that defies all time and space and tries to walk beyond the body; I could feel my soul stretching out, leaving myself to be in Adam.

And I felt that my body had held me down for too long. It opened out like an envelope, carrying me inside it, the meaning of me opening out like a love letter. I've loved before. This happens to me, Adam can provoke it, I reminded myself. For the feeling was carrying me off, and I saw myself losing Adam, like the rest of them, like the way one leaves one's mother and father, as if it's inevitable, so time kneads one away from love, a wind coming between our bodies, as I clung to him like water, making me slip and fall from Adam. I clung to him in my mind, but someone was kneading my fingers from his shoulders, so I couldn't hold on. And I hated Joseph in the same breath, hated him for so much, as if he had pulled me away from Adam, made Adam seem small in comparison to his august person, made me despise Adam at times, thinking Joseph knew more than him, loved harder and gave me more. But that damn job that he'd got me and all the things he'd done for me were not what Adam gave me; but I saw Adam again, and his features were there, like Joseph's, like a seal that was filled with ink, whereas in Joseph the ink was running out and had gone grey and soft at the edges. It was as if Joseph had stolen into Adam at that moment, and for me to get rid of him, I would have to rid myself of my baby, my boy, my sweetheart, my Adam. I muttered all his nicknames to him like that, and ruffled his hair and put his head between my breasts and burrowed my head into his chest, and we played.

We thought of driving straight to Rapid City through the night, and getting a plane first early morning dawn, up into the clear air, into the big city where our lives would soon wash over all this and we'd leave it behind. I could see the plane leaving it all behind, leaving no more than a dot on the horizon and then nothing, convincing us just for a morning that we had actually forgotten the lot of them, or vice versa, but at least that they were no more. Just an Indian and his divorce, just some crazed kid living with some crazy fundamentalists, just people who didn't need us meddling in their lives, deciding what was right for them or wrong. I told Adam we had no right to know. It was their life, strange as it seemed to us, held together by a fragile balance, its own ecosystem, I said (and Adam laughed), where predators and prey have their own place in the daily routine. Who are we to know that perhaps it *is* necessary that Marta leaves Bobby and marries Blackfoot, and Minnehaha lives with her mum, Angel, leaving Blackfoot behind in a new scheme of things? But it's not for us to say. We aren't there for that. A pity that Blackfoot couldn't pay Adam, because then it'd be clear. He'd sack Adam and find a guy who didn't want to find out more than the lies and didn't have his own ideas about native customs. Pity that the poor have got to put up, always the same, with missionaries or other madmen, carting their own dump truck of culture or worship or whatever they want with help. So you had to stomach their conventions if you wanted their food. Always the same, I said so lovingly, still in bed, still playful in tone, kissing Adam from time to time, sharing a beer as the night went onwards into itself, darkly.

"I'm part of the picture now," said Adam. "We're part of it!" Now that Blackfoot was planning his big event, stealing the bison from Fort Robinson, taking his horses over to the Pennington farm, reliving the old days in front of the TV cameras (if he's lucky enough to get them there), Adam said he'd be called up anyhow, people know he represents Blackfoot, and if he left now it'd look like Blackfoot had no support, no one to protect him against the law. Of course, Adam said, we could leave, dump Blackfoot right in the middle of his publicity stunt, just so it really hurts.

"But Dad wouldn't do that. He gave me something, didn't he? Out of all the things he didn't give, or the wrong things he gave me, he gave me that, some kindness, misguided as it is. So I'll use it now, Dad. It's like I see him now, dying over me, asking me, what did I leave you, son? And I could say — a lot of junk — all the stuff you didn't know you gave — I could say that."

Adam turned to me.

"You heard the guy. It's his big-time event, next week, down by Fort Robinson."

"I didn't hear," I said. "No one told me."

"Over breakfast with Minnehaha? You were there."

"I didn't hear. I wasn't listening. I was thinking of him and her, dazed by their love."

"It's big time for Blackfoot. He's getting a load of kids from Wounded Knee Elementary, some hippies from the university in Vermillion, some Indians too, Marta from the Museum and her kids. It's Blackfoot's show. I can take the rug from under his feet. Say he's a liar."

"But you won't."

"It's Blackfoot's dream. Tread gently, that's what the poet says, isn't it? Tread gently on my dreams. I forget who. Just because I'm made of sponge, got no dreams, nothing naive like this, doesn't mean I'm gonna tread on Blackfoot's dreams. He's like a kid to me, a boy, something I was perhaps before it got knocked out of me. Cleverness got knocked in at an early age. You know how pretentious I can be. I got nothing crazy like this to fight for. Before it made sense to me, before his lies, all that American Indian stuff was great. It sounded like sense, fighting for rights, being the good guy. You got my number right where it hurts, below the belt. So it became my idea. Not a dream, nothing so soft, so warm, to go to sleep on, a dream, some crazy hope that defies the lot of us. Well, I made it my idea. Blackfoot's dream, taken from all those Westerns and a bit of American Indian lore; well, you can't justify now, can you? Now that we know he's divorcing Angel and throwing that Snake Boy out, ostensibly because of Minnehaha, dumping all *my* ideas, MY ideas, can you believe it, out of the window. As if Blackfoot would defy my brilliance! My superior wit and knowledge, particularly on his life and on American Indian lore. I know better, don't I, honey? You think I should tread on his dream?" asked Adam suddenly, as if he had woken out of his frenzy and were asking a casual question.

"I don't know," I said. "You're glued to the place, to *him*," I said sadly.

My own life had left me behind. What I was here to Adam and Blackfoot didn't really count at all. I was an onlooker at best, an appendage to Adam, some kind of support at times, but what did I do here? I didn't really care about any of them. I hated them then and wanted to be with Adam, even as he was making me choke down all his madness, his Blackfoots and Snake Boys, as a punishment for being with him.

"Do you want me to leave?" I asked. "I can."

So I'm nothing, like the Snake Boy said in his very first game with me outside the Rosebud Cafe. Nothing.

I can live with it. It's just a dull sadness, nothing more. It doesn't even feel too unusual, feeling like this. I can be here without a motive, not even the wish to help. Just because I need Adam. That's no reason. I could meet him back in New York. I don't have to hang out here with him.

"You know I can leave," I said.

But I can't, not for the moment. I remember driving away from my parents one evening; I must have been eighteen. I was off to Brighton, somewhere nice for the weekend. And I went away with this bucket of tears. I felt so heavy-hearted. I knew I'd lost them, the way they spoke to me, like a stranger. I was grown up then. I'm not now. I could drive away then, but I can't now. I can feel Adam tugging at me, so I can't leave. I'll just think about him all day and night, and twist and turn on the plane leaving, wanting to be with him. But there's nothing for me here. This place renders me useless. Not even a home to clean, something to get on with while he does his work. It's like being a fly on the wall.

When I got to Brighton, I remember now, I felt so sad. I wanted to have a home. But there was no room for me to stay. You're too big anyhow to stay at home. But I'm tired. I want someone to give me a rest just for a moment, so I can get back on my feet, and then I'll face the world. Just a helping hand. But that weekend was filled with something else. Some boyfriend in a hotel room, sex late at night, and more driving. The salt air on the beach made me cry; it was winter. The man didn't like my way of showing too much emotion, about things that didn't concern me. I didn't, I suppose. Such indifference everywhere. It would be easier if I could care for Blackfoot, love him, even want him.

If I could *feel* for him.

"I'll try," I said. "I'll try."

"Try what?" asked Adam in surprise.

"Oh, nothing," I said.

"You're looking better," said Adam. "But outbursts worry you, don't they? My moments of knowing what I'm about. They come with such pain, like flame or something being thrown through me. As if I can't help but see what I'm up to. You know, it's like Dad. Just like Dad. Thinking you're doing a great job with other people, giving all you can give, and ending up being like some petty dictator, wanting YOUR IDEAS to live on. Like a genetic monster, wanting your mind to pass on its rambling brilliance to a kid, not just in general, not just the capacity for brilliance, but the ideas that make you brilliant, the very thoughts, time worn out of date, wrong for the next generation. Such stupidity from such a great man, like wanting to impregnate me with his sperm, leaving aside my mother."

17

He treated me like a girl, wanting me to receive him, be fucked by him, by his mind, so I'd just lie there passive and take in his mind. But that mind was limitless. It stretched across the worlds. At least he said it did. No escape, he said, it covered the planets, even at night when you looked out of your window and couldn't see any further than those stars, some fuzzy and some bright like icicles of gold, all of it was his domain. Other people didn't know anything about it. They just looked at it sometimes, if they went backpacking. But he lived up there, his telescopes saw the planets talking. He knew their birthdays, when they were buried and who mourned them. He knew their love life, their national holidays, and when they burnt out he smelt it, said Adam.

There was no way of getting away from him, and why should I want to? Because I was his prince. I would become him, and walk up there at night, where there were no climates, just a perfect night sky filled with cool stars, without heat or cold. Just those blessed night ways that no one knew of. It went on and on, and no one could take it from me. It was too far to go. No trains went there. Once or twice people go to the moon, but she was a whore. She lived too close to earth, not knowing how to hide from ordinary men. No one could buy those night ways. It was all his, and she was pure, she wasn't bought. She only made herself known to those who love her. Dad was her lover, he never strayed. He was faithful to her. Not to Mom. Mom went away. She was a woman. Everything reached her. She got upset. She wept and wept all night before leaving with some man, Dad said. He told me later. I saw her a lot. But Dad kept me. You know the story. I don't have to tell it again. I saw her during those weeks when she left. She was in some small apartment, it was her nest, she'd been getting it ready for years, I think. It was furnished and a little sexy, with a fur rug, and in the bathroom was a silk dressing gown, ivory silk, like skin, like flesh, so soft. When I went to the bathroom I clung to it and covered my head with it and just sat there with it. She called to me. Her voice was sad, not like the dressing gown. I wanted to take it with me and leave her behind with her sadness. The dressing gown would be soft and calm and not cry to me like she did. But I came out, and she said she'd see me next week, she'd pick me up from Dad's. I didn't ask questions. I stared at her, wanting her to hear in my silence she was hurting me. Funny, how kids can be, wanting you to hear their thoughts. And then she came back a few weeks later and stayed. She didn't leave. I don't know what happened to the apartment, nor the man. But she stayed.

"You could say she stayed," said Adam.

The way people are together, the way we spend our time together, it ebbs and flows. We touch and then fall back, as if repelled by each other like waves meeting the shore, reaching for land, and falling away from it. There's some force that keeps the balance but it's not the right force. It's not working. I'm here with Adam, but I should leave. As he spoke of his mother, I kept thinking of ending up with no life, just watching Adam's life. His mother stayed, he said. Nothing more and nothing less, a presence, with her mind elsewhere, thinking of how good it would have been in that flat with the man.

"But she wasn't all there. Sometimes she made Dad feel she was sacrificing herself for him, staying on without loving him." I knew the story, sensed it all before he spoke. He didn't need to tell me. It was inevitable. A common story, nothing unusual. It's not even sad, staying on with a man you don't love; it's so common. And then who's to say she didn't love Joseph? Perhaps it was her way of loving, not from desire, but duty. Perhaps she would have turned that sexy apartment into the same sad place after a while, once the rebellion had died down and sex had died down. She would have stayed from duty, the only way she knew, in the long term, of being anywhere. But not I. I know better, am from a different generation, can't stay on with Adam because I owe him something when I don't. We're not even married yet. No kids, nothing to make us glue ourselves in for the long haul for duty's sake.

But Adam wants the good life. I see it now. He wants something different with me. He wants it but doesn't know what it is, and neither do I: we keep falling back, like waves, sucked back into the sea, relentlessly, licking the seashore for a moment, deliciously met with, in each other, the foam like sperm giving life, a magical fluid we touch. Then it goes, and we're left, me with no life, watching Adam, and he with his Blackfoots and Snake Boys, his do-goodism and ideas, his goodness and faith. He wants it all, me and his faith, within a larger life, but it's not here yet. He can't create it yet.

"I don't know why I'm talking about Mom," said Adam. He yawned.

"I don't know if it really helps to know each other," I said.

"I'm working it out," said Adam. "I'd like to do this for a long, long while. Just sit here and tell you about it. The life back in New York seems like a sham now that we're here, talking about things."

"I don't know if it helps, talking about the past," I said. "So much that people tell you is about some kind of confession that no longer bothers them. They tell it proudly, pretending to reveal themselves, and I'm sure at one time it hurt, but now it's self-congratulating, this unearthing of the past."

I doubt if Adam cares about that silk dressing gown, or those months his mother spent in that flat in Boston. He just wants to go back to his childhood, pretend things haven't changed, like Blackfoot does, wanting to ride his horses across the plains and shoot white men down who stole his burial lands. This place does it to you. There's nothing here to distract one from the past. The emptiness of the sky leaves room for nightmares, and you feel isolated, thrown back on yourself if you come from the city and aren't used to fitting within the land. Adam and I don't know what to do with her, how to till her or hunt in her. We won't tame her, or be in her. We can't become her. She leaves us to ourselves, as we watch her, always at a distance. But you don't have to be alone here.

You don't have to live off yourself and be thrown back

into your past, like Adam is. Blackfoot showed us he knew the land differently, the way he swam in that pond, catching fish with his hands. He takes the land as if she's his. I don't even think it springs from some intellectual idea of Indian rights. He touches the land in the same way he'll make love to Marta, taking her, not caring what the law says. I want Adam to make love to me like that, just feel me with his hands, confident I'm his. I'd like him to lick every part of me, like a fruit.

So we made love. It was as if everyone was strewn on the bed around us, all our conversations of the night evoking them, and they were there in some big orgy, so drunk that they didn't care what we did. So Adam licked my feet, and the spaces between my toes, and he licked my breasts, and sucked on my nipples as if they had milk, and then he pulled open my mouth and put his fingers in, and he licked my cunt and I licked his prick, but it felt almost funny, because we couldn't keep our balance, and we had to strain to keep everything in our mouths, and we ended up laughing. But I wanted a new beginning, some kind of spring when we could feel all of each other, and each touch we made on each other's bodies would be a sensation we'd hear. It'd be a piece of music, and like making a sculpture. We'd make new sensations out of each other because we'd listen and do nothing but touch and listen. But Adam got on top of me and moved backwards and forwards and backwards and forwards inside me, you know, almost like a seesaw. I'm not allowed to do this to myself, I said. I can't just lie back, feeling cradled. But I did, and we slept quite easily. It's so easy not to feel too much.

CHAPTER

19

You can get caught in a situation and think that it's all that life's got to offer you, said Blackfoot, but *he* wasn't like that, he told us as he drove me and Marta into Fort Robinson to watch the bison. They were quite pretty from a distance, but close up they looked ferocious. Blackfoot said they were his favorite beast of all the beasts in the plains. "They're prehistory," he said, "before all those kings and queens got going and phony movements, these bison, buffalo, roamed around in great herds, the kings of the plains. We knew how to use them. But the white man came and killed them, to take away our food and clothes from us. You see, in Europe you guys thought you were above it all, civilized, not just animals, like us primitives with no castles and no mines and no cars. But then comes the Second World War, and you're worse than shit, the lot of you. All those perfumed wigs and designer clothes were nothing, just like a camouflage for evil."

Marta was stroking Blackfoot's forehead as he spoke. Against him she looked like a wilting plant, perhaps a weed twisting itself around the bark of a powerful tree. His blondness was not a form of pallor. It was like a crown, illuminating his chiselled cheekbones. His eyes were outlined with brownish eyelashes, so they looked large, almost made up. "I know how to drive these lot over to the Penningtons' farm. I'll have to do it at night when there's no rangers. I know the two guys up here, graduates from the forestry school at USD, or dropouts, I don't remember, but they didn't want a university life. I might even tell them my plans. They'd give me a hand probably, take the day off, so I could do my business."

"It'll be wonderful," said Marta. "It'll bring back *your* glory. Just imagine how it was — with the spirits of nature roaming across the plains like a paradise on earth, a garden of Eden, where man and woman just loved each other."

"Like we do," said Blackfoot firmly. "The way we do," and he stopped the car, leaned over to Marta and kissed her long and carefully on the mouth.

"Let's get out," said Marta.

It was a mellow day with orange light softening the distinction between things. The grass would be cold. My feet were bare. I put my ballet shoes back on and followed them into the grounds of Fort Robinson. No one was there, not one tourist. We walked for a while, saw some horses feeding quietly in their paddock.

"We're filing the papers," said Marta. "You know that Adam's doing it."

"Yes," I said.

"There'll be a fight for the kids. But Angel won't fight for Minnehaha. I couldn't live without her," said Blackfoot. "I need her and you. Just the two of you ... an' your kids too."

Would it all shift over so easily? Like a small migration with no bloodshed, just musical families, almost, except that Bobby and Angel would be left alone.

"I know you don't like Marta," said Blackfoot, looking at me. "But you're not a man. You don't see her breasts, so small and perfect, like two small strawberries. You don't see the way she goes with a man. She's not so good with women, I'll admit that. She's a bit standoffish," said Blackfoot, as if Marta was a possession of his whom he could sell like a horse.

Marta smiled to herself proudly.

"Her breasts 'ud drive any guy crazy. The way she wears them. Careless, like she doesn't know she's got a body. Like she throws down a mink coat on the ground, careless. She used to be nervous with me, the first times making love, didn't you?" said Blackfoot menacingly.

"Yeah, I did," said Marta.

"Then she went wild, couldn't get enough. I unleashed her. She'd never had it like that; in that body of hers it's hard. It can leave you behind. You gotta go chasing it; she's immaterial at times, so you got to grab her from the start, make her feel quick before she leaves you behind."

I liked Blackfoot.

"Not that a guy likes going round talkin' about his bed life, but I want you to know she's got fire. You can't look at her like you do, like she's some weakling. In front of Adam she is. With some guys she gets caught in a mind trip. Then you can't reach her she's so damn scared. You gotta be forceful, bring her out of herself. Then she moves like the wind."

I wanted Blackfoot.

I wanted him; just then a shudder went through me, but I laughed at myself simultaneously, thinking of the noble savage I had turned him into, a Lawrentian figure who would make me come alive. A man who would feel deeper than I felt my own desire. But it wasn't that alone, or his eyes, or the way he walked so gracefully and the sun falling on his hair, illuminating it, absorbing somehow the stateliness of the Fort Robinson grounds, so he looked as if he owned it.

Blackfoot went rambling on about women. There was no fear of punishment in his voice, no sign of anxiety or even the slightest shame as he spoke of Marta's lust, or the way he bathed in it, making her his. He was still stately, growing taller as he walked backwards and forwards, recounting her breasts again, and now her thighs, so slim and white, almost deathly white. And I thought again that he was doing her a favor, this pale outcast, this white woman from a dead civilization. (I thought of Christianity killing the body with its crucifixion and killing the soul simultaneously, because one cannot split up man, cut the baby in half and divide him between his parents, say to one's loved one: "I love your mind but not the head that holds it.") You cannot do this, and Blackfoot knew it. He was so calm as he spoke, delighting in those breasts, those thighs, and I couldn't blush, for he made her beautiful. Even as she walked, she became what Blackfoot said she was, and I envied her, imagined her in bed with Adam, and with Blackfoot, and wondered if I would come to life with Blackfoot in my bed.

Blackfoot had taken us back past the stables and the picnic tables, the dappled shadows, the clean lawn, back to the bison feeding. And I felt so sad, as if I had lost some part of the world always, that I would always be without it (I didn't know what I had lost, but that did not lessen the sadness), as Blackfoot stood by the barbed-wire fence holding back his bison; and he stood in silence. There was an immeasurable distance separating the world from what it could be, and I was a culprit in my own way with Adam; we had lost our joy in each other. We walked round and round in our thoughts, like a horse in one paddock, doing the same exercise each day, turning and turning to the whip, to get our punishment. It was long drawn out, interspersed with memories of another time when we loved each other in the flesh.

"You look kinda sad," said Blackfoot, patting my shoulder, and I cried. His sympathy for me unlocked the tears, and they fell with relief. I could cry with him there; he didn't mind. And he held me, gently, so as not to watch me like a freak, but to comfort me. He knew I wanted to be held. The tears stopped, and I just liked being there in his arms. He was soft, incredibly soft. His arms seemed to fit around me, and Marta eyed me questioningly, but I turned away from her and looked into his eyes.

It would be possible with Blackfoot, the other life, the one I'd lost. I could see Blackfoot doing it with me, cherishing me. He'd kiss me on my lips when I woke up; in the morning it'd be the first thing I'd feel, his lips brushing mine. Some days he'd put his tongue in my mouth; I'd close my eyes, he'd lean down over me with his tongue playing with my tongue, my lips, my throat. I'd feel calm and quiet; he'd press down on me and cuddle me. I'd smile. I cried again. For a moment only Blackfoot could do this. He had proven it with Marta. I'm not an immaterial being like Marta. My body's strong and I don't hide it. I show it off, even. But with her he did it, and with me. Just imagine; we'd be unstoppable together. So I cried because it wasn't possible. I had to go back to Adam.

"An' the bison roamed in great herds. They had their migrations. No one stopped them. This was their home. They don't like man. You can't tame them. I saw a program on educational television about buffalo. They tried to round them up when they were dying of some plague, to give 'em shots. But the bison died in the pens. Once they were trapped, not out in the plains, they just lay down an' died. Their spirit was broken. Nothing to live for being locked up, near man. Like a fish out of water. Being near man jus' killed them off. You could see them lie down, not out of sickness, but despair. No hope left. An' the Indians is like them. When you lock us up in suits and those perfumed wigs and all that stuff you call civilization, we die. Sometimes we get your number and we take you on, man to man, and fight. But we can't win. It's not our world. We just got to do it even though we got no power. We got no power in government. No one cares. Jus' a few senators here and there. But I don't go feeling sorry for myself. You don't win wars by feeling sorry for yourself. You get your own ways of fighting back."

Marta was looking a little bored. Perhaps she had heard his speech before. It rolled off his tongue like waves. Blackfoot could hold an audience. His certainty was charismatic, unlike Adam's sudden bouts of confidence.

Or perhaps Adam's sudden certainty was attractive, and I had been a bitch, knocking him down, trying to make him feel small. For I found Blackfoot's confidence drew me to him still further. Marta's like I am with Adam, pulling him down, with that smirk on her face when he makes his speech. Does he worship her because she's not Indian like Angel? Could I love him even better than her?

I doubted it. You end up doing the same things with people. I'm old enough to know that now. I'd end up like I am with Adam, doing the same things in bed and out. I knew it but it didn't matter. I said it to myself, like a teacher repeating a lesson, the right answer to some math problem, while outside the classroom window the sun is hot, the parks are open, there's lemonade in the fridge at home, and all one wants is to leave the classroom, stuffy and musty, and be out in the feel of a summer's afternoon. Regent's Park, that's where I'd go, sometimes into the rose garden, where the roses would droop with their own scent. They drowned in themselves.

And my childhood; just this glimpse of it was so nostalgic. I could feel for Blackfoot's vision of the West, the buffalo wild and free, and the plains open as they are now, dotted with men in bright plumes, song, the smell of campfires, some childhood of our race he wanted back. It's gone. It never was.

We gloss over images, fuzz over the edges, and clean up the shadows, so the past can come to us like one of those images of Mao that used to adorn China. His cheeks were soft like a baby's, and his smile was everything. He was father and baby and husband and god. So this is how Blackfoot sells his past. It's a lie, but I don't care. I ought to be ashamed of myself, letting myself fall for his cheap images, but *he* is beautiful. He sweats slightly in the sun now. I could rest in his arms; tell Marta to get lost, and we'd fall right there on that patch of Fort Robinson, no tourists around, just the clouds, large and bulbous, and the bison.

But sex was perhaps not what I wanted, because I wanted my childhood back, when I could be cuddled and calmed with hugs, and it had gone. I wanted the childhood of America too, not this derelict place that Adam had taken me to, with all the scars showing of what the first settlers did. You do smell blood, the pure viciousness of land appropriation, the way they came to middle-class the place, leaving nothing of beauty, just bits of towns here and there, practical places with just enough to get by, and it had been taken away from Blackfoot, so he was part of the drabness, really.

I wanted an overall childhood, where other people thought of consequences, stopped you from swimming in the big waves on Calais beach, or swam with you to the right depth (in fact, I almost drowned once off the French coast, or so it felt, when the salt waves covered me and took me out too far). I wanted Blackfoot's big arms round me and his bison to dance to his voice like an Orpheus, and the days would come back when I would feel awe at the smallest occurrence, the shifting of clouds across the sky. Blackfoot did bring this back, this urge to return that I had kept buried.

And I suddenly feared for Blackfoot's life. I thought, he is an endangered species, perhaps he is one of a kind, and if he dies, if the bison kill him when they stampede over to Pennington's farm, or if in a fit of rage Marta knifes him (there was no reason to think she would, but it occurred to me then, like a nightmare), if Blackfoot dies, the spirit of the plains will be lost. They'll be barren, just wasteland with grain silos, and fields and fields of alien corn; I was filled with terror that he might die. And I wanted suddenly to hear his secret, know what it was that he knew about the sky and the land and Marta's body, so I could pass it on, write it down, or just tell Adam to do something, for God's sake, and stop messing around with Indian rights. Learn his story, Adam.

But Blackfoot hadn't really said anything to me about what he stood for, and I couldn't just ask him, like some TV person, to tell me there and then (as if you can tell that kind of truth in a phrase):

"What do you stand for?"

"I got to give the bison back to him," said Blackfoot suddenly. We were walking into their field, over a dip in the barbed-wire fence, and were unafraid. Blackfoot's voice led us, and the bison were calm as they ate, stuffing themselves with grass, lazily eyeing us.

"My Grandad wants to hear them roll over his dead bones, and the old war cries. I taught them now to some students in forestry and anthropology at The University of Vermillion. Nice kids that Marta gave me. They love the sounds," said Blackfoot, and he let out a melodious yelp, like a coyote.

"I been tryin' to figure out a way. A bit for me an' a bit for him. Keep us both happy, me an' my Grandad."

"But he's dead," I said. "Why bother? He's not going to hear a thing."

Blackfoot smiled.

"He's in that earth an' he's in my head. He's in more places than I am. I don't inhabit two worlds like he does. Except when I talk to him. Then I'm in two worlds. You can close the door on your own mind. Like you do, stop listening to those conversations. My Dad lived over by my Grandad, near him, most of his life. When Grandad died, he went out into the plains and talked to him, sent his soul off so he wouldn't fear. They'd hated each other in ways for years, but my Dad was scared when he died because the spirit becomes more powerful then than in the lifetime. Living in two worlds gives you that power. My Dad stopped fucking around when Grandad died an' became a man."

Blackfoot was within twenty feet or so of the bison. Marta and I stood behind him. I was frightened now. The grass seemed blue, like in a dream, covered with water. The sky sent cloud shadows over the blue grass, like whales swimming through the depths. The bison stood very still and stared at Blackfoot. With the speed of the wind, they left us. We waited until the sounds of their hooves had gone.

'm beginning to understand how images are handed back to the past, as I spend time with Blackfoot. He wants some recognition from the Dead. In his own eyes he can travel backwards and forwards in lost time and alter it. In one hand he carries his grandfather's corpse, alive and listening, and in the other hand he holds in his grasp prime-time America. It will happen, he's told us, when his grandfather wakes to the sound of the bison's hooves pummeling his grave in Pennington's farm. Grandfather's spirit (Grandad was always on his side and trusted in him, unlike Dad) will steal over to Marta's pond and regale his son with tales of Blackfoot's exploits. This would have been enough perhaps for Blackfoot, to wake the dead and have them happy with him, treating him like a man.

"We all have our initiations," said Blackfoot, "both us guys and women. And it's often the guy who does the initiating of woman. But for men, it's not his woman who makes him a man. We got other ways, through fire, hunting trials, doing stuff with men that makes us men. It's a challenge, something big you do yourself that makes you a man. You may have screwed around a lot, had big success, but that don't make you a man. Only the Dead can give it to you. Without them, your ancestors, you're nothing."

We were standing on the mound of Wounded Knee, with Marta and Minnehaha bickering in the background. Minnehaha didn't want Marta to lead the parade with Blackfoot. "Everyone'll know what you're up to," she said maliciously. "Mom'll know.

She'll grab you an' pull you off your horse."

"Oh, shut up," said Marta absent-mindedly.

The two of them bitched in a casual way, as if they were used to it.

Blackfoot didn't take any notice. He continued to read from a typed sheet of paper, his speech for the cameras.

"When the Dead die, we burn their spirits out of them so the smell will wake their Dead, friends and family of any nation who come to meet them. Their eyes turn blue first, then yellow, and the whites go bright like flame in the heat of the fire. Faces from their nightmares come, their old fears, like the God of Rain swallowing up their fields or the snakes biting their flesh, but we are singing. Our voices sound sweet, but to an enemy it's death because of its sweet melody.

"The fire goes through their body but warms them. Nights come and go, twelve nights. Then we let them be. We've done our work and kept them safe to cross into time. We can't go any further with them. A wall stops us and send us back. Some of us knock on the wall, asking to be let in. But we can't. We've done our work," said Blackfoot.

Minnehaha giggled. They were walking to avoid the gravestones and trying also not to trip in the heavy undergrowth. They were silhouettes against the sun. Then Minnehaha turned round to face me and I saw she was me. I saw in her face a look of adulthood, a knowing look mixed with how-could-you-do-this-to-me? and a little resignation in it too. This was my face when I was a child. At first it seemed that I was back in my childhood and that nothing had changed; and then I was me again, and all the years in between rushed through me and left me as an onlooker watching my childhood sink and disappear, and I couldn't even remember a moment of it. Minnehaha knew it. She held something that I didn't have, despite all my grownupness, my lovely shoes, my tight skirt and my breasts (no doubt she wanted all those things, I thought). But my childhood was in my past. It was quite the opposite of what it seemed. Blackfoot was right. For my childhood was old. It was the oldest part of me. It was a veteran and governed me even though I thought it had gone.

And Blackfoot took my hand and led me up onto the wall from where I could see the two churches of Wounded Knee and the clouds, empty, like cotton wool, to cover the wound of an empty sky that God had vacated. Only nature remained, replacing other kinds of destiny. But we got rid of her too. No destiny. Wounded Knee isn't sacred. The gravestones aren't sacred; only the other day someone dug up some bones in another farm to sell them. Indians have always known that money would eat them up, like a disease. Now that their ancestors' bones can be sold for a few thousand dollars or stuck in some museum. Who cares? The land has lost its soul. But she takes her revenge. Last year the Penningtons' crops were wiped out. Sleet came and hailstones followed by a strange sun that tempted the seeds to grow up for the light, and then, just as they were showing their little heads, nodding in the wind, more hailstones came and knocked them out of their skins. That was Nature's revenge for digging the soul of America out of the land, said Blackfoot, but all his thoughts I felt as my own thoughts, as if there was no wall between us, as if we were one.

Because I suddenly want to have children. There seems to be no other way of altering the balance. For life falls in and out of my hands, and everything has been in the wrong place. I can see it now, after a few weeks with Blackfoot. Adam could have taken my own self from me. I see it now because I am sensing joy in Blackfoot's presence. Time, in particular, is moving. It's disconcerting for everything to shift, for the fences around my eyes to fall that stopped the rush of life from moving me. And the wind that's growing, sounding loud, is actually time moving.

I know I'm not limited now in the way I was, trying to suck something from Adam and not getting it, and when I did get bits of love, piecemeal, I shrank from it so that the pain of it being lost time and again would fade. Time took love from me. But Time is opening up. There is my mother who died and my father who lives; there are friends too. Lovers I now remember. I can call on the dead and forgotten to give me what I need. Blackfoot has taken the wall away. I thought it was "real." I thought, I really did, that losing was the way things are. Love is here and gone forever. You lose the dead. They don't come back. Life was slippery, like some crook trying to steal into one's home and steal one's heart to hurt one. Some vengeful god let loose on the world, ransacking lives, preying on feeling. I am holding Blackfoot's hand over Wounded Knee, watching the two churches below us emptied of God, and the cemetery ransacked last week of Emma Bluegrass's bones. The blue sky like a painting now, for the church is red and the fence is pure white. A horse is nuzzling the fence, and some Lakota women in the distance are talking.

And I told Blackfoot as we sat on the mound of Wounded Knee, as on the dome of the world, surveying it: "It must be hard for you, living here."

But Blackfoot said nothing. He held my hand, and I let it lie in his, like Rodin's sculpture, "The Cathedral," where the praying hands are the gothic rise of the cathedral; but our hands were like a solid house, nothing grand, a house of the first settlers, made into the hillside to protect against the wind.

I wanted to help Blackfoot, because he was helping me. But I couldn't. He was bent on his project, not just as an act of imagination, but as a piece of magic. It summed up everything and would transform everything: the damn bison rumbling across Pennington's farm. He imbued his Event with every kind of significance. It became like the Resurrection (to a believer), or some other Biblical moment when God's grace unfolds. I couldn't say anything to make him listen to me. I kept saying that when you unleash those hefty beasts with their small eyes (a sign of small intelligence) and the TV crews, all you'll get is a circus show, not something befitting an Indian Warrior Chief; it wouldn't be mystical; It would be crass. I said all this respectfully. But Blackfoot made his phone calls every day from his antique shop where the costumes were stored. Feathers and plumes and wonderful beads and blankets were strung up in the barn that had almost been converted into a shop. He rang newspapers, radio and TV stations across the country (and there were thousands), the Farmworkers' gazettes and the Bagmakers' newsletter and the Agrarian something-or-other's newspaper. He went through the lists from two fat encyclopedias he had charmed the librarian at Wounded Knee to give him. Marta made calls too as Minnehaha gave instructions.

She had cajoled and scratched and blackmailed and cried for Marta to give her one of the war bonnets from the museum. It had eagle's feathers, wooden beads painted ultramarine and turquoise, ermine tassels and pink suede fringes. "I got that bitch to gimme the feathered crown," she told me. She had cajoled Blackfoot (and it wasn't hard work) to buy her a shocking pink swimsuit and turquoise tights onto which she had sewn feathers and buttons. Marta wanted Minnehaha to wear the war bonnet respectfully, with its buffalo-skin dress, but that wasn't sexy. American Indian clothes weren't "cool." Where's it gotcha, Dad? she'd asked Blackfoot.

"It's a chief's war bonnet," said Marta, "from your tribe, from the Sioux. You should be real proud wearing it," and Marta showed Minnehaha how to place the war bonnet in traditional fashion, but the child screamed, "It's a crown." She squirmed and sweated, fighting off Marta's hands as if the war bonnet were an insult to her. When Blackfoot called it "her crown," she quieted down. Blackfoot hardly ever tried to make her proud of being Sioux, like Marta did, with an almost evangelical tone to her voice. (It would have put me off, her self-righteous way of loving Native American culture.)

"I ended up like some midget under my Dad and Grandad, like Adam is under his Dad, lost in the shadow of warriors. But they are old hat, like Minny says. What am I gonna do with war bonnets? You gotta mix and match. A bit here and a bit there. You can't just follow their path. The present won't let you. She taught me that, Minny did. And I'm not gonna stuff it down her throat if she don't want it. Am I, little honey?" asked Blackfoot, hugging Minny until she laughed in delight.

"She modernized me," said Blackfoot one afternoon as Minnehaha danced a rap dance in her crown and sang some song called "Wild Thing."

"But who wants to be modernized?" asked Marta. "We've all lost our roots in America. All we've ever had is that phony culture that Minnehaha likes. You don't understand what you're losing," said Marta angrily, "when you think your MTV people are hip and Dad's old-fashioned."

But Blackfoot didn't care if Minnehaha valued her heritage. "It's for her to decide," he said.

Blackfoot told me that he stood in between Minnehaha and

the Dead. He had to keep them quiet, give them what they wanted so they'd leave Minny alone. It goes down in generations, and if one generation doesn't give satisfaction to the elders, then they wait patiently for the next ones to deliver.

"To deliver what?" I asked Blackfoot one night when we were alone. (Adam was off to Manhattan on a case and wasn't due back for several days).

"To deliver pride. That's what it is, self-respect. Each generation, they wait for the children to show respect to themselves. But first they do it by trial, particularly with the men. You have to prove yourself in battle, show scars on your face, prove your manhood."

"You haven't done that yet?"

"Not yet," said Blackfoot.

"Through violence it's done?" I asked.

"Through facing the Dead," said Blackfoot. "Knowing them, if you like. They're scary. Larger than they were in life now, and they roam where they like, in your mind and your bones. They're leaving Minny alone. They're onto me now. That's why I got to do it, this show. I got to show America something, win a war or two, do something big, so they'll let her be."

You can only do that in your mind, I told Blackfoot. You can't prove anything by some clumsy show on TV that'll make a mockery of your tribe. Actions overtake one. Perhaps that's why I'm wary of doing things. Certainly I think I've got something to give to Blackfoot now, to teach him that he doesn't need to go to such lengths to prove himself. His love for Minnehaha is enough, a reason for the Elders to leave him alone. As a feeling it's sufficient to itself. "You don't need to give a girl diamond rings to show your love," I said, hoping he'd understand that. But he didn't. He said it was all lies if you couldn't see it there in the flesh. It wasn't real if you didn't do it and it just stayed in your mind.

"It's just lies," he said angrily. "White man's talk," he added.

I didn't want to lose him then. I thought he'd ask me to leave. We brooded over the first anger that had come between us.

"When's Adam back?" he asked. "Don't he mind, you spending all this time with me? That's what I mean. That counts. Don't that mean something? More than your talk? All this time you're spending with me?"

Well, it does, I admitted.

Are you here to spy on me?

Underneath it all, no, I'm not. I want to be here with you. You understand something — about life, perhaps that's the reason. Perhaps I just like being here with you. I don't know, I said. Do I have to have *one* reason?

Blackfoot stared at me, in pain, out of his blue eyes. They were knowing. He'd been had by enough people like me. Confused motives, people who don't really know why they like him and aren't really friends. It's a fascination perhaps with him, just erotic.

Perhaps it's just erotic, I said, sadly, wistfully.

Well, that's okay, said Blackfoot.

Limiting, I said.

If you think erotic's low-down, dirty, sure, it's limiting, said Blackfoot.

He was surrounded by his tribe. Their feathers and wooden beads that must have been carved by hand (the hands were there in the room, I could hear them, stroking the beads). There was suede taken from the hunt, sewn by hand. Everything had a person who made it; each object, like a child, was made over time with love, with the body, through sweat and the mind. How I loved him then, surrounded by his family and their arts, in the death of it, trying to do something about the end of his culture. Perhaps it had already happened. Perhaps our world, this America, had rendered his culture useless. There was no place for it except in some museum, like the Byzantine madonnas and child, but they have more meaning, even the ones with their green faces and big gnarled hands and the flattened perspective, because some people still believe in Mary and Jesus.

What are you thinking? asked Blackfoot.

That's what all these wars are about, people holding onto

their culture, I thought.

I should leave, I said.

I don't want you to, said Blackfoot.

I don't want to, I said.

Let's be happy, I said.

We had some wine and turned on the local radio station. They were playing a country-and-western song called "Distant Places" ... "I'll leave you in distant places...."

We smiled at each other nervously.

So what are you doing here? asked Blackfoot. "You're spending days with me. Lots of time."

It doesn't feel like a lot of time, I said.

I walked over to Blackfoot and put my hand on his.

I like you, I said.

You got to love someone, said Blackfoot. Liking isn't enough.

I can't love you, I said.

I know, said Blackfoot. Even if you could, you won't do it.

I just see the consequences, I said. I can't get drunk on the present anymore. I did it too much. But it stretches out. It goes on and on. You think it's over. One night. You can forget it. But it's more than a simple thing, even when you want it to end there and then.

It happens when you don't make love too, said Blackfoot.

Not often, I said.

No, said Blackfoot, it goes back to the Dead, and they hold it out to you as your life, taunting you with it. They're the ones that give it long life, when you don't make it sacred. Two peoples sacred, said Blackfoot. Together, they're sacred.

He's too beautiful, I thought, to live. He's like a flower, perfect, and so colorful. Here, all they like is plastic. Beauty's an insult to them, reminds them of their bad taste.

You're too good for this place, I said.

It's my home, said Blackfoot.

You'd like New York, I said.

They're always watching, no matter where I am.

Who?

The Dead, said Blackfoot.

"Everyone round here lives in the Other World," I said. "The Penningtons do. They can't wait for Heaven. And you're talking with your Ancestors as if they're on the telephone."

"Everyone in the big city's running away from here. This is where America is born. It's like running away from home. The kids just get lost. Same in the big city. This earth here never stopped being alive. It's God's country," said Blackfoot.

"They thought they'd kill us, but they haven't. I'm still alive," said Blackfoot.

Then I wanted a child with Blackfoot. The thought of making him live, and his world and the ancestors watching, and being happy as we made love, because it would be sacred then, wouldn't it?

My body would carry him on.

Good night, I said, picking up my handbag.

Walking out of the door. The last time I torment myself like this. I won't spend nighttimes alone with him in this junk show. I want just to touch him, be held. Nothing more perhaps. I'm not going to stand it. It's all I want. I'll see you tomorrow, I said. Like cutting myself in half. The door closes. Half of me's gone. It hurts so much, all over my face, tears are springing up, in my cheeks. My eyelashes, my forehead, all of me is stinging with tears.

Moving from being a tourist to a feeler, that's all it is. That's why it hurts. It doesn't need to. I didn't lose Blackfoot. I never had him. That's what hurts perhaps, that I never tasted the fruits of some passion that rocks me in two and that heals me when I'm with him. Perhaps I'm just touching my own depths. But I'm walking around wounded, belonging to this place now, just one of them, carrying around this gaping wound of something lost that was never had. Look at Blackfoot, for instance, resurrecting the bison rolling across the plains. It's his fantasy. It was never there in his lifetime. I'm one of them, English as I was, or am. But my pride has gone. Blackfoot's changed me. Adam never did. It's only here that I think I know for the first time how it feels to be American. I couldn't discuss it with anyone. Obviously Adam wouldn't want to hear what my passion for Blackfoot had effected, the epiphany of Blackfoot in my dreams, how he walks godlike, and I need him and wake up hot and tousled as if he's made love with me on good nights, and on the empty nights, he's been killed in my dream, eaten by the Snake Boy, mutilated by Minnehaha, shot by Joseph, a Christ on the cross.

Perhaps this is my Epiphany, painful as it is. The cold, withdrawn me has gone and I'm a mess of feelings. I always thought Americans wore their hearts on their sleeves and didn't know what it was to have that *sang-froid* that I owned before Blackfoot.

I had a sense of irony. When I came here I thought I saw it all clearly because I was an outsider from a different culture.

(People say that you do see a place more clearly when you haven't been stuck in it and taking it for granted for all your life.)

You know, you have a sense of comparison and can define. You notice what people actually do. But I'm not sure recording what people do tells one much about who they are. I think I know more about Blackfoot, now I love him. He's named all the places around here, so I know the massacre took place at Wounded Knee. Women and children and unarmed men were shot with guns and cannons, helplessly sent into death. And the church is where the survivors were taken, wounded, thrown onto straw-covered floors in the middle of the night. That was the end of the Sioux uprising.

Blackfoot goes out into the Badlands for two days to meditate on his Event. He communes with the Dead and won't take anyone with him.

He says in his Dream the answer will be shaped, but he comes back and has no answer. He asks Minnehaha to tell him how to run the show.

So, when it happens, it will be Minnehaha's scenario. This reenactment of the old days will come from the mind of a child who doesn't really care much about her heritage.

CHAPTER

The sun came in a shaft of greenish gold through the storm clouds. That was on the right-hand side, over Fort Robinson. There were banners and horses, and those long war bonnets streamed down from the riders like a bloody horse's mane, or a bird that had been shot down and fell in the wind, dead. Blackfoot, Minnehaha, and Marta were on white horses. The students from the University and some archeology majors (who held posters saying "WHOSE GRAVE?") had ghetto blasters playing very loud rap songs. Some were on foot.

The Snake Boy began shooting. The bison stopped for a split second and bolted, like waves from a waterfall, through the crowds. They were heading for Wounded Knee. The Snake Boy kept shooting. People fell. The sun went in. It came out again. The Snake Boy couldn't stop shooting with his rifle, up in the air at first, round and round at the sky, screaming "Jesus." Blackfoot saw it happen before it did. He knew it would happen because he was there to stop it. I watched him. He was in slow motion on his horse, following Abe's horse, to get the gun from him.

Abe pointed his gun one more time at the sky and then at the crowd. He shot someone. Blackfoot was on top of him on the horse that reared and fell; they fell all in a heap, the gun fired of its own accord. From someone. We couldn't see. I went running towards Blackfoot. Adam tried to stop me. He held me back. I kept running with him on my back, like a dead weight stopping my flight to Blackfoot, who lay motionless on the ground.

I got rid of Adam. I was suddenly very strong. I was at

112
▲▲▲

Blackfoot's face. He rubbed his eyes. The bison were there. Abe was dead. The grass was red by him. He wasn't making a sound. I realized with a terrible sense of relief that Abe was dead. The thought made me want to thank God. It was him and not Blackfoot. I got what I wanted.

Blackfoot was up. He didn't notice me. He carried Abe in his arms. Minnehaha was white with fear. The cameras from the local station were there. Blackfoot didn't notice them. He said nothing when they came up to him. We saw an ambulance making its way through the horses. The bison had left. They were on their way to Wounded Knee. Afterwards Minnehaha admitted that she knew that Abe had a "real" gun.

I told Blackfoot my dream a few days after it happened.

My dream would come into my mind like a shameful memory. It felt, when it appeared (an image or two was enough to give me that sensation of shrinking away from myself), that I had actually orchestrated the death of Abe and Adam's disappearance. I'd be doing something enjoyable, like driving through the cornfields or going for a ride on the Fort Robinson pony trails, and suddenly it fell on me, the shame, the pathetic call to God, thanking Him for getting rid of my enemies. He did it, in all his glory, for me, because I was faithful. He was on my side, in my dream, because he killed when I asked him and preserved Blackfoot. The world was a good place because I had won out.

That was all in the dream, those feelings. But to my conscious mind, my being in the dream was despicable. I was no better than the Penningtons. I had become like them, I told Blackfoot. My religion was medieval. And in any case, I explained to him, I don't believe in God. I also added that I realized, of course, that my self in the dream was not really me, but Blackfoot looked at me with a sour distaste.

"You get visions, just like that. Big visions, and you talk — yack, yack, yack — all intellect — yack, yack, yack — all mind and no soul. Don't it occur to you that you been with the Dead? You got to go where I been trying to go for weeks. Weeks I go trekking in the Badlands; last year I did it too, to get the answers. An' you get a vision and yack-yack about it."

Blackfoot was angry with me, and a little jealous, and then he was afraid. We were walking by the lake down by Marta's farm, where Blackfoot's father's grave lay under a plastic sheet. (It must have been Bobby who covered the grave.) It was drizzling. We were to meet Adam at the Rosebud Cafe at lunchtime, but we were already late.

"We got to work out the dream," said Blackfoot. And then he grabbed me, his arms were round me. I felt so frail as he squeezed me. It happened so quickly and he was gone away from me, not holding me, and I had no time to hold him or feel him. I wanted to cry. I couldn't taste it so there was nothing to remember, just the moment of missing out, of not being there in time, to feel his body. Just my frailty, how small I felt, like a child.

"You seen the truth," said Blackfoot. "You seen both the future and the past, when the two meet, that time that repeats itself. It never ends. But I don' know what the dream means for us. We got to meditate on it, in sacred places. I'll take you there. I need you with me. I wish you hadn't had the dream," said Blackfoot wearily. "It sure complicates things."

But the dream is mine. It's private and it's shameful. I told Blackfoot that I didn't want him revealing clues to my personality, elements of myself I didn't yet understand. "The stuff about Adam, for instance. You can't tell Adam that I got rid of him to be with you."

Blackfoot was trying to rip the plastic sheeting off his father's grave.

"Whites," he said suddenly and stared at me with a sadness, a weariness.

"A dream is everyone's. It came to you. You received it. An' now you wanna throw it in the garbage. It's a dream that can change things."

"I'm no clairvoyant," I said. Blackfoot cajoled me, tried to seduce me into letting my dream be known. He wanted to ask some other Sioux to take the dream to the Badlands buttes and dream on it. But I wouldn't have it. I was hurt. I didn't mind being with Blackfoot, together dreaming on my dream. I even liked the idea. But I wanted to keep it private. Fine, for the interpretation to be known. I didn't mind Blackfoot using the "knowledge" he had gleaned from my dream, but the dream itself was mine, the worst of me.

Well, no, there is worse, I admitted to Blackfoot.

But what's so wrong about wanting to be with me? he asked.

I didn't say I did.

But the dream says it.

You can't take a dream literally. That's what's so damn wrong with your culture. With America. I'm sick to death of this place. Can't you see that the dream isn't "real"? It's not going to tell you what to do. It's just a fantasy. A sleeping fantasy. It might not make any sense.

Then why are you so ashamed of it? asked Blackfoot.

Because of Adam. I don't want him to know I got rid of him.

"So the dream is 'real.' *You* take it literally," said Blackfoot.

We were late for Adam, and the drizzle had turned into thick drops that didn't disturb us. We were intoxicated with our talk. I began to like my own fury.

I don't fit in here. Your culture's like a child's world. You think dreams happen, like Americans do. They think you can want something and then make it happen. But it's not like that, I said.

You confuse everything, said Blackfoot.

Adam wasn't at the Rosebud Cafe. He'd left a message with Jim to say he had to go back to the Penningtons to see some video that might help. So we drove, Blackfoot and I, back to his father's grave in a thick storm of rain. It'd wash us clean, I felt. We need to have our clothes clinging to us, our lips moist, then we'll be ready to know my dream deep down.

But I just saw Blackfoot's lips and couldn't see further. The dream was about leaving Adam for Blackfoot and killing off anyone who got in the way. It was my passion for him, murderous and full-blooded, that I saw when I closed my eyes in the falling rain by the grave, and concentrated.

I need you, said Blackfoot suddenly.

Me or my dream?

It's your dream, said Blackfoot. You were ready to have it. I weren't. I tried. I got myself ready. Every way I knew how. But you were there listening. So the Dead spoke to you. I need you because you can hear. Not just the dream, not just the dream. You can hear, he said again.

And I did. I heard the rain falling, hundreds and thousands of drops all at once falling on the corn. I heard the soil drinking it in, hungrily, and the body of the soil writhing with pleasure as the water came, transforming it into soft mud, malleable and wet. This rain was warm. It was fertile carrying prayers from the Dead. They liked the land even though their lives were buried there. They didn't take revenge. Only, Blackfoot didn't know. They didn't want to harm him.

And I told Blackfoot what I heard. "It wasn't really more than a poetic feeling. I'm not clairvoyant," I said.

And I knew I was talking about me. I was the earth, wanting Blackfoot to soften my body with rain. The image was blatantly clear.

"I'll remember it," said Blackfoot. "When you don't get visions, you do it that way. Bit by bit, you remember."

We walked down into the first edge of the lake, where Blackfoot had bathed and caught fish with his hands in the sun.

"When the first Spaniards came to South America, the Indians thought they were gods because they were riding horses. There was a myth that the Messiah would come riding a horse. So they welcomed them, and were slaughtered," I said.

"All places got myths that are sick. Americans are sick with 'em too. Filled with myths that stink, making it rich, finding gold in every fucking field, in anything they can lay their greedy hands on. We got 'em too. Myths that'll kill you. Fast times, stuff like that. Getting off on money, jus' money, no soul. Houses without family. Big gates. I been to those places. I seen them on TV. America's got myths like those dumb Indians had about whiteskins."

"Redskins and whiteskins," he said. But with me you can't tell the difference. I could be white, the way I look. You could be white too," he said. "But you're not, underneath."

"I'm English," I said, irritated.

"I know," said Blackfoot, "but that don't matter. My grandmother came from England. She married an Injun. I won' hold it against you, that you're white."

lackfoot would bring me offerings — a pipestone turtle that
stared at me maliciously with emerald eyes, bouquets of flowers,
wild from the plains, like wreaths on the graves on Wounded Knee
cemetery. I thought I'd seen the very same wreath, with pink and
yellow and blue flowers and ribbons, on Emma Bluegrass's grave.
He brought me perfume, lavender oil, and a small bottle of Joy eau
de toilette and asked if he might rub it on my wrists. I said no. He
was getting me ready to walk with him through the Badlands. He
treated me like a fetish. I felt at times he was worshipping me and I
wasn't quite human to him. He told me he treated me like this
because I'd walked into the Land of the Dead.

    Blackfoot repels me. I fight with him, in words, about
superstition, but I'm drunk on the notion that I have a vision. All
those charms, all that superstition, where did it get you? I asked.
Your people had no luck, just pain, despite all these dreams, I said,
but I had to fight the way I drifted into Blackfoot's moods. When I
sat still with him on the rocks above Wounded Knee, I could hear
the land. I could sense in the wind America. I was like a first
settler then, fearing the Indian ways, but drunk on them. I'm
fighting a passion, fighting the dream of Blackfoot. (For it's his
dream, now that he's chosen to own it. It has a new purpose now
that he's seen it. In private I am left with the dream and it's small,
just an ordinary thing you'd forget if Blackfoot hadn't made you
see it and remember it off by heart.)

    So we get in a trance from time to time, just watching the
land round Wounded Knee, even driving through farms and farms,

and the fields dizzying me with their multitudinous movement, always moving to the wind, and the wind has been dried of the sea and is like the bones under the earth, invisible too.

But Blackfoot always wanted more from me. It wasn't enough when I told him what came to mind, with as much honesty as I'd give a close friend. No, he wanted to steal something from me, asked slyly if anything dropped into my head "like thunder" (a sign to him that the Dead were talking). I told him (slightly embarrassed) about slowly finding a home in the earth and sky here. How, when I arrived, she'd abandoned me and left me wandering aimless through here with Adam, but now, even when I closed my eyes, I sensed her, I sensed her essence, the story she'd spawned, and the feel of the lives she'd buried.

"Puritan shit," said Blackfoot (furious, after a few days that his cosseting me like a baby hadn't worked, perhaps. Angry, anyhow, that I wasn't delivering the new dream.) "I seen them churches. They got no pictures on the walls. They jus' yack and yack an' talk an' more silence. It don't get you nowhere. It got to be the mos' boring stuff I seen. Invisible shit don't count. Minny taught me that. She don't say it like that: no. That kid's got brains. Smart like a demon for her age. She shows me by shifting channels on TV. Don' she show me — the way she dresses jus' like Madonna. An' the way she talks jus' like that Jamaican girl from your home town, filthy sometimes. Thinks it's cool. That's what Minny hears, like the other kids. Stick some Injun chief on TV with feathers on his feet, an' the kid'll start dressing like that. Thinking it's cool. That place is magic."

"So TV is a place, Blackfoot? Like the Land of the Dead?" I asked with my cold mocking tone, jealous of Minny that turning a channel on TV could be of mystical import to her father. But when I sat for days and days, trying to help him against my sense of safety, submerging it, letting my common sense be wobbled by the adorations of Blackfoot, when I *tried*, I was nothing. And when she didn't lift a finger to even talk to her father, she spoke the truth.

"So you want some screenplay you can put on TV, some dream from the Dead to set to music, rap music on MTV, something the kids will like, some perfect moment that will pass to Minny to give her back her heritage? Some vision of Indiana, native Americana, exemplary for all time?"

Blackfoot nodded, bewildered, taken aback by me, as if his game had been uncovered.

"Now you're a part of me, I got to be honest with you," he said, guiltily.

So, he told me he'd tell me the real story. But it came out in a jumble. It fell disconnectedly like a basket of worries falling. Blackfoot told me how we'd miss the deadline for his TV shows if I didn't dream "real quick." He told me the media across the States were waiting for him (all those phone calls and press releases must have cost him a fortune, I said). He'd set up a fund, he said, which covered his costs in full, and a non-profit company selling Wild West shows, reenacting scenes from the old Buffalo Bill shows, nostalgic stuff, family entertainment with a "liberal bent." "Kill two birds with one stone. Get them out for nostalgic shit like the stuff my grandad sold, worked in Hollywood, old Ben Rosebud Blackfoot, others too, uncles and aunts, selling the Indian cause up shit's creek, doin' 'em scripts where the Injuns got the brain the size of a pea, an' the white guys got all the tricks. Passed down shit to me. Took me years of watching those films before I saw it was lies. Minny watches them," said Blackfoot. "Can't turn the TV off. Spaghetti stuff. The Injuns small an' helpless or crazy with some dumb mystical stuff. You know the scene where he always looks serious, like he's above it all, an' then he gets screwed by some smart-ass gringo."

What was I saying? asked Blackfoot. He was sweating a little. He took my hand, reaching out (it seemed) for help. Drunk on his thoughts.

But I'm white, I said. You can't use my dream. You've got to dream your own.

Jesus, said Blackfoot. I hadn't thought of that.

Blackfoot kept hold of my hand and took me, like his shadow, through the fields below Wounded Knee. There was a tiny Indian farm, a backyard with clothes blowing in the wind, three children skipping rope.

I'll leave the reservation once I get more bread, said Blackfoot. This place makes me sad, he said. I pressed his arm with comfort, wanting some love to pass between us. I don't think I can help you, Blackfoot, I said to myself and kept it to myself. I don't have faith in dreams. That's the last time the Dead will call on me.

We walked past the kids skipping rope and glimpsed the mother standing in the kitchen, watching the kids from the corner of her eye. Blackfoot knew her and smiled. She waved.

"We're always in the same room, you an' me, now. Now, you're part of me. You don't understand. You think you leave people behind. Forget them. Close the door an' they're gone. One-night stands. But we're all in the same room, me an' those Hollywood moguls that screwed my ancestors, me an' Minny, an' we keep adding new people, like you — more an' more people to the place — but sometimes the Dead won't come. They won't help. You can go looking for them, but they'll stay away. Jus' like them to give a dream to a white. I'm too small for them. They don't respect me. But *you* — you're like Dad, or Emma Bluegrass. They'll give it to you. That's why I give you the wreath. I thought you were like Emma. I gotta tell you the truth, now you're part of me," said Blackfoot, again repeating a mantra to drum it into his skull that he mustn't lie to me.

"I could hate you," he said suddenly.

"The way you behave, I think you do, turning your kindness off and on, like a tap, wanting something from me, not me, trying to twist my common sense into superstition."

"I don' want no revenge. I don' want 'em kids from the University killed, an' Abe tossed off his horse onto the dirt, an' Abe dying all in blood — like you saw. You saw the future an' I don' want it. You gotta believe me. You gotta give me a new dream. I don't care where we get it from," said Blackfoot. "We'll search in the day and night. You can have dreams of Thunder walking upright, you can have them listening to a Walkman, on a skateboard. You can daydream," he said.

The sky was hazy with twilight. Of course, I could daydream. I could do that now. Dream up some image of tranquillity where Blackfoot gets his cake and eats it. I told him that.

"You mock me," he said.

It went through me like a knife. That I could mock Blackfoot, try to make him feel as small as he already feels because I'm white and am given the dream, it hurt me to think of myself hurting him like that. There was no way out of this. If I love him. I'm not going to alter his world-view now, persuade him that mountains don't become men, and the childworld has died. Our thoughts don't create themselves. Our dreams aren't real. And the TV might send them out to millions of viewers but there's no saying if Minny will want to keep her Sioux heritage just because there's some Wild West show on Channel Five once a week. This simplicity does not reign in the modern world. Perhaps it did once. Perhaps once, a long time ago, heaven would be waiting for the Penningtons, and they'd listen to their airport music and eat forever their German bread just as they'd imagined it. But I doubt it, Blackfoot. I told him all that, giving it one last try, so he'd see that my dream was *my* dream, about *my* life. To put this dream simply, Blackfoot, it's about getting you and killing all who stand in the way.

"You're lying," he said. "I can see through you. Why do you lie to me? Why do you fuck me over like this? What's in it for you?"

"Sometimes you can't win. No matter what you say."

"You had your chance," said Blackfoot. "You don't take it. An' you say you want me."

We looked pure disgust at each other.

This is a good way to end this game. The only way. If I feel anything about Blackfoot, I'll want to help him. Now, I don't.

"I'm drivin' you to Adam, to Rapid City, to meet that plane," said Blackfoot.

"Thanks," I said.

"I won't go back on my word."

"Of course not," I said.

"I said I'd drive you," he said sullenly.

It rained and rained on our way to Rapid City. We drove through some towns with just two or three homes, one derelict and the others falling apart. This wind looked as if it would rip open those wooden frames. How people lived here I can't imagine, without electricity. Without heat. In the old, old days. Blackfoot nodded. The heavens were very black, blue black, like the ink spilt out of a bottle signifying chaos on the page. No words. Just a mess of anger. Lightning shot through the sky, in a split second cracking it open. Then the wound was covered over by the black sky. Blackfoot said nothing, stopping off to get us a beer and some chips.

Back with Adam. We're in the back seat, holding hands. Adam talking nonstop about a piece of paper he's got to take Abe out of the Penningtons' home. Blackfoot interrupted him.

"We gotta protect Abe. We gotta get him away from here before the Event. We gotta keep the buffalo out of it. Use cows instead. (They don't stampede like 'em buffalo.) An' we gotta have a safety check before the thing starts. No guns. We gotta keep the whole thing off Pennington's farm, because they got guns. Lots of them. Heard 'em shootin'. You name it, they'll shoot it. The hunting season's on. Killer Christians. That's what those dumb-ass creeps are. Killer Christians. I don' want no dream of revenge."

"What are you talking about?" asked Adam.

"Her dream," said Blackfoot.

I told Adam about the dream, and Blackfoot's belief in it.

"Pretty Freudian," said Adam.

"Yeah?" said Blackfoot threateningly. The beer had gone to his head. "You tryin' to make a fool of me?"

"Are you looking for a fight?" asked Adam.

"You wan' one?" asked Blackfoot.

It happened swiftly. The car's brakes jolted us out of our seats. They were out of the car in the rain. I ran out. It was my fault. My dream. My violence that got them out there, screaming at each other.

I took a stone from the road.

They shouted at each other at a distance, their fists covering their face, but neither of them looked as if they could fight.

I took the stone and threw it down on the ground between them.

They looked at me like lost boys.

"It was my dream," I said.

"You bitch," said Blackfoot.

Adam screamed something about me. It was to do with loving me. Like a wind it sounded. I was deafened by a sudden rush of rain, thick like the jet of a shower. Adam was shouting about giving me respect. You're the bitch, he said to Blackfoot. D'you think a man talks to a lady like that? I couldn't make out the sense of it. Like conflicting winds, all of it, crisscrossing, Blackfoot's worship of me, and viciousness to me, and Adam's absence for weeks and his sudden homecoming strong with a new love for me. But it could all have been momentary, like that bloody knife-wound in the sky, always there, but illuminated only in moments of drama, when thunder strikes and the Dead want the score. Then it comes out, bright and clear as if it were there forever, his love for me. But it's gone.

They ran at each other, wrestling down on the wet stony tarmac, like madmen. They'll kill each other.

Then the thunder came.

Blackfoot let out a scream, like a coyote. Adam let go of him in fear. Blackfoot muttered something in Sioux to the sky. In the pause created by the thunder and the sudden gnash of red racing through the sky like a knife-wound, they grew calm.

Their own violence seemed small and useless.

"We can get killed out here, both of us," said Adam. "Let's get back in the car."

But I didn't. I couldn't move. As I told Adam later, I was back in my past. It crept into me, in my body, the sadness. A woman was shouting at me, and then she went away and my father was facing me with his anger. And then I was walking alone down Mayfair in the rain. Completely alone. I was all dressed up, trying to look as if someone wanted me. No one could tell I was so alone. I'd die from loneliness.

Adam grabbed me and stuffed me in the back of the car.

As I told him later, I didn't even feel his arm. I was somewhere else. We all stopped off at a motel, a Best Western.

The car was rattling to the sound of thunder, like huge drums in the sky, thudding, reverberating down on earth. Blackfoot was silent with fear. He sat in the driver's seat, holding the wheel like some crucified Christ, punished by the heavens for something like overweening pride perhaps. Adam was calm. He got out and made reservations, leaving the two of us together.

"I'm not mocking you," I said. I was crying.

Blackfoot was in a trance. Not just a dream, for when I leant forward to put my hand on his shoulder to comfort him, his body was rigid and his eyes were glassy, his lips apart. I recoiled. He was smiling, not in pleasure but in pain. His lips pulled apart like a puppet by invisible strings. And I saw him then, like the husk of a man. My Blackfoot dead, and in his place, just for that moment, all due to that smile, the death-mask smile, poked into place by an undertaker. And I knew who Blackfoot was. He was the Jolly Indian Chief, all dressed up outside the Rosebud Cafe, smiling to tourists, welcoming us to Pine Ridge. He'd been had again, just like his warrior chiefs before him. This time by me. Modern with sex; was that what floored him, made me a bitch and killed his dream? Did I reduce the Land of the Dead, their call to me, just to dream of sex? Was this the legacy we had for Blackfoot, Adam and I, some chic sense of desire? Oh, yes, that's it. A

Freudian dream. Oh, yes, we know.

But how it catches me now, sitting in between Blackfoot and Adam like some devil entering me, leading me to temptation, desire. It pulls me in two, so I feel that one of them has to go. I'll sacrifice Blackfoot, leave him lying like that on the front seat. He gets in the way, owning desire, as if it has to be jumbled up in a world of confusion, magic, an underworld of the spirit. In me it won't come clean. All of it goes to Blackfoot, and Adam gets what's left. Blackfoot gets in the way. Before our times together, I thought that Adam had all I have to give. He squeezed me dry, needed my understanding, like a lost boy under his Great Father's Shadow, needing my understanding. I gave it all, listened for nights. You know, I told you.

But Blackfoot knows I lie. Half of me lies buried under a chain of thought, like a convict whose ball and chain is obsession. I'm killing Adam, in my dreams, and loving Blackfoot, running to him, all reason spent, love flaring, desire all I am.

"Let's go. It's late. Adam's waiting." I said gently.

I'm sorry, I said to Blackfoot. I'm sorry this happened.

And that night Blackfoot was next door to us, drowning our talk with the sounds of MTV (Steve Winwood's "Higher Love" and "Talking Back to the Night"), drum beats from so many times thudding through the wall, as if Blackfoot had turned on some memory machine, so it all came back to me, the men before Adam, and the incongruousness of Adam. For one thing, his earnest goodness and the way he'll torture himself to find something true (helping Blackfoot's a good example and so is the way he's taken on Abe) but still tortures himself to find out his own motives. And now with me he holds back his anger, tries to understand what I'm doing with Blackfoot, our dinners together, this dream that's made us like one. So Blackfoot needs me, but I can't explain to Adam what I need from him.

"Half of me's buried like Emma Bluegrass," I say, telling Adam about the wreaths Blackfoot gives me and the way we start our walks at Wounded Knee, just by her grave. "Half of me's dead, dream-walking in Blackfoot's world. I've given you nothing."

But Adam tries like some joker in the pack (someone I never lived with before) to hear the mystery of it. No, he won't leap to conclusions, turn it into some cheap romance or some tale of possession (in a moment of fear, I asked him if he believed that Blackfoot was animating the old spirits in Wounded Knee). But we don't make love. We talk, tired, into the night.

Adam sleeps as Blackfoot plays my old life through the walls of the Best Western Motel. All those songs of lost love, chasing love, looking for love in all the wrong places, Baby, I need your lovin', oh, got to get all your lovin' ... on and on through the night while Adam sleeps. Adam's the New World, lying by my side, almost mine, if I could love him now, get rid of Blackfoot. Blackfoot's the Old World across the ocean. I left it behind, I thought.

Dawn comes, and I imagine stealing into Blackfoot's room, with the stone grey light, and still the sound of Madonna and all, and we'd make love so violently, without caring if Adam hears or the world wakes up to watch. Because we won't fight anymore over my dream. Our bodies will be one with the same dream, so restful it would be to share the same dream. We'd rest in it, as in death. Sleep would be heavy, so weighted down with the end of trying. No struggle against desire, no tension, just the fall. And after it, when we awoke, half of us would be left, the part we call ourselves would be gone down into Emma Bluegrass's grave. Because I can't make good with Blackfoot. I can't have kids with him, and I'd ruin my chances with Adam. It's not just that, not only the practical side. It'd be like ditching my future, here and now. I mustn't be near him. The wall between us makes us still so close. He doesn't love me. Nor I him. We're drawn together, like Blackfoot says, by the Dead. Some force that would pull us backwards in time, to live in the past.

CHAPTER

Abe was returned to Blackfoot on a crisp autumn morning. The sun was out with the wind, exhilarating, painful with its new season, but it smelt good, of the fields and the herb garden behind the Penningtons' kitchen. We watched videos of Christ's birth, crucifixion and resurrection, set to airport music hymns. Abe clapped whenever someone was killed and screamed Gotcha. "But his mildness will come," said Mrs. Pennington. Mild like a lamb with God's grace. She kept crossing herself. She wept.

"His love will change the boy," said Mrs. Pennington.

Jesus was taking his Father's place. He stood on a golden throne that rose up into the sky. Where was his Father now? Well, you worshipped Father in the Son. Didn't you?

The three in one.

So, you don't really send him off into some Siberian corner of the sky. Jesus didn't really try to kill Him off and take His place and then kill off, later on, centuries later, all those who hadn't joined His club. I couldn't work it out, how to get round the fact that Jesus was going up, like some Son of a King, replacing his Father, taking the crown before his Father's breath went cold. Killing him off. Couldn't work it out. Why they chose some wimpy, hippie, long-haired boy to play the part. Yet his eyes were sick with rage, made like a killer. Why would the LTL (Love The Lord) choose such a crazy face for Jesus?

But the Penningtons wept. Adam and Blackfoot sat in silence, drinking their coffee. Mrs. Pennington said:

The Lord will make him good and pure. You give him to

me. I'll make him good.

We'll all be swept up in this one day, I thought. It never abated, the swirling flames of God's breath, burning the flesh and taking the spirit up into some semicircle of angels. It just won't end. For a decade or two Faith falls down into forgetfulness but she comes back. Faith, Hope and Glory, all those girls come back, allegories abound, and the meaning that's given to life comes from some old story. We just accept it.

It's here and now, in this modern age, in modern America, but the spirit's a millennium old, sick with it.

But what happened to Blackfoot's culture? How come it's dead and gone, and the Penningtons' Jesus story on videocassette had taken its place, will heal Abe and quiet the Dead? Why not the spirits of Sun and Moon and the River? Why this madman killer stealing his father's throne before his breath is gone? Why some guy with nails in his hands, bleeding, bleeding for our sins?

"I likes Jesus," said Abe.

"You *see*?" said Mrs. Pennington.

"The car's waiting," said Adam.

"I'm in no hurry," said Blackfoot.

You can't wrench parent and child like this. "It won't work," Blackfoot said in the car. "Abe don't want me. You can see that."

"I'm behaving as if you care about Indian rights," said Adam, and I laughed. Some abstract theory (like Joseph might have) to cover up his contempt of other's feelings.

Damn bastard like Joseph with principles taking the place of feelings. Indian rights. What does Adam know about Indian rights? What if the Indian in question doesn't want his nephew living in his home? What if one hour of Buffalo Bill's Wildest West Show on MTV gives back to Minny and Abe, in one fell swoop, respect for their Indian elders? What if TV will do the trick, Adam? Not some principled *legal* gesture — the legal gesture having a history of killing off Indians. I hated him then, and more than Adam (who became quite suddenly just a receptacle, just the place where Joseph hung out). I hated Joseph. I hated the way he helped me, made me do his research (I never had time to do my own, his mind was so encompassing, like baby's needing this and that), like some nursemaid to the great mind (man). Tending his prick. That's what it was like. (I didn't tell Adam all of this, but I told him what I could, like that last bit of my thoughts.)

Tending his prick. His mind turned women on. Why it should, who knows, since most of them couldn't understand one first line of his math puzzles. But I did. To get my foot in the door? To get my papers? And a nice job from which I could take off and become me — just *me*, describing *my* ideas. Eventually that would happen. But it didn't, and I stayed stuck there, with Adam's father, wanting to get rid of him, and his prick, the two of them so full of themselves, and *I was* so much in love with them.

But that "love" was just cover-up. Like the bait, all bright and luring, made of metal, that sticks in one's throat later when one takes the bite.

That "love" I felt for Joseph, gratitude, filial affection, all of it was an infatuation, and what it hid was the true story, that, underneath, I just didn't want my own ideas, didn't trust them (at that moment I thought I had some, and that I wanted the time, the freedom from Joseph and my job as handmaiden to him, to plunge headfirst into this sea of my own imagination). I wanted to be the one reading the telescopes, dreaming my own vision of the night sky. And as Adam sat there piously, driving on the right side of the road, with his principles, *knowing better than Blackfoot* (as Joseph always knows better than me), I thought I would have something to say, something of my own, not a hand-me-down to flog, not that constant lecture explicating Joseph's theories so I knew it off my heart backwards and forwards, like a cassette I could pick up in the middle and rewind.

This was what I was to the world, an ambassador to Joseph.

Poor Adam. Poor me. Swimming daily in the shadow of the father. Poor Abe, fatherless, with only a red-nailed, bleeding Jesus to hold his hand now. Blackfoot won't spend a minute with him. You should know that, I told Adam later over dinner in the Holiday Inn. In between Minny, his passion for her, and leaving

Angel, meeting Marta secretly and the Wildest West Show, do you think Abe will get a father?

And did I have one?

We were sitting in this goddamn fake Italian restaurant in the Holiday Inn (which could have been anywhere). They are eternal, timeless, these American institutions. Like the Soviet Houses of Culture, the same in each city, in Poland (where I lectured on Joseph), in Czechoslovakia, in all the eastern bloc, the same vicious building looming over the city center (I said to Adam). The chandeliers were Pyrex. The fake vines in the latticed window display were lime green and violet. There's probably the same display in the Holiday Inn in Sioux City. And Iowa. And Kansas City.

Did I have one? I asked Adam. A father?

I never met him, said Adam.

But the way I am, do you *imagine* I had a real father?

What would he do? asked Adam warily. How would I know?

So you'd invent it? Make it up from scratch, watch it on the TV, the Bill Cosby show, "Kramer vs. Kramer" perhaps, and "Three Men and a Baby," to see what I do?

I got an idea or two on the subject, said Adam, stroking my hand.

I said nothing, shy at the thought of having a child with Adam. And for what seemed to be the first time, I felt fear, because it seemed possible. To have one with him, to imagine him having the wherewithal to be a father.

"My parents hide in the background. They don't play much part in all this. Not like yours. What they do is hidden in me. It's not obvious, like it is with you," I said.

"But it isn't obvious," I said, correcting myself, looking at Adam, and for a moment I thought I had passed out. My breath went. The features in Adam's face disappeared. The look of the nose, the black eyes, so dark brown they seem black, the receding hairline, the aquiline nose, so strong, so like Joseph's, had gone. The configuration returned. And I saw Adam. Without Joseph. No longer inhabited. He was himself. Young. I mean you would have known they were father and son. Or would you? Joseph is short and stocky, and Adam is long and thin and that extends to his face. His cheeks are long, the chin points down, whereas Joseph's face is stocky like his body, square and hard the chin, so determined, deathly strong.

And I reached forward for Adam's hand. I didn't tell him what happened then. I just stared at him.

Adam took my hand. He laid it on my head. His palms were wide, like an oak leaf, cooling. His calmness made me want to cry. Why he seemed calm now, I don't know, but he was some stable presence to me then, someone who didn't worship me, someone who didn't hate me too much. Someone who wasn't Blackfoot.

Blackfoot's helped you, he said.

You were reading my mind, I said. But not all of it.

He's made you stronger.

You're jealous, I said. Don't pretend you like what's been going on.

I trust you, he said. I believe you.

I was silent.

Well, you're right to, in one way. I'm not going to fuck him, I said. In other ways, I don't know. He makes me wild, brings out sides of me that aren't really mine and gives me things of his imaginings. He gives me powers, almost as if I'm a god. Some nymph or dryad, some Grecian thing skipping off the plains, a plains god, a household god, I don't know. Not a Jesus or Mary. Nothing like that. Just the sense of being one of many deities. He says I've walked into the Land of the Dead.

You never take yourself seriously, said Adam.

I don't want to worship myself, I said.

I know what Blackfoot is. I've known him for years. Don't forget *I* represent *him*. I do it despite all. He's special. He'll go far with some help.

How's Joseph? I asked.

I didn't see him. He's off to Rio, speaking his mind.

You're making me feel better, I said. I missed you.

I missed you, said Adam. I'm pleased you came here, to see this place. It always brings me back to my senses. Back to myself. I don't know why.

A touchstone?

You know what I'm like when I'm here.

Well, you worry. Incessantly.

There's nowhere to hide here. Perhaps it's the plains. Nowhere to hide, said Adam.

CHAPTER

29

With Adam's blessing I went off into the Midnight Walk with
Blackfoot. You have to stretch yourself, walk into fears
sometimes, because they can lead out of themselves, said Adam.
Blackfoot's no madman. He won't get you into trouble. He just
wants his dream. That was Adam's reasoning, and he, too, thought
I might come up with something from the "unconscious," which
was the way he talked about the Land of the Dead. For me, it was
the Night Sky. And at night you see the stars, you see where the
world is placed, who its friends are, who warms it and who holds it
in place with some strange dance. When it's dark you see not just
the busy world of appearance, the sharp spotlight, the world's way
of pointing to what it wants to sell you, those neon signs above
strip shows and Spanish delis; things to sell are lit up and you lose
your way reading them. You can live your life like that, watching
for where the world will lead you, into the bright lights. But if you
look up (and in Manhattan I can't see them, only out here I can,
tonight) you can see the world being held in its dance, all its family,
and the dead ones and living ones there for me to see, all in one
place. The dead stars still talk to me.

▲▲▲

And I thought of this as I walked with Blackfoot into the
wrinkled hell of the Badlands. Moonlit, so deathly pale was the
light with Blackfoot's song leading the way, some sad song of lost
tribes, dead in the earth, please come to me. He translates for me.
Please come to me, send me the steps of my life. Tell me the steps

of my life, the moons to watch for. And I went very cold. The sky was black, there were white clouds that shouldn't have been there. Like those spotlights I was talking about. So it was unnatural, the way the clouds were lit up, almost like daytime, but the sky was black.

Take my hand, said Blackfoot.

The wind of the past, I can feel it. Its cold. The breath of the dead is cold. You can't just live like this, in the night, placing the Dead first, Blackfoot, I thought. When people have left, you can't keep calling for them. It drives you mad. I remember. I remember well, calling out, but I'd got on the plane already, stepped on the gas, I was gone, but still calling out, torn in two, regretting every move, because I didn't know what you do when they leave, the loved ones.

"They'll come to you. You're like Emma. You're white. So gentle, so much a lady. You jus' wait an' see. No beating the whites, even the Injuns come to them. Makes you bitter, don' it?" said Blackfoot.

The moon bobbed down over the careful pencil curves, up and down, jigging and zagging so abruptly, and she was lost behind one of the peaks.

"No jokin', there's spirits in them rocks. The shapes of them looks like people. When their lives were ended they came here. They live in those white clouds and the rocks. You can see them," said Blackfoot.

And I felt my Dead there in the rocks. Not just the ones that had died. Friends of mine, one was blown up by a land mine in the Nile Valley down in southern Sudan, nothing left of the body; people, rebels who didn't know him killed him. Probably he did a good job of reporting on them. Didn't carry a gun but was blown away, as they say here, made into wind. And another died of a heavy heart, never getting his life on the road. It kept pulling him backwards. He had no energy, no life, really, and then life left him; once and for all his heart stopped. These were young people, I said.

Like Emma Bluegrass. Never had a chance to blossom. It ends, it's over, nothing left.

I wanted them there, sentimental or nostalgic as I was. I wanted them there, in those rocks, and I wanted to believe Blackfoot: that the Dead could be seen in the clouds. Something would be left.

She's in you, said Blackfoot. I can smell her. Come here. Come close, he said.

He grabbed me. I smelt his breath, thick with beer.

I can smell her. Emma. She's in you.

Come closer, he said, and he held me tight and then pushed me back away from him.

You're fighting her, he screamed.

But I couldn't. I caved in.

And then my mother came to me. I hadn't thought about her much. Not for a while. But she came to me crying, asking me for help. I'd said no. I remember it clearly. I can't pretend I sacrificed myself. I didn't help. I walked out. No, I'm too old for this. I'm too young for this. I won't look after you.

She was fifty-five. Leaving my father. Why should I help her? Wanted me there to be with her while she waited for the new man to propose. Why should I wait like some nursemaid, holding her hand when I was the one who needed love. Seventeen, needed a home, a mother and father, a mum and dad, the dinnertime conversations, even the rows. But it went. She left. She wanted me to come with her. I said no. I left home, went to the seaside with some man. Tears in my eyes, all of me dead, but the hands moving on the steering wheel. I didn't crash the car. I drove all the way to Bournemouth, watched the sea. The sea healed me. She did. I promise you. Some man was almost there. But the sea showed me, the ebb and flow, like a hand stroking me, easing away the pain, rocking my eyes. Backwards and forwards she, in her infinity, went with her waves. All of her showed me my own strength. She was in me. I had more thoughts than her waves, but why quibble over infinity?

I had her in me, this sea. She was simpler than me, in a way. I was not just alone. Not just dead. This moment was like a long wave, striving, crisscrossed by millions of waves. One after the other, all in me. I contained it. Goodbye, Mummy. I didn't help you. I know. I'm cruel in my own way. It wouldn't have helped you anyway to have me. You'd have wanted me gone a few months later anyhow when you moved in (he proposed); you got what you wanted, and I was alone. No man. No home. Just that sea in me, taking the place of it all. And my mind working away, interpreting seasons, waking at night to work on the sky, brilliance in me. By then I had gone into my own world. My university, my doctorate. Goodbye, Mummy. I have my own mind. Goodbye, Mummy. I grew up, didn't need you much. Goodbye, Mummy.

But the memory stood there in that South Dakotan sky so alien and wide, and shapes I'd never imagined even were its background. My mother came out of the place where Emma Bluegrass was meant to be. My ancestors, my mother, my parting from her stood like a pillar holding me up.

"I can smell her," said Blackfoot, holding me. "She's in you now."

But I laughed. A small laugh.

"You're crazy," I said. "Imagining things."

It's Mummy who's here, not cuddling me, not giving me love. But here asking for help. This is the truth, Blackfoot. This is the truth, Adam.

There was no doubting it. I was not Emma Bluegrass, could not metamorphose into what Blackfoot wants me to be. I've got my family history, there, right in the center of me, ingrained in me, each year marked on me like on the bark of an old oak tree, defining me.

I can't get up one morning and change my roots, pretend I'm entered, washed clean, made sacred by this or that demon from Blackfoot's world or Pennington's video imagination. I change slowly, over time. I can't change this game of yours, Blackfoot. Though you believe in it. That I'm sure of it. It's *your* world.

I said this with such relief that I wanted to dance. I was full of joy, knowing it hadn't been all good, had marked me for life, in a way; all those moments I closed the door on my mother. Good reasons or bad reasons, who knows? I'm sure it made me. I'm sure it broke me. The anger is still there, crisscrossing in the sea inside me of waves.

And Blackfoot sensed it. He wept. He knocked on the rock where Emma was hiding and called to her, like an animal wrenched from its mother, being weaned; too rushed, too rushed. Emma. Three moons dancing over the plains. Emma Bluegrass.

The body of Emma stretched across Kansas. I could see the blue haze of her body sweltering in the heat of the wheat fields, and the dry land where the cattle graze flicking their tails in the flies' faces. I could see her out there, but not in me.

I'm sorry, Blackfoot, I said.

But he didn't hear me. His grief was terrible. He lay down on the rock, all twisted and torn by the wind like a stalactite, so pointed, so unnatural, and the moon bobbing up over the peak to show me his grief. I couldn't help him. I can't lie to him. I can't be someone else for him. So I watched, in pain, my heart pounding and hurting, throbbing like a toothache, as Blackfoot scratched at the rock like a dog, scratching for Emma's soul.

But I waited for Blackfoot until it was over and dawn came over his mad grief. The stars were pale and the moon and the sun were lemon colored, so all of them hung there, a bit dismally, but returned to us, coming home into our sky. They'll never leave, not in my lifetime. And I just sat, thinking about the sky, the patterns and the dances and the perpetual movement of the planets. And this was permanent, untouched by the inconstancy of love. So abstract it seemed now in this odd landscape, all I'd done, like some expression of human failing. How imperfect it was, because I was always caught in memories that turn and toss you backwards and forwards, from pity to fear, with odd showers of love, sometimes love, but not enough to make a life of it. But I wanted Adam. I wanted him so much to be there, to catch my mood, to know when I was soft with love I thought of him.

But what is the worth of that? To think of love after a wild night of holding the Dead at bay. Wanting love just as a comfort, not as an offering, not as magnificent thanks to the loved one. To the sky for existing? Not as a daily thanking the loved one?

Fuckin' cold here, said Blackfoot.

You want to leave?

I'm talkin' to Adam's old man. The only guy who's got savvy. I'm communin' with him.

Not Emma? Not your Dad?

You gotta have modern answers, said Blackfoot. "My world's dead. They don' come to me when I need 'em. They jus' couldn't keep pace. No savvy. Like Minny says, they ain't got what makes things tick.

So the childworld died in Blackfoot that night, not once and for all, but something started dying in him. I could see it in his eyes, how they stared like his friend Jim had done. That look of hopelessness, and the comfort of despair. When no one comes in that dead night, not even a memory of anger, a mother one way or the other, nor me, no one from the living came with what was needed to make Blackfoot warm. So something died because it got no food, no water, no loving. I don't know what died in him precisely. But Emma killed it by not coming to him. He wasn't good enough. And I wouldn't take over and be his Emma. You can't save people like that anyhow by giving up your roots, your center (let's not be abstract), by giving up yourself.

But Blackfoot's going to do it now. He'll give up his ancestors, now that they failed him. No one will notice the difference here in America. He won't have to make much effort to *be American.* He'll just stay the same. And no one will notice he's lost his ancestors. And I said to Blackfoot, there must be something she said to you, you can remember it. One thing she said when you were a baby on her knee, something you imagined her saying, just a word, a lullaby.

I dunno, said Blackfoot, what you're talking about.

And I hated America.

And I knew the difference between my country and this land I'd so wanted to live in. I told Blackfoot, I too wanted to come here, to live here, take part in all this obvious optimism, all the things that keep ticking here. Nothing changes much at home, like the clusters of stars; friends are the same, hardly move jobs. It's very unmodern, I said, where I come from. We can't just join in, become one of the crowd. You know when you give up your ancestors you just need new ones, Mary or Joseph, born again this or that. When your center goes you get a plastic refill, something like a fake limb or something to take that place in yourself, of that spine that holds you up, that odd variety of emotions that is you, and the anger, and I can tell you, Blackfoot, I spent a lot of time just remembering how much I hated Mummy.

There's nothing to remember here, said Blackfoot. They'll dig up what's left to get gold. Uranium. You don' know. They dug out the spirits. Now there's only money left in the land. Real estate. But here it's worth shit. Dirt land. The ghosts trashed it and left. Took their revenge. No one's left. They vacated it long ago. They dug up the graves. You don' know.

Blackfoot took out a beer from his rucksack, a beautiful beaded rucksack with pink suede tassels made by some Navajo tribe for tourists, I expect. He drank slowly on his empty stomach. I could hear it rumbling, irritated by the brown beer.

We come from the same place, I said. Places where the past holds weight, traditions are carried down. People still wear wigs in court. At university I wore a gown and studied in the same libraries, surrounded by the same worn leather books that centuries of students saw. The same smell came from the trees that fell in the same position, and even when the sun slanted through the stained-glass of the Bodleian, I saw it just as centuries before they did. Everything was the same, I carried it on. I fell into place. But made my own way a little. Not yet I haven't. But I will. I felt it with you. How I'd go my own way. Adam noticed you'd helped me. We come from the same place. We're not American, don't start out from scratch each generation, almost from scratch, I said.

"I gotta dump my trash can," said Blackfoot. "I got given the dud heritage. Nothin' that works," he said, drinking his beer.

When I get some bread I'll leave this hole. Like the place wants to kill ye. Freezin' through your bones. You jus' gotta stay at home when the snows come. They'll be here soon. Fuckin' freezin'. I was talkin' to Adam's Dad about it jus' now. He escaped from Nazi Germany. He should know. I asked him why 'em Jews jus' kept on and on, no matter, like he said on the TV show, if it works or it don't, they jus' keeps bein' Jews. Millions of 'em go down, like with a plague of Nazis, like buffalo, like you'd think it's the end. Why bother? Who gives a shit anyhow? But they keeps goin' on and on. I'm goin' to see that guy. You know him, don't you?

I smiled, a little bitter smile that left me almost immediately.

For I was proud, suddenly, as if I owned Joseph, as if he was part of me again, not haunting me, filling me crammed full with his visions, no, just a friend, one of the family I was privileged to have.

You works with him, said Blackfoot, as if waking from his dream.

I wasn't going to tell Blackfoot much, but I said, yes. That was enough.

Like your Dad, isn't he? said Blackfoot, eyes sparkling again, resurrected by Joseph, flush with his beer, igniting pleasure in his eyes, alive again.

No, I said.

Yeah, he is. Come off it. Adam told me. How you love him, he can't say a word that's wrong. You'd think Adam is jealous, the way you love that old guy.

He isn't, I said.

Yeah, he is. I see him, he's jealous all right. That guy's got more savvy than the two of you put together, and you know it.

He's cleverer, perhaps, I said.

"You love that guy," said Blackfoot. "I would. I do. I'm goin' to see him. Go on a pilgrimage up to Boston. You can organize it for me. Adam will if you won't. If I don' see that guy, I'll never know how you do it; when they're killin' you off, how you keep at it, livin'. That guy knows mystical stuff. In the skies he's livin' right up there, man, with planets, real modern too. Can't get more modern than him, no one's thought what he's thought. He's the newest guy at it, got the first ideas on the earth, prizes an' prizes."

"Galileo was killed, you know. You don't always get prizes, Blackfoot. He'll tell you that."

"I wanna know how 'em Jews survived," said Blackfoot. "I tell you, man, I'd just give up the ghost, say forget it. Who's havin' me on? Lettin' my whole tribe die? You think there's no message in that? You think that don't mean something, like yer into the wrong trip, man, into the wrong God. Bit slow on the old uptake, ain't you?"

Blackfoot opened another beer can.

Bit slow when yer whole family ends up dead or broke, stuck on some shit-hole reservation. And they all forgot. May as well be dead. They forget we're here, that's where they came from, all of them that's what they are, thieves of our land. But they don' know. The world goes on like some circus, clash-bang noise to stop you from thinking. Like the news. More and more shit to stop you from thinking. I gotta move fast or I'll end up jus' like my Dad, dead drunk when he should be cryin'.

Blackfoot put down the beer can.

My Dad's even got 'em over his grave. Instead o' flowers. Beer cans and potato chips. Junk culture, like Adam says. His Dad's made him bigger than all that. He got something that don' give into this shit, this junk. Goddam fuckin' trash can, America.

And I watched as Blackfoot picked up the pieces of his soul, from here and there, anger fueling him forward, and I sensed some hatred of his father. But it all comes in useful, all the emotions, when you hold them as ingredients to make yourself. Then they fit into place. And Blackfoot showed me there, just as I thought he would die, that something else died, a kind of mania (well, the mania is still there to this day), but some distortion went out of his mind, bringing despair, and in its place he wanted something true, something that would help him live, some notion of living that would make him stronger than America. His father didn't have it. But Emma did. She didn't love him, wouldn't give it to him. I'm sure that was all true. But I wasn't sure that Joseph would have an answer. He didn't for me.

Damn Blackfoot, taking me back to Boston on some pilgrimage. That's where I started out here, and that's what I'm leaving behind. This very minute. I'm leaving Joseph behind. I've been leaving him for a while now. But I felt my running was over. I couldn't even feel much anger in myself. Just irritation, a sort of lethargy coming over me at the thought of being returned, again and again, by hook or crook, to Joseph.

"I told you," said Adam later on, as we walked through Marta's farmlands by her home. (Bobby had left, packed his bags, the ignominy of being cuckolded by an Indian was too much to bear. When Adam filed for Marta, he left. Betrayed by his old friend. Sex always wins out, he said. You fucked everyone to get your own way. Marta told us he said that, and then he packed his bags, said she'd be hearing from him and his lawyer, and didn't even check the plane times from Rapid City. He left.)

"I told you. This place takes you back to yourself. That's why I come back here. This place is like a scar on America's face, but it hasn't healed. Keeps on bleeding and bleeding. It's like the backstage in the theater. That's where you see what goes on, rehearsing for the show in the big cities. But this is where America comes from, I told you that when we arrived. You don't believe me," said Adam.

We caught a look in each other's eyes of knowing. It was true. I don't believe him much, not that I think he'd lie to me. I just don't think he's got the truth. Searches, yes. Makes a brave effort. Now I've admired that paltry effort. Other men don't even try, and they hold the truth. I thought Blackfoot or Joseph knows it, godlike, and I go, like some magpie, picking up pieces of wisdom they drop for me, content with that. We caught that look in each other's eyes, and it hurt us. We knew Adam was right, but he wasn't angry. It might have been easier if he let fly as he did with me, or tortured himself as he does. But his look was steady, and there was beauty in it, such boldness and confidence mixed with sadness on those carefully outlined eyes that are colorful like a butterfly's wings. The brown of his eyes has color, it's not some muddy pool. I saw the brightness there, the flecks of green and yellow, patterns on a butterfly's wing, diverting me from the sickness that fell on me, knowing I didn't listen to him, he was second best. Though we lived together, he was given a little less credence than others. Joseph or Blackfoot, was it a similar story? This time in the Badlands, mirroring weeks in Boston I'd spent with Joseph waiting for wisdom to fall? Believing it did, while my body slept with Adam, and my mind slept with him and awoke, its awareness so acute, so waking when I was near Joseph. Through the corridors I followed him, pen in hand, taking notes from his genius while my body slept with his son.

You don't have to look at me like that, said Adam.

How? I asked.

Oh, I dunno. Shiftily.

"I need time to think," I said. "I don't want to" and then tears came.

I didn't say more than that. I didn't know if I could do it, alter the way I was, giving body and soul, not one thing to one man and something else to another. And was the body a lesser form of giving? So Joseph got the best, more love, respect, and——

What's the matter? asked Adam.

But I cried. I couldn't tell him. There's no point confessing that you don't take someone seriously. It's an insult. You just have to change it. Do something about it. One day something will change. One day I will, I'll know how, I'll will myself to change. I'll put the two pieces of me together, my body and soul, and only be able to give it to one man. So I won't leave one behind, drop my body from fear when I'm with Joseph, and drop my soul away from Adam so I don't give him credence, so he falls short of being the loved one.

"Perhaps it was shocking," I said, watching Blackfoot. "Perhaps it made me think," I said, belatedly, in answer to Adam's question.

And as we walked over to Marta's for dinner, to her new home which had an open door to Blackfoot now, so he could come and go like a husband, we let the dusk sky, humid with late dew, clinging to the skin, hold us. The air was thick, like a hand it felt, brushing us softly, God's hand as always in this damn land. Who owns the sky here? God. And who the earth? Man. And we planned for the pilgrimage to Joseph, who would take Blackfoot, and who would ask Joseph, without ever doubting that it was necessary to do so. Blackfoot had made it clear that his sanity depended on a journey to a man he had only seen twice on TV.

So Blackfoot went to Joseph in Rockport. I could see it without being told, those eggshell skies and the derelict seaside town, tourist town, with its pretty boats and pretty harbors made full with beauty by the roughness of the sea. This Atlantic that separates me from home, but is just a mirage, really. Water and waves will take me away, but not inside. I could see Blackfoot going, just as I had gone to Joseph, wanting not just a job but an answer. Joseph has a way of providing for you with his odd ideas, a contact here, a seemingly useless remark there. For Blackfoot, it was a woman who worked for CBS in Manhattan; he should try for a job, get him away from the Badlands, back into the swing of things. "You never know. Pitch your idea of the Wild West Show. Dance for her. I like her. She's got style," said Joseph. So that was the first gem that Blackfoot brought home.

The two of them had walked by the ocean off Pigeon's Cove, watching the waves. "Sometimes he looked straight at me, through me, with bright eyes. But most of the time he was in his own world, musing on things," said Blackfoot.

You don't have to tell me, I said.

▲▲▲

If I had a father, I'd want him to be like that. I dunno why it ain't helped Adam.

Nor me, I said.

That's different. You're a woman. Sex is in it, fires it up between you. If I were Adam I'd keep you away from him. That guy got the devil in him.

He was better than anything I'd known, I said to myself, tears coming into my eyes, welling up with recognition deep somewhere in my bones because the tears made no sound. They were just like blood from the heart rising, beating too fast with emotion, pushing the sea in one out. He was better than my father. He gave me more in two weeks than my father. Talk about being distant. My father lived with a wall round him, so invisible, but you couldn't hear him. Everything he said was stopped by the wall. It must have been sad for him to live like that, in a fairy tale where the prince never awakes, but there was never a happy ending with my father; the spell never broke.

"So he slipped me two hundred dollars for the fare down on the Boston shuttle. Said he'd give her a call."

If he hadn't been like that, softened me up a bit (God, was I on the make, brittle and hard on top, career mad, that was all I had to hang onto, I thought): but he softened me up, let me trust a little. I kept crying after I saw him. The tears kept coming out of me when he was kind.

"So I went. Damn bitch. Kept asking after Joseph. Not one word — didn't give half a shit for me. Except at the end. She took my number. Said she'd call. I had a nice face, she said, like you'd say of a chick. I told her. Babe, I got my show. Not my face for you. And she stared. She looked scared. You think you'll meet some chick with brains up there on that twentieth floor, big time...."

He softened me up, so I was ready for Adam. Perhaps he planned it. Did it all for me and handed me over on a plate. Almost ready.

"So he said I'm right. I won't go nowhere, won't get shit out of the world unless I stop believing in magic."

You'll never stop, Blackfoot. That's the way you are.

"So, I asked him about the Jews, and he said he didn't know why they survived. He wouldn't presume, he said, to know. He's no God. No man is."

"Is that all?" I said.

"Yes," said Blackfoot, "but I gotta convert. I told him. Asked him how. Two years, he said. Full study. I can't afford it, I said. You can if you want to, he said, but I don't advise it, substituting one religion for the next."

"I don't believe you," I said.

"I am," said Blackfoot. "Them Jews is stronger than this shit culture. I seen 'em. They're bigger than it. No one can get them. I dunno why. They don' go down. They jus' keeping swimming, centuries on."

"And Joseph didn't say why?"

"Why what?"

"Why they survive?"

"No. He said he wouldn't presume. I told you," said Blackfoot, irritable with me.

"And Marta?"

"She'll do it too. It's about time she said for spiritual growth. Since I gave up God, I'm lonely, she said."

Lonely? I asked, with you?

We're all lonely, said Blackfoot. People ain't enough. People is shit half the day and sun the next. There's demons in them. But I gotta eliminate that, said Blackfoot.

Thinking like that? I asked.

Yes, said Blackfoot. Yes. Time an' again. You lay hold o' someone, have them in your arms, they're yours, an' the next day you hear they're off with some other guy. Like the weather out here. Freezin'. You can be sure it'll freeze the pants off you in winter, sure of the cold. Them demons come into you, live in you, leavin' no room for no one else. You can shout and scream for some space, but there's nothing for you. I wan' God. One God. Always the same. I don' want demons in people, demons in the sky, moons that sing, visions on mescaline. Last summer I ate too many mushrooms, trembled four nights after that, jus' with the cold. Yer body stinks with it. If you hold out yer hand for help, people fall away, like in winter. You push yer finger in them an' the reflection in the water goes into mud.

I told him about that night we had together looking for Emma, continued Blackfoot. You wouldn't hold her in you. You're a bitch, I said. Joseph laughed. "I love her," said Joseph. He stared at me. Don't going sayin' bad things about her, said his eyes, but he was saying nothin' aloud.

"She let me down," I said. I was there for the truth. I ain't goin' to lie. Those minutes was precious. Each minute with him I felt it tickin' away like in a taxi.

"That girl's got principles, backbone," he said. "Why should she pretend she has powers she don't possess. You're asking to be hurt, when you go to a woman like that and ask her to lie. It's a waste of her mind."

"I love her," said Joseph. Again.

His face went funny, a little red, like he'd had two beers or three, and he flushed up. "How is she?" he asked me, a bit shy. So I says you was havin' trouble with Adam. There's somethin' wrong with your son, I said. Not that I wanna be bad-mouthin' him. He done great things for me. But he ain't happy. Why's he unhappy? I asked.

"He wants to kill me," said Joseph.

Oh, come on, I said, mockin' a little. It sounded crazy there an' then with the wind blowin' in our ears. (Why the hell we had to chat in this freezin' wind?, an' I hadn't come prepared like that with a hat, so it went through my ears.)

"It's fine if he wants to kill me. But the trouble with Adam is that he wants what I've got — the fame, that kind of nonsense. It seems to be so important to kids, the fame, and he thinks he can get it by killing me. I've seen it in his eyes. I'm not imagining it," said Joseph. "Of course I'm at fault, young man." (He called me young man and young fellow too). "Sometimes I want what he has." (An' his face flushed again. He was thinkin' of you. I knows it, his voice went like it did the last time he talked about you, an' he flushed up again, like he's drinkin'.)

"He's faithful," said Joseph. "He can stay with one woman. I've seen his constancy. It's quite remarkable. I would like that. But I don't have it." He laughed, good natured.

"But when he has anything," said Joseph, "he thinks he's stealing it from me. He really believes he's killing me to get *anything*: there's tremendous guilt in the chap, every time he achieves anything. I remember it at Harvard. Every time he won a boat race, every time there was a little limelight on him, down he went, moping for weeks."

I made notes later, sitting on the rocks when he walked away, so I wouldn't forget, word for word. It stuck in my mind, all he says, like it's written in stone, with a knife. I repeats it again an' again to myself, said Blackfoot. "So why he wans' to kill you? I says.

"It was just a thought," says this old guy. You'd never know he's seventy; sometimes he looks young, too young for his age, like Adam, like he's a boy.

"Adam doesn't look like a boy," I said. "He doesn't look like Adam anymore," I added, firmly.

No, that's changed. He doesn't inhabit Adam's face anymore. He's gone back into himself. He's not wandering for the moment into others. Not that he really wandered, but I imagined it, projected it, like a movie projector onto the wall. When all was dark, some nights in bed I saw him clearly as Joseph.

"An' me, you think I wan' what you got?" I asks Joseph.

He says he don' know me. "You thinks people who want what you got wanna kill you?"

"Metaphorically, young man," he said. "Not literally."

"What d'you mean?" I asks.

He says it all comes back to my hangup with magic. He says if I thinks of killing someone metaphorically it ain't no big shit. It's not gonna happen. The trouble with your way of thinking, he says, is you think it'll happen. So you become scared of the action. You pitch your Wild West Show to Gaily. You have your limelight. It won't hurt a soul, he says. An' I take notes on that while he was speaking. I wonders if it's jus' my shit culture, or everyone's like this. That guy got savvy. He *knows*.

An' I felt kinda sad, sittin' on the rocks after he left. He's the kinda guy you don' wan' for breakfast, dinner an' lunch, givin' you ideas. I'm tired. So much is changin'. Mart's livin' wi' me now, an I'm her man, an' the demons left me. They asked for it. When you abandon someone like that, treat 'em like shit, why should they come back, worshippin' you? Like I'm masochistic? Keep comin' back for more? No way, man. I'm gettin' one God. One that I knows is a long-term thing. Not some pushover. No. You gotta study to be with him. But, he'll see you through. He saw 'em Jews through everything, didn't he? said Blackfoot, a bit nervously.

We crossed the road to wait for Minny by the yard of the Wounded Knee Elementary School, with its modern totem poles, eyes of gods staring at us like the gods who left Blackfoot, and the tepee-shaped turret, all of it kindly preserving this old way of life in decorative form. At least it's prettier than the oblong slab of concrete down the road, and that chapel nearby that Blackfoot never worshipped in. Why? Because it got stuffed into our throats. Mary or the knife. The whole of South America filled with hymns an' shit they don' know their grandfathers were forced by the knife to sing. You know what I mean?" he asks me.

Wounded Knee Church. The Madonna is white, as if drained of all life, all blood went from her long ago, and she was frozen like a wedding cake, so white, icing and all (little lace frills on her dress), she married death. And her skin is so smooth, like a bar of Ivory soap. She's looking so sad, her baby gives her no pleasure (she looks away from him heavenward, perhaps, but she's not even squeezing him in her arms). Her baby is already old, having to find his own way. He's really an old man at birth, huge responsibilities fell on him. He's white, too, and so cold. No comfort came from her. Just a vision of some form of death, the end of giving, the reverse of the natural cycle, where children have no time to frolic. Adulthood falls on them like a curse, so early, there's no room for joy.

And I went right up to the Madonna and Child, and Blackfoot stood a few steps behind me. He was scowling at her. She was his Emma, perhaps, who left, dead in the rocks, unmoved by him. But for me she was symbol of all that had gone wrong with Adam and me. Our lives went backwards in time, not forwards enough.

"She's a bitch," said Blackfoot of the Madonna.

I can't end up having a child with Joseph, I thought. But the way I feel about him, it's as if I should. Backwards it goes, my life, into an old man. Backwards goes Adam, wanting to leave him behind, every day wanting and wasting time leaving him.

"She's late," said Blackfoot. "She's out at two-thirty. It's three."

I don't want to have a child and burden him with this sort of pain, the pain that Minny has, and Jesus in His cold mother's arms, and me, perhaps me too, I said to myself.

"I'll look in the school," he says.

So he went and I stood under this frozen mother, not wanting to be like her. So cold, the way I can be, the way I left my mother, saying no to her. The way I did things to her, said things to hurt her, the way she hurt me. So cold I can be, like the Madonna. Wanting to have my child with God, too snooty for mortals.

But Blackfoot came back alone. He said that Minny skipped school all day, and no one knew where she was. And I caught him eyeing the Madonna as if blaming her. But he turned away from her, eyes hot with disdain, ice hot and blue, like the burns that come from ice, that char the skin, so he looked at her and away.

And it was at that moment I realized why I couldn't leave this place, or why I was here, perhaps. It was when I saw Blackfoot's shift of expression, in his eyes, how one way of thinking was suddenly replaced by another that I became aware I could see his mind changing. It was like watching history unfold in miniature. Nations change faith or lose faith like this, I'm sure, some matter of deep concern, a lost child or war, something that goes to the core of you is broken, destroyed, some storm falls on your home or fire burns it. And you change. You walk out of the flames growing a new skin. And though Blackfoot's change of direction would not be mine, watching him helped. I see you can do it in your life. Just a flicker of change, and it can come from ashes, from the stone face of mother and child, the night out in the cold land, badland. And Joseph was wrong. I don't think Blackfoot's substituting one faith for another. Who can be sure? And is it merely a question of changing faith? No, I can see him move, get on the plane to New York, on the twentieth floor of CBS or ABC. Who cares? Doing a song and dance for Gaily. Give me a ring, Gaily. That's a move forward, I thought, exhilarated by it all as Blackfoot drove me home to Marta's house, by his new home. He's moving freely now, swimming between cultures. Choosing this or that. It might not work. Who knows? You can't predict. But Blackfoot's doing it, making the move forward out of past time. Leaving Emma behind wherever he finds her, cold in stone.

And I turned on the side light, because the shutters were

closed and the light was soft, and I saw Adam's body (he's in Manhattan, but I saw him still in my mind), the sensation of moving over him, night after night. I could hear our flesh touch. I could feel his tongue in my mouth, under my tongue. I'm one with him now. And I lay on the bed, and the light was soft. Next time we make love we'll start like this, his hand on my breast, sucking me, like a baby, sucking me hard, and I just stayed like that with my hand on my breast, my left breast, pretending to be Adam's hand.

But as I lay there, finding for a brief moment some resolution, some easing off of thought, some movement towards sleep in this, my hand went heavy, seemed like an object of fun almost, and I came down on myself, asking why this image could make me content, feel as if all is done, my love for Adam true, and it will all end well. Just a hand on my breast, a finger in my cunt, is that the happy ending? And yes, it makes me content, helps me to sleep, and the face is Adam's tonight, not Joseph's or Blackfoot's, thank God. In that there's reason for peace. But this image, is it enough to say I love him, ask him to fly back here, come to me, come to him, so that we'd always be the homecoming to each other. Is this hand in my cunt with Adam's face enough? And I hated my own mind for ruining it, the soft sensation, the thick sensation of sex, and I hated myself. The reasons unclear tonight, the reasons for hating this movement down to my breast so it dies. The pleasure and the way the question of love is asked makes it unanswerable. Body or soul? As if the two don't live in each other's arms, inseparable. But I knew in myself, turning over, taking my hand from my breast, that it wasn't enough, that resolution in sex, with or without Adam. And I needed something else, some action I did, some feeling I felt, to turn to, not just his hand on my breast to evoke him.

And it came to me, Blackfoot's words taken from Joseph's mouth, saying I love her. The way he turned red, said Blackfoot, suggesting I turned him on, but I thought for a moment that Blackfoot was wrong and Joseph loved me entirely and made me feel loved, as if his love had been given to me at the beginning of time when I left my mother's womb and my mind and emotions were being formed, and it created them. The kind of love that changes one, that Blackfoot feels he will get from God. The kind of love that feels like a hand molding one's self, so it touches me fully, not just my breast.

rang Adam at dawn, after my dreams of my father, one after the other, so many images of him, waking me from sleep, on a Rolodex, he was so many persons, all with the same name, but different faces, and his emptiness had disappeared, and instead he was full with so many identities. But it frightened me that he was the only one I knew. I had no friends but him. He had filled my life so from A to Z, he was there, his photo turned up, never leaving me. And his emptiness in his life seemed like a fraud, his way of saying nothing of import and the deep anger or sadness that never came out; but in the dream he was everyone, and he had expressions, and so many I was awoken by them, running past me, in the wind, blowing over, one after the other in my Rolodex. And I wanted Adam. I truly wanted him, for him to appear, to interrupt my father, prove to me that I'd lived another life outside my home, that my time away from home had not been a mirage, and moreover, that being here in America was not the same as staying back where I was, in a small town, never moving from Oxford, the same faces, never changing, stuck, in a word, but running.

So I rang Adam, saying I miss you, I want you. Come here for the weekend. Be with me. I love you. A little stilted I was, but not much, considering the way I've been with Adam, pent up, half eaten up by other loves. And he'll come. My life is starting. I heard him smile. My life is starting. My man, he'll come to me.

This I asked for, this I deserve. So the dawn came through, like a wedding dress, all pale white, not stark, but the softness of lace on a wedding dress against my skin, pinching me a little in at the waist, and I lay there, hearing my life start, and the dawn with me, to welcome me. She's opening up the room, killing off shadows, so all is light. And I walked to Marta's kitchen in the dawn. No one would be up. I could have my breakfast alone. So I walked on the stubs of dried-out grass, mixed with the soft blades of young grass, the smell rising up of greenness, and the sky was pale blue now, but white at the edges. From every point in her circle she soared up, in strong silence, so strong I could hear it and the coarse shout of a bird, and another breaking the air's calm. The sun was still cool, still a bit sleepy, rising out of the golden corn. And Adam had taken me here, to come back to myself. I thanked him. He didn't know it but he's drawn me inward, so I can see myself a little. Not much, just a glimpse through a once-closed door, the images of people in me. I thought I'd left, but they stayed, because I had lied and not heard my own voice talking in their tone. And it didn't feel bad. I wasn't to blame, not this morning, anyway, not now. It'd ruin beauty to enter blame into this frame where life begins.

And I went to the kitchen and opened the fridge to take out the food I'd bought, but the fridge was empty, just some cans of beer and a bottle of wine, half drunk. And the kitchen table was strewn with chips, empty beer cans, an ashtray of cigarette stubs. I called out but no one answered, and I walked to the bedrooms but no one was there, not a soul. I felt so alone. Cold water poured on my dream, I'd been left. The morning was ruined. They'd walked out on me, taken my food, perhaps even my car. But the pickup truck was there, and I ran to it, wanting to get away from this place. And I drove.

Night came. I booked into a Holiday Inn and ate, thinking and thinking, and so alone as if I could die. Something like this would always happen, a terrible cycle of being left in the lurch. And part of me didn't believe it at all. I knew I was mad. But still it hurt, like a wound, a wound from generations, handed down, some stigma on my flesh marked by it for life. And I slept without dreams, thank God.

It was cold waking at dawn, and I drove again in the still

greyness, past Interior, into the buttes. And beauty returned. The land calmed me, the sky. God's country came to care for me. I wept in the fields. I was overcome.

I'm walking through myself at breakneck speed, through the circles of the inferno, waves and waves to step through. But this is Adam's place, he took me here to come to my senses; he told me so. I can hear his voice. We were driving down by the Lutheran church. We stopped, the corn was high, to hide us. We hid in it. Here we made love over the graves; nearby they were. So white. My wedding dress would have been white. Last morning I felt it snug on my waist and saw myself walking to Adam, married in flesh and spirit, before and after death, for all time. And I found myself sitting by the edge of the Lutheran church, under the bright clouds, a little frightening, moving so fast with the wind, those cities and great gods (I saw them with the fear I'd have as a child, seeing demons in the clouds), knowing this was all my own making, my despair.

It was not Adam's fault for taking me here, nor Blackfoot's fault for leaving early one morning (God knows where), nor was it writ in the clouds that love could end like this in one of those empty rooms with smells of late-night parties, drinking, cigarette ends, the way love ends in adolescence, blues always the day after, love never consummated, always a hope that dies. But that's my story, my despair, not Blackfoot's doing. And I sat stupidly on the corn, uncomfortable, with the ants crawling by and the sun beginning to beat down, blinding a little, and I rubbed my eyes, coming out of my dream, knowing it was my dream. Not Blackfoot's, not Adam's, this dream ending in despair.

It was the way I wrote life, always the same story. I'll see it everywhere, even in this field, and I saw the emptiness stretching, all those blades of corn becoming one great mass of desert space, no one to talk to, and the death clouds hovering, no one to be with, all alone. And the corn stretched out into an empty sky with only God sitting there over his church, saying he'd fill the emptiness. There where my father lay, empty of truth and so featureless, there in that place where someone was meant to be. Hug me, Daddy, tell me a goodnight story; laugh with me, Daddy; but no, there in that empty space God will walk if you give him half a chance. But I won't. That is Blackfoot's dream, not mine. And Abe dreams differently; those who have no real fathers dream like this. I'm sure of it; drunken spells of hope become faith.

And I won't. Here in God's country I won't. I'm not Marta needing some spiritual growth, nor Abe killing, killing, nor Blackfoot needing a way outside his magic, demons, visions of deities confusing life. And the land came to comfort me. Some rhythm, perhaps the imperceptible sound of the earth turning, faithful day and night, day and night, rhythms I live in, sleep and wake, deep in my blood. The moons dance, suns wake and fall, and I'm part of it. Get up and go. Start again. Try once again. You know, you can do it, fish in water, breathing the cool sea, this is your sea, swim in it. Life was made for you. Not a bad time or place to start. Here in this field again, not so alone. Adam'll be here for the weekend.

And I picked myself up, took myself to the car. Down I drove myself to the Rosebud Cafe. And it felt good, driving slow; at the steering wheel, whistle a little into the air, turn on the radio, turn it off, step on the gas, down we go. Gravel and stones rock my way. I'm singing a song. And the Rosebud Cafe was dark, smells of beer and toast, breakfast with beer, eggs on whisky, drink yourself to death. So I walked in and sat down and realized, after my second glass of papaya and milk, that I was waiting for Blackfoot.

But I don't love Blackfoot. I never have. I watched the shadows on the wall. The sun was slanting so bright, making the shadows darker, like ink drawings splattered across the wall by a child. Darkness holds light. My love for Adam came out of my love for Joseph. Darkness and light. My love for Adam comes out of my hating Blackfoot. Waiting for him, following him around, feeling he's not quite one, splattered all over the place, changing faith, not quite Blackfoot. I can't quite trust him, never know what I'll find. He's so many people, husband and father to two women or more.

And how I hate him now, watching the shadows on the wall, the fool I am to him, wasting myself away, waiting for him when he's got nothing to give. And how I don't care. I'll see it through, loosen the reins on myself, trust myself a little, wait for Blackfoot, look for him. Out I go now, on the gas, old love songs on the radio, sentimental tunes of lost love. I don't believe them now. But I'm looking for Blackfoot, no good reason, wanting to find out where I'll go when he's found. And I drove.

The afternoon clouds were low and I drove through them like a god, flying so fast through time. And I drove to Marta's farm but the place was empty, and I drove to Angel's home but the place was empty, and night came, and I wanted to be with Blackfoot so bad it hurt, no reason why. He's someone else. I know he is. But I don't know who. So I drove wanting to find out Blackfoot's disguise, who he is to me, some lost love returned. I don't know.

And I went to the ANTIQUE BARN to be with his things from dead warriors, suede tassels, and war bonnets, the things I loved about Blackfoot that evening when we talked about us, as if I was human, neither God nor dolt, neither Emma nor demon, but me. And his voice broke a little, it was true, when he said, "You have to do more than like to make love. You have to feel more than sex to make love," as if he felt it for me, and I went to the door wanting to relive the time, one instant where Blackfoot saw me, felt for me, stopped his feelings because it wasn't fair to me then. He felt so strong, but he stopped to save me from eating myself up in him, mangled in his arms because I love Adam, and he has Marta. And I wanted to think of Blackfoot well. My hatred of him was tiring; it's better to have some love going inside you.

So I opened the door and the light was on dimly, in the background, some candles perhaps, for the light was a warm glow, peach-colored, and the war bonnets were made peach, and the wooden warrior wearing his suede dress and his fur boots with black tassels. And the spears were moving, like blades of grass in the wind. A war was going on, the spears moved. I heard not the "shoosh" of the wind, but a human voice. Shadows on the wall, moving. "Shoosh" said the wind. The light was peach, a glow of warmth over the room, the log fire crackled perhaps. I heard it giggle. I walked over behind the spears. The shadows of making love moved on the wall. The four-poster bed sent its shadow across the wall, and I saw a woman splayed out, her legs tied, the ribbon around her ankles wild in the flickering light, and a man, over her, moving up and down, up and down, like a horse rider, and the light went out and the wall was dark. But the wind was up. I heard "shoosh," an old wind.

I'm leaving. Blackfoot's spirits are here. I'm leaving, seeing things on the wall, starting this morning, just like a child, reading people into shadows. I've got to stop seeing things, like a child, with all that fear, trying to go to sleep at night, but I couldn't alone.

Mummy, come hold my hand. I'm frozen with fear. The darkness is on me, suffocating me like a blanket. Mummy, come here. And she came. She ran through the corridors, down to my room. I stood there. The dark was over me. Mummy, I'm here. So she came. Her arms around me. Mummy, I'm here.

34

Abe stepped out of the darkness, Snake Boy's evil eye laughing at me. His thin legs trembling, naked from head to foot, still a child, harmless it seemed for the moment, his being naked.

He laughed. "It's her," he said.

"Oh, her," I heard, dismissive voice of a girl.

So I went to see, half a child with Mummy holding my hand, half me, alert, wanting to see where Abe's nakedness led. And Minny lay there behind the spears and the Navajo blanket, Abe leading the way with a candle. Legs splayed out, tied down, her arms, ankles, and the four-poster bed holding her down; and she laughed hard and cold.

"It's you," she said, dismissive. "Looking for Dad?"

And the two of them laughed at me, coldly, Minny naked, pulled apart on the bed, Abe moving to her, sitting down on the bed, placing his hands on her cheeks, closing her mouth.

"Shut up, you bitch," he said to her and to me too. He had me under him just as he did right from the first day. I walked into his game, like a victim, sparrow and snake, the way he bewitches me so. I watch him in fear, this small boy, touching Minny, putting his hands on her breasts, so I turn away.

"Stop it," I said.

"I seen you wi' Dad," said Minny. "*You* shut up."

"We seen you wi' Dad," said Abe.

Doing what? I wanted to ask, not trusting myself for a moment, wondering if they'd seen something I never saw, something between us I'd missed.

"I seen you wi' Dad," said Minny again. And she laughed, pleased with her nakedness, her legs open, splayed out, pleased with it all, showing her body off and Abe touching her.

"Don' preach to me," she said like an adult, sullenly. "I knows your type. Angel tol' me, your types like that. Tryin' to get into my Dad's pants. Sit here tryin' to get his fingers in you. I knows," said Minny. The Snake Boy, pushing his hand into her mouth, tightening the cord so her arm hurt, pulled to the bed post.

"My Mom knows. She says they're like that, with Dad. I seen it."

The Snake Boy stroked the inside of her thighs and pushed his finger inside her. Showing the pink flesh, he parted the lips of her vulva, gently. He stroked her clitoris, he did. I saw it with my own eyes. I was not seeing things. And her eyes closed, smiling. He knew, perhaps she'd taught him, and he knew what to do, quicker and quicker his fingers went, and she let out a little scream, and her mouth opened, and I watched.

You knows they've gone? said Minny.

She grinned, like an old woman her face crinkled up into wrinkles.

Marta and Dad. Looking for me. Thought I'd gone into the Badlands. Chased me out there, dumb ass. Think I'd go out in the cold like you, Dad?

Shut up, said Abe. Don't go talkin' about him.

My Dad, said Minny fretfully.

He went, I said. The place was empty, two days. How did you hide? Down here. No one comes back here into 'em shadows. Dad was here yesterday. We hid under those blankets down at the end. Heard 'im talkin'. Then he left.

I looked for him, I said.

We knews you was waiting, said Minny. We saw you waiting. Why's you waiting for Dad? He don' want you, she said. Dad's got me. He got Marta. He don' need you. You're extra, jus' hangin' aroun', makin' a dumb ass in yourself.

Why don' you go home? said Minny. Leave us alone? You're extra, she said with such relief. You don' count. For nothin'.

But I stayed.

Get down, I said. Get off the bed. You've got to stop this.

Minny laughed.

Jealous, she said. You'd like Dad's fingers up your ass. I seen him, does it real good with Marta. I saw him. Dad knows how to do it. Not like you, you dumb ass, she said to Abe.

You don' see him, you don' know, don' go tellin' me stuff, she howled at me, suddenly caught in a fury, almost in tears. I thought she might faint, her eyes rolled, the pupils up, showing the whites. Abe pulled on the rope.

Stop it, I said, grabbing his hand.

Small boy, small hand, harmless, so sudden his body tells me he's harmless, but his presence stings. I remember him now. He's just a boy, without a Dad, Adam's helping him. Pull him away. He'll never hurt you, too small, just a boy. But he lurched round, pulled on my hair, and I screamed.

Nights of violence, nights of slaughter, coming back in my dreams. I remember now, nights when the house was ice cold. No one spoke, so much hatred in the air, chilled and iced with silence. If they'd spoken it would have sounded like this. If they'd moved it would have hurt like this. Nights at home, frozen.

Abe ran.

His shadow grew large against the wall. I watched him. Minny screamed. Come back. Abe laughed. Come back. I'm here. Beat me, she screamed, desperate. Come back.

So he came back running. He yelped like a dog.

Bitch, he said.

And she laughed.

Here, she screamed, and he came, pulled on the ropes. Her wrist was bleeding.

Stop it, I said, grabbing his hand, blood on my hand, stop it. But Minny screamed. Fuck you, to me. Leave me alone. Beat me, she screamed, mad like a dog wanting water. One of Abe's dogs yelping for him.

Then I cried. I burst out like a child, just in tears. No thoughts for a moment, nothing to think but tears to cleanse me.

Blood on my hands, so helpless, standing here, watching Abe's eyes, my father's eyes, bright with hatred. My father is smiling in Abe, happy in pain. He drew contentment from it, the cold silence, the never giving of emotion. Here he comes, blood on his hand, blood on my hand, Minny's blood, bleeding for our sins. Here comes my father, pulling at the rope, tightening the pain, not a word he'll say tonight. Nothing, not a word, just a look of pleasure in pain. We're waiting for it, emotion to fail, just a word or two. "We love you. Goodnight. Sleep tight, my pumpkin, sleep tight." But the silence came, and he liked the tears, silence like blood, the bastard knew we were calling out, we wanted emotion, love and hate.

Fuck off, said Abe.

But I stayed. Very calm, the memory came and it went. I'm calm again, dealing with two kids.

Get down, I said. You two get down. Firm as an oak tree, standing so strong.

Get down, I said, voice from heaven it seemed entering me. My better self came from my heart, wanting to breathe.

I'll call the police if you don't get down.

So they did. Meek like two lambs, a little contrite.

I'm taking you home.

We *are* home, said Minny.

Get in the car. Get dressed, I said.

Outside, night fell down on us, but some lights are on in the town. Some of these kids have homes, if you're lucky, but these don't, so you take them by the hand, place them softly in the back seat, under your wing, nowhere to go, Blackfoot's away, Angel's away, there is *no* home.

So I drove into the night, two kids under my wing, blood on my hand, strange how warm I was through caring for them, feeling them there, slumped in the back seat, now in my care, helpless they are, needing my care. And Blackfoot's no use, after he's let them be lovers like this. *He* could have stopped her from watching, he could have heard her waiting for him in the hall, seeing her mummy tied up. He won't understand when I tell him to close the bedroom door so no shadows stray onto the corridor wall. She's learnt from them, watches at night by their bedroom door, this kind of lovemaking.

So we drove away, white clouds lit by the moon. She's so heavy out here and so ripe, she'll fall from the heavens, land on earth one night and empty the skies.

We stopped at a Holiday Inn. "French fries, please. Coke an' cheeseburger, ice cream with chocolate topping, for me," said Minny, just like a little girl. "French fries an' chicken wings," said Abe. "Regular coffee for me," said Abe. And we fed, under the bright lights.

We booked into a suite and slept as if they were part of me, children I'd left, lovers taken away from me, limbs gone numb and returned to feeling, so our being together healed me. I was put together, of one piece, as the dawn came and I heard their breathing.

So I lay there in my own bed, as Minny and Abe slept in separate beds, peaceful and sweet, returned to childhood, resurrected, no longer nipped in the bud by sex, like an early frost on young blooms. Sex can be that, as cold as a killing frost. I had to hide it. You have to. You can't go out, wild on the town, wetting your pants in public. That's how it came to me in those old days when my world was caught in a circumference, so small, and outside there was no news, nothing of other worlds that counted, just me, all alone, hiding upstairs in bed, imagining sex. This way and that, sideways, upside down, he puts it inside you, like Abe did. You move up and down. It's so warm, sometimes Mummy holds me like that, so tight. I can see it in Daddy's eyes, the way he looks at me, sometimes I think he wants me. When I'm all dressed up, pretty and sweet, everyone wants me. I dance for them, legs up and down. I'm showing my thighs. No one cares. I'm just a little girl, but I see the men watching. It's coming over me, ruining it all, the terrible shame. It's ruined it all. Such shame. But Minny will dance in the bars, in her swimsuit. Just like a virgin, she dances. You'd think she doesn't know sex. She's just child, with her hips swaying. No shame. While his hands are in her and no shame; nothing stops her, oil on water, shame on lust, no brake stops her coming, just a kid.

But shame helps, I can tell you. Your cheeks go red, and tingle. And your body hurts a little, if a belt is squeezing you, all over. It's all being squeezed out of you, the sex. So you lower your eyes, pull down your skirt. Sometimes I cried, feeling despair, so young, as I danced and the men looked at me. Daddy smiled, but he didn't like it. I saw in his eyes, he was saying "Stop" while his mouth smiled, giving the impression he loved me. It had to stop, so I cried. And then, it was over, Mummy came running. Daddy was calm. No emotion. He looked on in silence. It was her job, bringing me up, so she held me as I cried.

And I cried and cried, despair coming, ending pleasure. It worked. It was so strong the way the tears fell, over excitement, over the river bed of sex, hiding the mud. So you put one flow of sensation over another, like a cover over a bed. No, like cold water in hot. The cold goes away. I tell you, it works. Despair is strong, and it falls over pleasure, ink in water. My mother held me when I cried. She was so sad, it calmed her to hear me cry. She heard her own tears flowing. She held herself. She comforted me, not knowing the way I saw her, so young, knew her already and my own games, building blocks of emotion, one brick over the next, coldly. I cried sometimes just for the sake of it, so she'd come running.

But Minny's got no mother. Angel's been off in Tucson, lonely as hell since Blackfoot left her, selling rugs and stolen arrowheads. Now she's on her way to Cheyenne. Blackfoot's left to be her Mummy. He's Mummy, Daddy, and lover all in one. And she waits outside the bedroom, watching Marta's shadow coming, held so tight in Blackfoot's hands. But no Mummy comes to hold her when the blackness fills the wall. Marta's shadow's growing bigger, bloated, blackened, burnt with sex. And she shrieks as Blackfoot comes, filling her with all his loves. All his dead dreams come inside her, Emma Bluegrass becomes her as he comes.

She's the last woman in a long line of women, lying there, all joined, they're all hiding in Marta's shadow. It's so huge. One woman couldn't be that big. Grandma's there from Wounded Knee, crying. Angel's in her, tearing her eyes out. But she won't leave. She's stuck to him. She's him, a monster on the wall, trembling, ready to pounce like the cat, ready to pounce, on all fours, waiting. And she's got it all. All Blackfoot's love flows into her. She'll have it forever, inheriting everything, she's crying out for him. The ropes tighten. Like ribbons on a wreath, they flutter in the wind. They're soft really. They don't hurt her. The rope tightens. She's smiling. The rope tightens. Round her neck it goes, making her smaller and smaller so she's one person. She'll die like this when the rope gets too tight but she likes it; listen to her like a bird at dawn chirping.

Henry, Henry, my baby.

Henry, my love.

And the candle flutters, so they're wiped against the wall. Minny's taken her hands and has swatted them, like flies, but they rise up huger than before, a tidal wave of bodies, love, so big it's ruined everything, love so strong, now it's emptied all homes, and Angel's wandering, selling buffalo pins, stolen arrowheads. Last month she hitched to Tucson. Love so strong it's like a fire, burning homes.

Henry, fuck me.

And the candle stays so still, so you can see it clearly. She's under him, lifesize. Her eyelashes, you can see them. The shadow has color. It's so real, like being in the room. Don't look that way. If you look through the open door, you'll turn to stone. Remember the story the teacher told you. About the girl who looked back. Her lover's a singer. And she turns to stone.

That was the only thing she had to do, to look ahead onto the wall. You can see it all there. It's in color now. They're moving on red and green and blue blankets, shining like gemstones. The shadow is real. If you look through the door, you'll see their dead bodies. They're not real. Grandma's taken them. If you look through the door you'll go with them too, down into stone. Cold, so you can't move. Always frozen.

Henry, stop it.

She's screaming now. He's telling her off. He's eating her breasts. She's his Mummy. He's eating her breasts like dinner. I'm hungry, I want some food. If you look one way, you can't touch her. She's got nothing for me. On the wall, she's just empty. If you run to her through the door you'll turn to stone.

I heard a scream. I'm coming from sleep, climbing out of it. I can't see out.

Angel, Angel.

The shadows are back on the wall in black. They're moving across the wall. They've come running. Blackfoot's arm is around me.

Daddy.

He's carrying Minny into their bed in a dead faint. He puts her between them so she'll sleep soundly. I hear the soft sound of her breathing. I'm all of a piece, healed, the birds are chirping. I'll wake up now, and it will be morning. The light was filled with the sun. Minny was still asleep.

The light is glorious. It's not too hot, through the windows. It's light-hearted, so dazzling, like the light dancing on the top of the sea. I'm moving with it, happy after my dream. Though it frightened me, I am seeing it myself. The door is ajar. I saw how love burns. It's larger than life, like this sun.

Huge as a mountain, but made of flesh. Minny's nightmare perhaps, but mine, for sure. I've been through this once before, taking my dreams back for myself, knowing from whence they came, to whom they revert. And I saw the monster from whence I came, the Minotaur roaming always in the back of my head. Last night he showed himself to me, Mummy and Daddy all in one, stuffed into my throat so I'm coming too, dying with breathlessness, trying to breathe, but I can't. It's killing me, their sex. It destroys me, their love. It burns down houses, mountains move with it, forests grow from their hair on the nursery wall, and the world is thunderous with their breathing.

Slow and stealthy, the monster made of their bodies returns. I'm welcoming the return. The light is on in the skies, so I can see so finely, drawn into his buffalo skin (that's how he's shaped today, huge body with a small head), my breasts. And there in his rump is my heart, beating so loudly, coming under him, tied by rope to his side, so I come to the sound of stampede.

I am moving through the plains on this monster's back, hair flowing in the wind, battling fear. For when love falls, you become nothing. You'll go underfoot, trampled to death under the monster's tracks. And when love falls they'll be everything. Light and darkness meet to make shadow. And when love falls, you'll become them. Love always becomes them, clinging and fighting in each other.

And I daydream, like this, while Minny and Abe sleep. The endless shapes they make together, enough to last you a lifetime. You can spend your life there, stuck, thoughtless in front of the TV set, never moving away to live your own life. This kind of love excommunicates you from life. So you don't do it. Your hand drops from your breast, when desire comes. You deal with the things you can, step on the gas, drive away. When love comes. I suppose you can keep living like that, on the border of life.

CHAPTER

Minny, come here, let me hold you close. I love your hair, the way it falls like a red shaft of sunlight over you. It's so tangled. Let me brush it soft and glistening. Your eyes are big. If you were mine, I'd love you, never leave, never run, like Angel. If you were mine I'd do my all for you. You break my heart, just watching you in the back seat, eating your peanut butter sandwiches. (We bought a jar, and some raisin bread. That made her happy, making sandwiches as we drive.) I bought her ice cream with so many colors in it, all the colors of the rainbow, while Abe eats chicken wings, day in, day out, and dries the bones out in the cool sun that hardly warms the back seat. The smell is terrible, but I can't throw them out. He cries, silently, each time I make a move to clean the car, trying to take just a few bones, not all of them. In the end, we buy some dishwashing liquid, stop off by Powder River, and wash the bones of meat. We put them back in the car. Abe trusts me now just a little. He'll leave his bones in the car when he wants to run in the fields or go off alone to church. Every so often he wants Jesus. Jesus waits in the church for him, and if the door's closed, he kneels outside, puts his head down on the earth or gravel or stone, digs his nails in, and prays.

Minny and I wait for him in the car. "Dad don't like Jesus," Minny told me. "'The guy's real big on suffering,' says Dad. 'He's a 'mastic'. Got no balls. I like a guy that's got balls. I like Eric Clapton. Not like Jesus. Jesus got trashy songs. Real soppy stuff with no beat."

Abe is now lying flat on the gravel outside the Assemblies of

God. So far he's prayed in Presbyterian, Catholic, and Lutheran churches. "It don' matter," says Abe when I tell him. "Jesus waits jus' under the cross. You see where it is. Jus' under there. He flies down. He sees me comin'. I tol' him I got the chicken bones for him. I share 'em with him. He don' eat meat because he's dead. But he likes bones. People's what's dead like dead things. He likes fish bones too. I asks him how Dad is. Dad don' talk much because Jesus keeps him busy. Dad's gone off fishin' today. It ain't much differen' in heaven. You jus' eat differen' food an' you fly, you don' walk. Minny don' understan'. She'll go to hell. She'd better keep livin'. When she goes to hell, she'll be burnt all day. An' devils will eat her for breakfast. Jesus won' give her no water neither."

"Minny, don't listen," I say when Minny scowls, a little scared.

"I'd kill her," said Abe, "if Jesus wanted her in heaven. But I don' wan' Minny to go to hell. She's better off here. So I'm real careful. I don' hurt her real bad. Those ropes can kill. I know. I killed a pig with my hands. I killed a bird that frightened the dogs. Mum an' Dad says you mustn't kill. But Jesus killed Dad, I tol' 'em. Jesus can do anything. He could 'av killed me. But he don' wan' me yet. When I'm holy, says Mom, I'll go. It'll be nice. But I sees a lot of Jesus. Sometimes I ain't sure I wanna go."

Minnie kicks Abe, lying prostrate outside the Assemblies of God.

"You two stop it," I say. They fall quiet.

"You don't know much," I say, "not yet. You've got to grow up to learn things. So stop talking as if you know everything, Abe," I said. "And Minny, you stop talking as if you're a woman."

They fell quiet and their faces smiled, not a smile from the mouth, but all the muscles in their face relaxed. I'll give them a break for a while, so they don't have to grow up overnight, understand heaven and hell, learn of sex and the disappearance of homes, passion that breaks the soul in two, the death of God. Each day, I see it in their eyes. Too soon, these kids were asked to know the boundary of life and death and to take themselves on, be their own teachers, no one to say stop. But I'm here. I know shame. I have brakes on all day. I know the look in my father's eyes that says no. And under the no, he pleads, Don't disgrace me; and under that is another layer of pain. Don't dance for life. I'll cry if you dance too much. It disrupts the house, this strange joy that's in you, this sex that pours from you. I can say no. It helps, I know it does. Daddy held on with his might to all his emotions. So few came out whole. No, he said in his eyes to so much. I know how to say no, Minny. You'll listen. But for you, it's like a holiday, to hear me say no. You're ready to go to sleep from relief. And Abe is too. You're so tired. I'll pick you up, Minny, if you'll let me, carry you back to the car, back to the Holiday Inn. You can watch MTV. But not more than an hour. Then you'll sleep, have some food, not just ice cream and peanut butter. I know best. I'm your Mummy now. I'll give you a bath, comb your hair when it's wet. My love will heal you.

It'll go down into you, this small trickle, down to your being. I know it because I can sense it now, coming from Father. I'm searching in the way he said no for something else, and I think I can see it sometimes in the way he held himself back. He didn't scream at me. He didn't say a word. He shuddered when my small thighs leapt up into the air and the sex poured out from me. He didn't know how to tell me no so he kept quiet, shrinking from me, losing his balance within, feeling so hopeless, so unlike a man. My thighs leapt up, wildly, I could have turned an audience on, I could have won them over, a circus full of men. It was so strong in me, like a skill I'd learned in the womb, some female power I owned from birth, coming out in my eyes too, glistening. I was like you, Minny. I had sex in me, spilling out of me. I know you, just a little. I don't want you to lose out on life, be marred by Angel's going and Blackfoot's strange passion for you. I want to give you what was passed down to me. It came out all wrong. It didn't happen for the right reason (wrong or right motives, who knows?) the way I held myself back. Later on for a few years I was out of control. But I came back to myself, taking a firm hand on desire. When it came on me, I'd jump on it, kick it to death, for a month or two. I don't know how it happened, that some sense of self-control was passed down. I can't tell you. I don't know if it was because my father's eyes were stinging, as if he was going to cry, when I brought my first boyfriend home. But he didn't cry. He walked out of the house and came back late in the night, smelling of wine. It'd made him sick. I shouldn't do this, bring men into the house. I was eighteen. He wanted to hold onto me. He couldn't let go. And I couldn't let go of him. When I went away from home, I cried all the way, put my foot on the gas, speeded so fast, in tears I could have killed myself. I didn't. I don't know how these bundles of love are passed down from father to son and daughter. They're so mixed up with shadow you often can't see the clear definition of love. It's eaten away by mould, forgetfulness.

Minny, I want to give you something my father gave to me. He didn't give it clean. Nothing comes clean in life. You've got to clean it yourself, so you can see what it is.

Minny was picking wild daisies down by the Assemblies of God. Abe had his plate of bones ready to offer to Jesus. He was singing a song.

The Lord is my Shepherd, I shall not wan'.... He leads me in still pastures. Though I walk in the Valley of the Shadow of Death, I shall fear no evil, for you are with me.

The Lord is my Shepherd, I shall not wan'...

He sang and sang, sticking his bones into the earth. Then he took his fork and spoon and began digging a grave. Minny handed him the wild daisies to bury.

And I wondered what in me would go to waste because it's so lonely living like my father did, fearful of saying much that mattered, always hidden under the joke or the right remark, the urbane river that covered him, so you hardly knew what he was. I knew, so he didn't go to waste. I know what he would have done, had he spoken his mind. It scares me, the violence that he held down, and the rage. And also his love for me. He worshipped me at times. He kept going for me. I was his *raison d'etre*, he said. Otherwise he would have left my mother long ago. I was the glue that held the family together. Take me away, and they'll all fall apart.

It was a lie, Minny. They got divorced long before I grew up. They shifted the meaning of me just like that. Suddenly I was a new word in the dictionary. But that's useful. Later it's useful to see you can change the meaning of someone just like that. Well, it doesn't happen overnight. But, you can.

Minny smiled and looked at me, big eyed, with delight.

You're talkin' real strange, she said.

I remember being like you, I said. Moving from home to home, backwards and forward, never staying in one place. One week Mummy, next week Daddy, both had so many problems they don't have time for you. Have you noticed how useful it is to have problems? You never have time for people, and they're meant to feel sorry for you? Sympathy? Well, I didn't. I wasn't like you in that. I just waited to leave. Another four years, I was gone. It happened quickly. I was out in the big world, alone.

I'm ten, said Minny.

Perhaps she'll get a job. Leave home at fifteen. It doesn't matter. You need someone to love you during those years. Even when I left I was always looking for someone to love me.

What's up? asked Minny.

Nothing, I said.

But I wanted to tell her. I'm just as I was before. Impotent. Nothing I can do to set her free. She's caught in the prison of Blackfoot's inconstancy, Angel's sadness; she'll dance on the tables nightlong in between two houses, no home in sight. They won't care. Blackfoot likes her thighs. He'll watch them, fondling Marta. He'll put her in their bed, wet with semen. She'll swim in the aftermath of their sex, caught in the river of it, teaching Abe how to do it the next day.

I can't help her, I thought. I'm just as I was. Helpless. Caught in Blackfoot's inconstancy. And I wanted to kill him. It came to me, the thought of killing him. So I could take her, and he'd be gone. I'd adopt her. Stop her from hurting herself. Give her the love that heals.

So I held her, there outside the Assemblies of God, in the vaulted sky, like a painting by Van Gogh. The clouds were so full

of thrusting brush strokes, like a scythe, each one, cut off in pain
and started again, so quick, avoiding death, so the strokes are wild,
each one striving for breath, each one replacing the next, in some
hymn to life the painter's hand moved. Each time the brush stroke
died it was resurrected. And I held Minny, for dear life. I picked
her up. She was heavy, but she flew up, like a bird. She rolled her
legs round me, clung to me as she had clung to Blackfoot that
afternoon in the Rosebud Cafe, when she passed out. But with me,
she stayed there, completely conscious. She cried. And I thought
of Abe's God, imagined him watching over us, flying down from
the church spire, whirling with the weather cock, arriving down in
my head. And I wondered why he'd left Minny like this, so alone
until she found me. And did He put it in my head to love her? Or
was she alone when He was roaming the skies? And I thought of
this as a puzzle, since I don't believe and stopped probably around
Minny's age when my Grandmother died (that was my tragedy, and
then I couldn't trust Him after that, and then I stopped believing).
And I knew it was Him or me. My mind free, to choose to love, or
His mind telling me what to do. And I saw Him as a kind of
Blackfoot, as someone who wants to possess you, use you for his
own ends, as a follower, as someone to spread His Word, not your
own. And I saw Him as a kind of Joseph (although Joseph never
asked me to spread his ideas. It paid for me to do so. That was my
specialty, the way I got by in the world of universities).

And I looked again at the vaulted sky and asked did He
paint it? And I thought, No, Van Gogh did. This sky is his. I
would have never seen it this way had he not shown me one rainy
afternoon in the National Gallery, when I was just a kid, taking
time off from two homes to stray into his paintings. I'll live there, I
thought, in his world. It's got color and light. My life is grey. So I
entered his paintings and this sky is his.

Each time he saw a flicker of light, he painted it. In
between those strokes is death. Sometimes murder. Those lights
are born from the darkness. That's why they look so bright, almost
frightening, the way those fields are bright and the furrows thick
with true darkness of death. A palette knife cuts through russet

and green and gold and grey fields, smudging them, so the mixture appears like darkness. All the colors in one make mud. You'd think he destroyed his own work, cutting through those colors to make mud, his palette knife making all colors one. But look. Over in the corner of that field the ears of corn are showing. And there is barley and rye coming out of the dark loam, becoming itself again from darkness. We watch, Van Gogh and I, his eyes in mine, just as we had when I was little and lonely. I had long conversations with him, in the National Gallery and at night read his letters to Theo. And I want to give that book to Minny and his paintings. I don't want to give her the no my father tossed at me that sent me running to my mother in tears. Such a long road away from my dance to life. He could have smiled, a little amused, just a bit appreciative. He could have watched me dance without the sex in him rising.

So I rocked her. She was awake the whole while. She sobbed and sobbed as if it would never end, all the thoughts that went rolling like waves through her head, and only my arms to hold her together. I was wet too, with her crying. I started to cry, too, with a sting of bitterness in my eyes, the feel of pollution in the biggest cities burning my eyes. All the sadness of a child's life to think of, all this pain I could feel ready to shape her bones and her flesh, so young, her posture, everything will be shaped by it. I have to do something to stop the pain setting. Now, the tears from this little life flow, and I'm sick with helplessness. I can't take her away from this pain. And I see her pain not just here, not just in my arms but in other homes as they break in two like mine did, and emotion, like broken limbs from a crash, survives in bits.

I held Minny, while her body stretched across Pine Ridge. She rose up like the sky and fell. The sound of her heart became mine. And I wanted to give her this, not the empty chair of my father's reprimand, because being alone and lonely pushed you out into sex too quickly. You'll do anything for a quick fix/fuck, I know you will, Minny. I know, when things go wrong you'll want sex, the pull of the rope too. Then you're not lonely. The pain enters you, becomes you, and keeps you not so alone. So I held her, and my body left me. It merged into hers. Our tears washed away any division between us. I'll love you and hold you like this. Don't let me leave you. I know what you'll do when you're lonely. You'll run to Abe for warmth that turns to fire and flame, burning you. There are burn marks on her neck. That's where they play, with hell fire, when Angel's off in Tucson selling arrowheads stolen from Blackfoot's and Marta's farm.

> *Come here my baby I said*
> *Mama she wailed Mama*
> *My baby I cried*
> *Mama don't leave me she wailed*

CHAPTER

37

Mama don't leave me, she sobbed.

It's like making love, being this close and crying. I never did this with Adam. There's no way to leave it behind, this kind of love. Even when Mama died, I still clung to her, when the body was lowered into the earth. The earth stretched out. It was her. The sky grey. It was her. When she left, she was in everything, too large to cling to. She evaded me, turning up in other places, hiding, hiding. I felt her in everything. I would have left the world to leave her. I wanted her to go, and come back differently. To be almost the same, but to leave me free. I wanted to leave the world for her. This kind of love won't go away.

When they lowered her into the earth, I screamed.

Mama don't leave me.

People came running.

They put their arms around me.

It was like ice. No one was there. Their arms were cold ice and wind, hurting me. Mama's arms were warm and soft when she held me. No one will hold me like that again and want me like that again. Their arms are cold. They were like ghosts in the restaurant afterwards, days afterwards, months afterwards, people were flitting, their words buzzing, nothing came to me and she hid herself in the land.

But she's back. All of her, drifting into me, into my arms, all in one piece. And all this time she's been hidden from me. All this time she's in hiding, she was untouchable (sacrilegious it was to think of the Dead too much, dig them up. When you're dead, don't you need more respect than the living? You'd better think good thoughts of the Dead or they'll get you, won't they?). Blackfoot knew that. He knew it for real, the way he walks through this Land of the Dead too. I did without knowing, I trod on her body, and saw her mind in the sky, untouchable, always there, but in hiding. She was the air I breathed, but I closed my eyes to her. Bits and pieces of her settled into Adam's face. His moaning and sadness were hers.

After they lowered her into the earth, half of me died. I couldn't love. Half of me looked for her and half of me ran. The gravestone has no flowers on it still because I can't look at that one piece of earth and see how small it is. I want her in everything, being the air I breathe, the men I run from. The ones I love smell of her.

She's passing out in my arms.

So I held her, just as she held me, all of one piece, all together. I was helpless when she died. No kind of loving could save her. I was helpless, watching her body smudge itself into nothingness, ink blot on the sky, whiff of smoke, mere emptiness, like the land you see here. Just the clouds moving, made of her soul, and the earth so flat, dotted with the markings of dead souls, wagon trails, nothing to see, just a dent in the earth. The path they made might have been imagined, almost invisible is the trace the wagon wheels left. You have to listen to the wind to hear them talk. Your eyes must be tuned to the smallest gust of wind to see their faces, women and children congregating in the sky, this is the land where they were left. Even when you dig them out and sell their bones, they own the sky. The sky, not the land. But the hidden earth is theirs, under the land, hidden are the Dead. This place, dirt track, end of the road reservation, streams abandoned by God, churches prayed to by the murmur of insects, this dead of the center, far-flung sky, peach colored, ultramarine, all white in winter, like a blank page, this place gave her to me.

She's back. I can feel her soft arms are mine. Her tears are Minny's. This land gave her back to me, invisible sky, cracked open by the smallest sound, so fragile its hugeness, so soft its invisibility, its clouds house the relics of Jesus. Mary lies in stone in the schools, and the children cry when they see her. This land gave her back to me. She's here in my arms, so small, the size of Minny. Nothing to fear. If I were to go back to England, I'd place some flowers on her grave. It would be small. The size of a child's grave. It would be small, like Minny's body, the way she flies up, as she cries like a bird mating.

The reservation police picked us up, a few miles away from Potato Creek. When they asked me where I was going, I told them. "Rapid City, the airport, I'm in a hurry, I'll miss his plane. I'm meeting my husband," I said, wanting to give myself the camouflage of belonging as wife to someone. It'd hide the way I drove, with Minny in the front seat, watching my mother's body roll by in the land. Blackfoot knew, he knew all right, the way the Dead live on in the land. In the city, you can't hear them, you have the impression the world is full of new faces. "Manhattan, yes, that's where I'm from," I said. The city hid my mother, I never heard her. But this Land is honest. It's bare and wide, and its shapes are made of wind. You can't believe that those gas stations stand for much. The wind will knock them down. Nothing is permanent here but the Dead, and we cross them, walking over their spirit, thinking we won't wake them. We're fools. This Land, white as a sea shell, the clouds curling and curling in infinite coils of a shell, the center receding into past time, all is reflective, all is made of thought. You can see how heartbroken the Land is, just now, as we stand here, trying to work out where I'm going, from whence I come.

"From England originally," I said to the small Indian, almost coffee-colored, his lips, but his hair bright black like a raven. "From England where monuments stand. Events are marked in stone, everything, every inch has a name belonging to some ancestor," I said, "there's no room for me. That's why I came here."

The Indian stared at me and laughed.

"You're driving too fast," he said. "You're drunk?" he asked mildly, as if asking about the weather.

No, I said. I'd like one, though.

Not in the car, he said. Not on the reservation. We got enough drinking problems.

It's the Land, I said. Who can stand this kind of Death?

They wander, he said. I know what you mean.

Mine do, I said.

Yours?

I have ancestors too, I said.

Here? he asked.

I nodded.

He whistled.

You slow down, he said. Fifty-five miles the limit, speed limit here.

His friend went back to the car and watched. He began eating a sandwich.

We don't get many tourists here, said the small Indian. He was sweating, although it wasn't too hot, the low wind was warm, but it brushed away the heavy heat that pounded the clouds and made them yellow at their edges, dark grey their center, holding a storm in now. They moved so quickly from white to grey, like my mother did. Her moods shifted, one minute to the next. But she was always sad, like this place. There was always a wound in her, as if hope had died or was silent, so other needs came in their place, needing me, always me, don't leave me. But the real hope for her own life had gone. You can't cling to your children. They'll leave or go mad. It's like falling in love with a married man, it's like wanting time to stop, it's reversing the natural order of things to cling to your children. That's why she did it, because hope was lost. That's why she wanted me so bad until it hurt her. I'm touching her now, seeing her eyes filled with tears. She was a little girl.

Yes, this is Minny, I said. Blackfoot's daughter. She was standing by my side, holding my hand faithfully.

Oh, Blackfoot, said the Indian guy.

And Abe, I said.

Abe, he nodded sadly, pitying the boy who sat in the back seat, humming a Jesus song.

You must be here for the Ghost Dance, said the Indian guy.

I asked him his name.

Nick, he said. That's the only time I seen tourists here. Most of the year you don't see no one.

I'm not a tourist, I said.

The Ghost Dance happens once a year. The buffalo come back. They'll come out of the Land and give it back to us. Like it was. That's why we did it. Now it's a show. Just a show, he said.

"The buffalo was like milk," he said. "Ma's milk."

I listened, calmed by him.

"Now it's gone, we drink. You gotta keep an eye on yourself here. When you're driving."

I was her wine. She drank me up daily. I kept her mood high, just a bit higher than it might have been had I not smiled for her, fallen into her arms and cuddled her. But I was, instead of life, like a drug. I suppose you could call that loving me, in a way it was, it felt so good, feeding her.

"The land's hard out here, the soil's not great for farming," said Nick. "We followed the buffalo, like milk. We lived off them. Then it was over. We got the Land, without milk. No food for us, not what we's used to. You've heard calves calling out, when they's weaned. You gotta cry out, shut them up. It goes through you. That's like us now. That's why we do the Ghost Dance, calling back the milk. The land's not worth much. It's dry in summer and dry in winter."

So the buffalo was milk streaming out from the plains, like a river, noisy as a waterfall, black as thunder, the milk came rushing in waves, unstoppable, wild from the breast of the Great Cow, the earth. They sucked her and more milk flowed. The more you drink, the more she makes, like Jesus with the fish. Nothing you do can destroy her, except the white man, who came and killed her for good. We killed their mother, I thought, and I said, "So you do the dance so they'll come back?"

"It's a symbol," he said. "The buffalo comes back in a different way now. It means good things. It's just like asking for good things. Now we couldn't live off buffalo if we tried. We likes stuff from the cities to buy. You know, TV, that sort o' shit."

But I couldn't take it, I wanted to forget, I wanted to escape so fast from this place, get in the car, and leave the land. No doubt ancestors of mine, someone related to someone, part of my larger family had come here, just like I came, murderous, wild with grief, saying goodbye to my mother shoreland, white cliffs of Dover soaring so high, blackened by hatred. In exile they came, or in search of something, a new life, but they killed this land, stopped her milk flow. Now she lies helpless across the plains, emptied of life. Even the Indians know she won't come back alive as she was, flowing with buffalo. Exiles, murderous with rage, came with old scores to settle, old visions to be maddened by. So, we came to take it out on this new land.

The land was flowing with milk. The buffalo ran wild just as Blackfoot painted it. And they followed like babes, the river of food stampeding wild through the soft land, baking in summer, ice cold in winter. It was always hard, said Nick, but they knew generation from generation the wisdom to survive. They knew the songs, the dances, and those who inhabited the grain and the rain clouds. There was someone to talk to each day in the land, hard or soft, blasted with storm, split into diamonds of light, falling on the grass, there was someone to understand in the Land. But we came, changing the face of their world, our way broke their way into pieces, there was no one to talk to in the land. We killed her, the Earth. And I wanted to run, to weep, to drink, to forget, to stamp out the memory. I'd fall down on the earth and beg forgiveness, anything but this dull thud, this ache of remembrance, of something I never did but am responsible for. You know, you can kill yourself over imaginary crimes, when they have no substance, just the feel of guilt, just the taste in the mouth you get after a bad dream, but you can't remember the images. So it came, the thud of guilt, as if I had killed their land.

Minny held my hand. I was trembling.

A blue rim covered the earth, like a river holding the earth and sky together. Around them the charcoal clouds wafted, outlined in orange and gold light. The sperm from the sky fell into the earth. Dusk let a blanket fall over the rain and mopped it up as it fell so a moist haze hung so delicately in the air, like a spider's web of water. You could lick it, join it, become one with the sky because she's waiting to be resurrected, says Nick.

You gotta keep her alive. It's a two-way thing. We don' look after her much. Not now. Some of us jus' like ta leave, pack it up an' forget her. You like New York? Nick asked me, a little nervously.

So I told him, as we walked. I painted the city for him, but my mother was in the sky. Her body was warm and wet, and I'd hurt her, she was crying. And then she went. And the land was empty. It was Nick's land, it was bare, so wide, so all-encompassing, from every angle its emptiness spread majestic, its throne abandonment, its triumph our solitude. She'd left us, or we'd left her, it didn't matter in this war between us, whose fault had it been that the bond between us was severed because she had clung so and I had to run.

I don't know if you'd like it I said to Nick. I don't know how you'd take the crowds.

In this war between us, I met Adam. I said he saved me from her a bit. But we did it too, our sudden anger bursts, we'll spite each other for no reason. I see it now in this land as the rain falls so soft, like a spider's web, night comes down, blue added to grey and purple at the horizon, a red streak slashed like a stab wound over her.

I've missed the plane, I said to Nick.

You'd be better off staying the night in Pine Ridge. Further on there's Scenic. Five miles ahead. Just a package liquor store an' a bar. Not much to drive for. It'll be dark in no time, said Nick.

I let him down, I said.

CHAPTER

We walked through Scenic: down on your left, the Church of God graves. Down on your right, the package liquor store. Next to it, No Indians Allowed. You see the sign over the bar? Just like it was, says Nick. "Old days, cowboy days. No Indians allowed. You see those skulls? Buffalo skulls. Great idea, isn't it? The jail's there, down by the post office. Two cells, jus' like it was. Can I get you a drink?"

So we drank. Minny on my knee, Abe out in the car, walking the graves perhaps, who knows? God knows. I'm leaving him in God's care.

I let him down, I said, I drove in circles. I let him down. So I drank. It cut my throat, awakened me. Each drop burnt me inside, gave me passion. I could feel what I'd done to Adam crowding the pit of my stomach. The whiskey washed it out. The memory went, and I saw how we'd be, each other's home, you know the rushing into each other's arms you see in the movies, falling into him, down in an old dreamt-of way, the gestures wild, magnificent, all longings, stretching out, finding flesh. Death would just be a lost thought. So I drank. Nick was talking Resurrection. Rodeo days, nearly died, fell off a bucking horse, hoof in the stomach, God came in, Christian cowboy woke up renewed. But it don't work. The Indian blood don't let it settle. A bad mix, says Nick, for an Indian.

Sawdust on the floor. The bar grows loud. I'm shouting too, to make myself heard. Nick holds my hand. It's red with sweat. But I like it, hot with sweat, smelling of rodeo days, the blood in the ring.

Like a bullfight is it?

Lasts all day. On and on. You make your home there and wait. People bring cars and kids and their dogs and wait in a circle.

Nick is holding my hand, red in his palms, a look of need in his eyes.

I drove the wrong way, I said. I thought I was near Custer.

But I lied. I didn't care. Adam came into my mind some weeks ago when I needed him. Now that I don't, the minute I got Minny and Abe in my care, I forgot. Memory like a sieve. Through it falls love, splintered. Only fragments, that's all I've got for you. But the thought was licked clean by the bite in my throat.

The whiskey came. Waking me up to something better, Nick's hand pressing mine, his hands down on my knee, pressing me. And I like it, like driving too fast round the curves of the road. It takes my breath away. The sweat is dark. He's talking resurrection. The buffalo skulls on the wall will come back, fleshed out, in the form of more TVs. Something good for the community.

Scenic needs some life. Not just a bar and a package liquor store. Minny is dancing. Up on the table. People are clapping. She's no longer mine. I wash my hands of her. I did what I could. I feel so right now, with his hand on my thigh, the puffy cheeks talking.

I fucked up over Adam, I said. I went in circles. I didn't drive straight to him to get what I wanted, to be with him, to love him. Him. Not you, I said sullenly. Angry now, it doesn't fit it. The logic is lost. The radiant truth is lost. God's message is just a billboard sign. Words without sense, something to trick you into making it with him. Lie down on the road and give yourself to God. Body and soul. Take it.

I do agree, I said. Christianity isn't the answer.

This is, I thought, but the thought died, and I wanted Adam. I'm so sad from wanting him. But I let him down.

You kill the thing you love, I read. Somewhere. From some jail. Oscar Wilde, I said. Down in a jail, he was. Writing this.

So I drank, my hand on Nick's thigh. I moved in. Into our circle, the smell was wild of whiskey.

Like a sweat lodge, said Nick. Where you have visions. It gets real hot in here, don't it?

You go deeper. You push your hand on his thigh, not in a friendly way, more like a gesture defying thought. If you go past thought you reach vision. You see, you'll get it. You'll be with Adam. So I put my hand there on his plump thighs. He liked it. He laughed. He bought me another drink. I drank it slowly, warm like a prick in my throat. Warm like love in my heart. Warm like food in my belly, taking away all thought, so vision is left. I'll know this time, I'll go past common sense. I'll get to Adam this way through his thigh. Like Adam and Eve, my Adam will be born from his thigh. He'll be one with Nick. There's no difference now. Just for this moment, God-given it feels, they're one and the same. When he puts his tongue in my mouth, the bar reels over. His tongue is a snake, crawling down, down to my cunt. It's heavy now.

She's heavy now. I didn't know she was there till he put his tongue down my throat, and he called to her. She's waking up, turning round, feeling of her own accord, fuck her. She's taking off like a car with a new engine. She's making me want him, I'm taking him down, letting him talk to her. She's alive, damn her.

So I took a sip, to drown her. It didn't reach her. It stayed like a blade in my stomach, killing me. More might take away the pain. More whiskey.

Another drink on me, I said.

I'll get it, said Nick. Are you okay?

I'm all set, I said. Ready to go. I've had it.

It's forty minutes to Pine Ridge. I'll have to drive you. There's a motel. I'll take you there if you want. You can't drive like this.

No. I can't.

Another whiskey. Another vodka for me.

I'll bring out the best of me soon. Push yourself to a limit. It works wonders on the soul, stretching oneself, going too far. I'm still in one piece. I can remember what it was like to be in one piece, at least, I laughed. It's funny now. He's so sweet. Such a gentleman, so kind. I made a good choice. I couldn't have found a better man on the road.

You're a sweetheart, I said.

So he talked. He put his arm round me, solemn now, and his heart beating fast. I could hear it, see it, it throbbed. It was too much to take, all that feeling oozing and beating out of his breast. I'm taking advantage of him. Sweetheart. He's feeling too much. He's telling me things about himself. Important things now, deep in the night, telling me things that make me cry. Rodeo stories, moments of triumph: he stayed on; he fell down; how he rode the wind. He's a man telling me men's stories, telling me how he's a man. And he is, he's no bastard. He'd take me home if I asked him.

In the end, I left it. You can't make a living of it. It's okay for a boy, proving yourself, day in, day out, how tough can you get? Who gives a damn? So I got a regular job.

How do you know then? I asked, laughing. I could see it in him, his prick. I know he's a man.

I'm only joking, I said, and I wanted to cry again, but the whiskey saved me, smacked me down in the place where tears come. It gave me a whacking hit and stopped the flow. I thanked it.

You're a man, I said gently. Even I know that.

Even I. Half dead inside, trailing lost women behind me. There's no room for much else, but he got it in. He pushed it in my throat and he'd ride me, easy.

I know you would, I said.

He smiled. It didn't make sense, but he didn't care. He likes me.

I know you're a man, I said. You don't need to prove it.

Blackfoot did, dancing over his father's grave. Adam did, circling round his father's fame, like a moth, to be burnt by it. But I don't really know about Adam. I never gave him a chance. His prick never came near as close. When he came inside me it went to my head, white clouds. I was up in the sky in God's country, my body faint, that sort of stuff. It went to my head. I didn't let him down. Down to my cunt, talking to him. She's alive now. The whiskey won't touch her. She's hurting. Aching away, with sudden need, as if she woke up from a long sleep, hungry. She's warm, and soft, and I like the feel of her. She's mine. I own her. She's mine.

I want you, I said. I looked into the bar. There were faces, call it humanity, always there, anonymous, all those lives never touching you, always watching, or stealing a glance, but never looking into your eyes, so they don't count. They've nothing, but I love them now.

I'm like them, part of them now, Indian, drinking up my inheritance, like broken glass in wine. You've got to pick out the pieces, and drink it down off the floor like a dog. You get down, till there's no more pride, and you rummage for it in dirt. You go out on the back of a bucking horse, tempting death, wooing her, fucking death, and end up down in the ring, biting sawdust, finding yourself, face down. When you look up, you're facing the clouds, there's nowhere to go. There's your broken body, meshed to your soul, crawling, crawling in dirt, but you won't give up. You want this earth.

Let's go, he said.

I stood up. Back to your place?

Oglala, he said.

I passed through it. Only a few houses there.

You can't miss it. Out on the plains. It's all you can see for miles.

I stood up. Minny comes running. Tears streaked down her face.

An' the kid? asks Nick as she falls down at my skirt, pulling at me, wild like a cat. I've seen this mood before, she'll pass out. There's not much consciousness left in me now. Some faint sense in the back of my soul, it's taken a beating tonight, been shaken up.

Don' leave me, she yelps. Mama.

Wild in the night, my cry. I've heard it before. I'm finding myself, don't get in the way, half of me says. And the other half, dead drunk, weeps and picks her up.

I'm here, I said.

The moon sits on the Badlands plains. She's heavy and ripe, oh my baby. The moon bounces up and darkness catches her. She falls back, easy, just a dance in the wind, no more, nothing to shake the heavens. Just a frolic, no more, my baby. The moon is white. She shows me Minny's face, white with the vision she saw of me in the bar, leaving, leaving. Will it never stop?

Out of the bar comes Nick, fills our bottle of whiskey with ice cold water, pouring my head clean. It's so cool. I can wake up now. Holding her in me, she's safe.

I'm here, I say.

The moon trickles white over her face.

I'm here, I say.

And she falls quiet, eyeing the moon on my face. It's a cold light, but reason is cold too, and I welcome it. Reason is milk white, bright as steel, moon colors that make the trees dark grey and silver. My world is gathered together in one hue, and the air is chill. If it weren't for her, I'd be off chasing this prick or that. I'd be gone to Oglala with Nick. But he stood there, quiet too. Perhaps his rodeo days were over. He's tired of riding the wild fillies, all night long, falling into oblivion the next day, laid to waste and forgotten on someone else's bedroom floor.

Don' leave me, she says, her litany of sadness unending.

I'm here, I say, breaking its rhythm and rhyme, breaking the silence she hears when she says it in her sleep to Angel.

If it weren't for her, I'd be off chasing the world round the bend in the road; the world's always receding.

I'd be off chasing my cunt down in Oglala, wondering where she went the next day, sick with fright. I'd be off and running, smashing my new self headlong against the world, sick with fright, looking for someplace to rest and someone to hold me. But I've got her in my arms.

I'm a good woman, I said. You can trust me, I said, with the white moon on my face, chill, the truth in it all, in my voice.

I won't budge from here till you give the word.

There's somewhere to rest now. I can hear a place to run to in my voice. It's calm, and it's calming Minny, rocking her sound to sleep in my arms, the cool tones, till she lies there, worn out by the long night, lullabyed into safety, on the roadside.

There was one church in Scenic, a crippled church, stocky and
flat with the spire knocked out by lightning's fire, the white
paint peeling, blackened like soot in the moonlight, like a snake
shedding its skin, over and over again, where the fire burnt it. We
looked for Abe in every crevice. We bent under the benches,
kneeling and kneeling, till we knew that church like one of the
faithful, and the floor caved in at points and groaned where we
trod; I saw a rat scurry out in the pew, and go back into darkness,
for the moon poured in here too, bathing in shafts of light,
crisscrossing the broken shell of belief, so fragile like the shell of an
egg, the home of God.

"You watch out in places like this," said Nick, "they've
been known to fall down on top of you, jus' like that. Foundations
don' hold, the roof caves it. You go slow," he said.

And we'd left Minny outside asleep in the car, with the door
open so we'd hear her waking.

I sat with her a while so Nick could walk out in the moon's
searchlight. I held her hand. My heart poured into hers. My love
poured into her. I knew it had, for she slept so calm, like a
newborn babe, one I'd carried in my womb and let out into the
world too sudden, so I wanted her near me. Part of me thought I
would break if I left her. She's given me fire.

I can't go back, I said. And it came to me in a rush, the
time I'd forgotten, the way I'd just dropped people, left them
behind, like Abe tonight, but they're still there waiting. All along,
Adam was waiting while he went out of my mind. My return came

to me, like a shoal of ghosts waiting for me, Adam and Blackfoot, and out on the Boston shores, Joseph would be waiting for me, like Abe waits, reflecting me, and the words I'd given to people and places could no longer fit quite right, for I called Adam my lover, but Nick really had me tonight because some fire burns in me now and some cool light allows me to see this fire I've kept under wraps. So I thought I was made of putty. That was all I was, another Adam, another version of Joseph, God's child, mouthing his words, but with no ideas of my own, no one I was, nothing in me, just a nursemaid, someone you'd pay to take care of you, nothing more than a whore.

And it all seems like a shoal of ghosts, Adam and Joseph and Blackfoot. All definition has changed now that I'm made of fire. Blackfoot says that he's Minny's Mum, but I know he's not. I'm more a mother to her than he is.

I can't let her go.

Then Nick came back, and I went out while he held Minny's hand and waited beside her dreams, and this moon-white, milk-white dream of a desolate town, this empty husk of another age, Wild West days, this empty Indian town was mine. I walked out like I owned it, knew it by heart, the brokenness of it, the way that it clung to memories never having the strength or the will to erase the remains of faith and build a monument to the modern world. Why not a real gas station with bright light signs, why just a hose in a garden, with a handmade sign saying, "Gas Sold Here," one you can hardly see in the night. Why not a Wendy's or Dairy Queen or a Howard Johnson or Taco Bell's? Why not?

But I walked as if this town were mine. She was true, telling a tale that the rest of the world has left untold, and in her face I see America. She's no clean, clean, spick and span cover-up with no past. This America just forgot, just like I did Adam, such a short span of attention, like a newborn babe; things don't change quickly here. This land has a soul though she hides it well.

And I walked in great joy, in the ecstasy of the moonlight, etching my thoughts so clearly. I walked, with fear gone out of me, because I was made of fire, and the fire in me had taken me down, torn in its flames my old life.

So I walked past the trailer homes, abandoned, I walked past the closed up liquor store, and the bar with its buffalo skulls and I saw the bluffs of the Badlands fifty miles off, through the open road, across the cornfields, and I came to the stone-made prison, small pebbles too, stuck together to make its tiny strong frame. This was a place that no storm could touch, it reached down to the earth, the blackened bars were over the windows, but the moon came in through a crack and I saw the Snake Boy, curled like a foetus, curled like a snake, fast asleep by the broken bottles and torn-up bed in one of the cells. And he clung with one hand to the broken bed post, and he slept so sound, as if he had found his home.

So I called to him softly, but I won't forget the thoughts I buried, one by one, as I woke him slowly, all the time, as I cajoled him, I wanted to leave him lying there where some had died and some were hanged. I wanted to leave him there, befitting a place that dwarfs man, makes him sick and so small, so carelessly evil with the things given to him, the wide skies, the moon falling across the plains, you can run and never stop, out in the street. You can hear the wind waking the corn and the sun smelling of earth, loving each minute of it as she burns on summer days, lifegiving. But this prison castrates man, takes from him vision and love and the sense of the sky that could give him hope. Here, men of justice and men of crime sat together, of one mind, waiting for death to fall, the hangman's noose or the gun. You can feel it here, how they made the place so there's nothing to live for and there he came and I wanted to leave him there. He's too far gone, too damaged, too lost to save. No one would know that I found him tonight.

Abe, wake up, I said.

He rubbed his eyes and smiled and he looked into my eyes this time, so sweet, as if woken from a good dream.

I dreaded picking him up. I wanted to leave him there and forget that look of sweetness curling his lips, so he's just a boy. Then I picked him up, against myself I did it. I wanted to vomit. I wanted to let him go out of my life.

But I picked him up and carried him onto the road and set him down, while he looks at me shiftily, hands into his jeans pockets, he's touching himself, rubbing himself erect. But he smiles like a girl, coyly, at me, seducing me to hate him, and I do. Each move of his, each rub of his hand, each simper in his eyes spurs me to fury. I want him out of my life because I don't want to hate so, I don't want to leave him there, have it written for years to come, for Minny to remember, for her to write down in her mind as the way people are and will be to her. I want to save her from seeing this side of me, and myself. I'll be sitting far from all this, and he'll come to me, just like he is now, part girl, part boy, part God, the way his head is filled with words of Jesus falling meaningless from his mouth. So he rubs himself, I can see him doing it now, and he smiles at me, runs to me, rubs his body against mine. Then he burns. His hand burns, flame let loose, a punishment from the sky, but I'm falling back, tripped by the flame in his hand.

He drops a match onto the gravel and smiles.

Fire, he says.

I'm leaving him here. He can set himself aflame and go up to heaven, the pain of the world burnt out of him, like a bird flying up, not made for this world.

You don' like fire? he asks, lighting a match, and he throws it down. Dead in the wind it falls before it reaches me, brushes my arm, no more.

You put them down. Give them to me.

They're mine, he says. Not yours. You leave me alone, messin' with me, like that dude o' yours. Quit messin' with me, touchin' my things, my matches, not yours. I'm makin' fire, he says. I'm makin' big fires runnin' through trees.

Give them to me, I said, or I'll take them.

"When the wind gets strong the flames go real high. I made a real forest fire last year. I put flame, all 'em matches, one-two-three-four-five, you can't count how many matches I put down by the fence on Dad's lane.

"I got matches and matches. The flames get real hot. It's all mine. It makes the sky red. It's brighter than sun. You can't get anything like it. It's mine. You can't put it out. And after the earth's all grey, like the sky. Dad likes the smell. It's a big pipe for him. He smokes pipes in heaven. He likes the smell."

I'll put you in prison, a real one this time. One with thick bars where the doors won't open. I'll put you behind bars, and the law will let me, the way you admit so easily to a crime, I said.

"I'll put *you* in prison, takin' me out like I'm yours, I'm not yours. Don' go talkin' to me like you own me. I don't do nothing for you."

"Give me those matches."

"My matches," he said.

"They're mine."

I'll get them from him if it kills me. So I ran at him, grabbed his clenched fist, too tight to open. The moon looks down and laughs. I'll save the world from Abe, that's why I'm doing all this, I tell her. It's for you, not for me. You heard what he said, how he sets the world on fire, burns it to the charcoal. There's nothing left. Last year I read sixty square miles were burnt; nothing could stop it. The fires have a life of their own. You can't get near.

The fires breathe. I've seen them. They take in breath, then they let it out as flame. They move like a serpent, spitting and biting their tongues of venom. Just one match can light up the world. They're magic.

He smiles, with his clenched fist poked at me, getting ready to punch me.

"You got nothin' to do with me," said the boy. You let go.

"I want to help you," I said.

"You get your shit out o' here. Shit talk!" he said.

"Bullshit," said the Snake Boy. "You an' your dude, the two of you's on my back. Like a monkey. You got me like a drug, like I'm shit, man. So get your own matches," he said, "you can buy 'em at the bar."

I'm saving the world from Abe. If I leave him now with those matches, he'll set the world alight. So I grabbed at his fist. He struck me. It didn't hurt. He burrowed his head into me. It didn't hurt. He stamped on my open shoe. I'm senseless now. I'm out of control. Wanting those matches, to save the world from those matches, hell fire, we'll go up in flames, like a nuclear war. The land will stink of smoke for years to come, there'll be graves everywhere. The prairie grass won't grow. It'll be yet another end for the Sioux. One of their boys burnt out their land, the buffalo went up in flames, ran over cliffs, so many souls were not saved.

So I fought him. The moon looked down and laughed.

The Snake Boy hissed and shrieked and swept his body against mine. His tongue of venom bit me. I tasted blood on the curl of my lips.

I'm not giving in. I can't. If I let him go now, he'll run out to the moon-chalked buttes, with their veins pink and yellow and blue. He'll run to the mudcaked land with its millions of years of wind, each wrinkle thousands of years of wind biting, each cornfield feeding thousands of lives, each farmstead made as a hearth against storm and stone and thunder. He's going to burn this world down, what's been made of it here, not much; it's done in enough as it is. I can smell the flesh of buffalo burning.

So I held him. I held on. He kicked and thrashed. I held on, riding the bucking horse, riding him into the ground, until I fell.

I fell downwards, onto the gravel path, saw church and moon and prison falling with me, crushed underfoot, like a pack of cards, falling. The town went out of my sight. A sharp pain came in my right thigh where the Snake Boy kicked me down. The box of matches was in my hand.

I don't care much more.

Have them I said. Take them.

They're yours I said.

He was standing over me, eyeing me, hopping from foot to foot, wary of me.

They *are* yours I said. You can always buy another box, down the road in the bar. I can't stop you from burning the town down.

Take them I said.

The moon looked down. She was waiting for me to hand them over. I know I can't be there, day in, day out, watching his hands to see if he lights the match that will burn down the plains and eat out the corn and wheat. I can't be there, a part of his body, an arm or an eye or a sense of judgment *in* him. If it's not matches, he'll take water. If it's not water, he'll take guns. If you want to kill, you'll kill, given no chance, not even the smallest chance, you'll find a way. And I can't be him, a part of him.

Then I wept. I don't know how I did it just then, with him standing over me. I wanted to be grown up. I wanted to do it right, hand him his matches like a mother would, saying take care, I trust you. But I don't.

"You're nothing," he said. "You'll get burnt down, too, when I throw 'em matches in your face. You can't do a thing when I make my fire."

"When I burn you down, you won' go up to heaven because you're a sinner. Mum told me, you're all sinners. You killed Jesus. You an' your Jew dude. You're shit."

So I stood up. The tears went. I have no reason to cry now. My guilt left me like a skin I had to shed all along. Nothing I do can stop him. He's a force, like the wind or flame, a force that governments use to kill. He's the lost boy who arises in each child-filled army of lost boys. I can see the Cambodian wars, peopled by Abe and his brothers, the wars in Iran, setting fire to the hearth and home. But here in America, he's of no use. No one is there to tap his violence. He'll end up outside the great movements of history. Here, in America, his crimes will be petty. They'll have no name to them. No wars will be fueled by his violence. And I was filled with a sudden love for this country. She'll give no grandeur, no common goal, nothing political will celebrate his violence. He'll stand by his crimes alone, perhaps be catapulted into the news, one day, if they catch him making his forest fire. But that's it.

And I bent down and I touched the soil of America, the arid, blasted, sun-charred soil that was given to Abe's parents. It's Indian country, reservation. It's yours, so you stay there, in hate, with the worst land.

But you can't go on and on all your life, seeing the land, like a piece of dirt, a dust-track, shit-filled hole, an empty path, presided over by heaven, and hell with nothing beneath, the world we know just a piece of garbage the white man left you. You can't go seeing the land like this, day in, day out, missing her beauty, the way she is, just because she was once the garbage can shaped by government treaties. This land wakes up in the dawn with more ecstasy than I've seen in Italian sunsets over the Arno, with more grace than the summer light dancing on Mediterranean waves. For now, the land is startling, mauve rim of the horizon, cutting the moon's huge face as she sinks, and the Badlands' buttes stretch to eternity, prisms of light making rainbow waves, one after the other, over her wrinkled rivers of still mud. You can't go on seeing the land castrated, sad just because they left her to you as a prison, a way of keeping you out of the fertile land, where the farms are white and Jesus prospers.

But poor Abe stood there, lashing out at me, threatening fire and brimstone and hell from a medieval world. He stood there, like a plant grown from the old roots of the land when she was made a reservation, and all the sadness ended in his frame, his burning eyes, but he doesn't know what he comes from, and has nothing to forgive and let go.

So I walked towards him, with no hurt anymore in my face. I sensed some pity, but a strength of vast depths in my bones coming at him, and I took the matches and handed them to him. I took his hand and he followed, suddenly docile, and we walked into the open road where you see the prairie always unending and the sky made one blink with its light. There was no history left, none in Abe's mind, none had ever been there, and I saw the land as if she had been wiped clean of the misery of her past. You can do that here in America, wash clean the past, everything's making you do it, even here in Indian Land, the past is waiting for the hand that cleanses and makes her new and changed, like a bird, able to fly free from the land that holds her down. And I wanted to dig out the grave I sometimes sleep in, so I can sleep in my own bed with Adam, not in the sweat lodge of last night, not to wake to the Snake Boy's charred eyes, not in this broken Badlands town I could belong in.

So I gathered myself up, with that hope in mind, woke Minny and Nick, left the Snake Boy in Nick's care. He'll take him back to Pine Ridge and drop him off at Pennington's farm later, for I asked him to. And Minny and I waved as they forked off, taking the crease in the plains, yellow and grey, the road to Oglala, and we went up to Interior, slow driving by the totem pylons, skeletal shapes hovering over the plains.

We drove into town well after dark and the moon was chill and the road was dark because she doesn't want me. All she wants is Dada. She's desperate for him, calling out, calling me names because I'm so late in getting her home.

"You stole me," she says as we brake in front of the Rosebud Cafe. "Don' go sayin' I left because I wanted to."

You can be hurt by a child. Even though she didn't yet feel quite like *my* child, yet here she was, for a while, under my wing, so that I cared for her (not in a way I wished, not in a way that I could, now), but I tried and my trying gave more to me than I gave to her. She's only a kid, you can't blame her for what she says. It's hurtful, yes, but that's what she wants and you'll give it to her. Dada. Back you'll go, taking her down to Blackfoot, warning him not to let her lie in his bed at night and watch, warning him not to leave her fucking with Abe, abandoned. He can't let the girl have sex whenever she wants it.

That's what you'll tell him. You can't let the girl have sex whenever she wants it. There have to be limits. No sex. Nothing at all. Let her grow up and wait for it. Let her imagine it growing inside a bond of love, you know, a loving bond. None of this sex flying free like a bird, always hovering, ready to pounce like an eagle, down on her, small prey.

"You're her father. Hold yourself like a man, not like a dog fucking in front of her. Blackfoot. You don't deserve her. Give her to me," I said over and over again as Minny and I sat in silence, drinking our milkshakes, waiting for Dada.

"Don' you lie when he comes in here," she says, biting her lips.

"Lie about what?"

"That I wanted to leave. I didn't. It was your idea."

But I didn't say yes or no. I waited for Blackfoot, and all the time in that smoke-filled bar, with the noise of laughter falling, I knew I'd let go. She'd slip from my hand. She isn't my kid. She's his. I have to let go. She wants her Dada, but he didn't come. So we drove down to the antique store in a thick wind that rocked the car, with the radio blaring to stop my thoughts, how I'd let her slip from my hand, and I don't have a kid. And I don't know how the human race will survive if it takes so long for maturity to fall, for love to snuggle into the soul, for someone like me to make a home, with a man to return to each day. So we'll have our nest waiting.

I don't know how we'll survive when to the mind it seems simpler to pick and choose from the world's toys, buying and not making, taking and not growing, so to me, for some dire mad weeks it seemed that Minny was mine, when she is Blackfoot's flesh and blood.

You're goin' in circles, said Minny, jus' so we'll never find him. You took me from him.

Yes, I said. I stole you. I thought I was saving you, but he's your Daddy. I know that you want him. He's yours.

And I stroked her head and some tears fell because I do love her in my own way and I want her to go to him now and leave me, I don't want to stand in her way.

I'll tell him the truth, I said. How I stole you.

Then she smiled, delighted with me, laid her head on my hand, and kissed me. Then she clung and she said—

Don't leave me.

So I stopped the car on the empty road with the wind, and the clouds yellow and vicious and grey, spitting rain, buffeting us, and I held her tight.

Don't leave me, she said.

And I wanted to hold her and take her back to me and tell her Blackfoot's a bastard.

You don't deserve her. Stop fucking like a wild rabbit in front of her, driving her out with Abe, playing S and M in your bed. Cut it out, Blackfoot.

But I saw, instead, all that love he gave her, pouring out, so she moves to people, wants to love, holds and kisses, cuddles too, with warmth snuggled in her soul. And I saw, instead, what he gave her, so she'll reach out to me, even to Abe to get love. She's hoping, still, she'll get love, but she picks it up here and there because there's no home, so you get it on the run, when you can, you steal love, when it isn't there every day to drink from.

So I held her, saying, "You don't really need me, Minny. You think you do, but you've got Daddy. And Marta. She's better than nothing. She'll be there, in the home, better get used to her, Minny."

I'm handing you over. Your parents are there, I said to myself, and I wondered how we'll survive when sex comes out like a parachute, stopping you hitting the ground. It saves you from total despair. For a moment you reach out, there's warmth, the face of love when he comes. You don't crash with the full hurt of an empty world all around you. So sex comes, to help you out, in the wrong place at the wrong age, all of you lives for it. But there's no love, just a slower fall to an empty world.

You'll tell Dad how I love him. I didn't leave him.

I'll tell Blackfoot, I said.

43

T hen I saw my life, all that was lived in silence, all that had been invisible, being sculpted now before my eyes. And my hands shaped the story, and Minny's eyes saw it unfold, my life, that had never been spoken out aloud, all those fears that my Father's cold boredom silenced, my Mother's subtle fears hid—all were revealed to me. I was shaping my past so I could see it, three dimensional, living before me, so it was no longer confusion, but my life at home.

If Father spoke, he'd speak like Blackfoot did.

If Mother spoke, she'd speak like Blackfoot did.

They were both in league to silence me, dull the sense of pain and joy, the opposites that meet and mate when you allow them. Man and woman was never said, and the sex of people was left like a dire secret to hide.

So the simple things, affectionate things, the holding of hands, were laden with fear that sex might grow from it, and the anger that fell was feared because of the burning volcano of hate that was at its source. We lived on the edge of ourselves, never saying "I love you."

Never saying I love you, and holding hands because of this sex that came from my body, making me woman or man, boy or girl, I never knew.

"You're behaving like Abe," said Blackfoot. "You're fucking her mind, beating her up with your shit talk."

"It's the truth," I said. "I saw her, lying there on the bed. You've got to stop it, leaving the bedroom door open so she sees your lovemaking. You've got to show her she can't have sex when she wants it. She's got to wait."

"You're crazy," said Blackfoot. "You're lying right through your teeth, just so you'll take your revenge because you want me. You want me like hell. I seen that look in your eyes, so you see it all night, me fucking you, you're standing outside that door, like a crazy, wanting to fuck me. You leave my kid alone."

And Minny cowered under his arm, like a broken bird without wings.

And I saw what would have happened had I spoken the truth, had I told my father of the violent desire he hid under his brilliant despair, the whole world of human emotion that lay there castrated inside the home, like a dead carcass rotting.

I knew it would happen like this. I imagined it, going to sleep each night, scenes just like this, but I thought I was mad until now, now that I see it, in Minny's life. I'm handing her over; she's almost gone now. She hardly looks at my face. She's crushed in Blackfoot's arms.

So you'll leave her alone? I asked, pleading.

You're crazy, said Blackfoot. You act like the truth's a sick joke. You're made of shit. You're not fit to talk to, you bitch, he said.

But I didn't move. I repeated myself, and the door opened. I felt Adam moving towards me. I felt him touching the air, like he does. I heard his familiar footstep. Then he was there around me, holding me, telling me, Come here. My sweetie. Sweetie pie,

While Blackfoot lurched forward, pushing Minny to one side and said,

I'm going to kill that bitch.

Adam laughed. He gave a bitter laugh.

Not while I'm living he said. Not while I'm here.

Then Blackfoot backed off, stared at Adam, and he howled.

"Why d'you bring that bitch to torture me? What's in it for you, with your pansy talk? All this homo talk you got with me, for days all that stuff about caring and loving me, pansy shit. So you got your man here with the filthy mind, talking S and M to my kid, teaching her all 'em lies, filling her mind with shit; is that what it is, pansy? Because your Dad's a man, and you ain't one? Is that it? So you take it out on a guy like me, because I got balls. You set this bitch on me, like the dumb-ass kid she is, like a boy. I wouldn't fuck that bitch if you paid me. That's why she's doing this to my kid, because she wants my balls, and I won't give her my balls, so she's trying to screw my kid."

I'm listening. I'm listening hard to his venom, because I've heard it before in my father's eyes, I've seen the hate rising, the war blood of censorship rising, the bedraggled silence in fascist countries, I saw it, the tawdry sadness in Lahore when I gave a lecture on Joseph's theories to rooms of men, just men. The women were stuck at home, never allowed to walk the streets for fear of desire. For fear of desire, the blade of censorship fell. So you can't speak your mind. You cover yourself in shame, each new emotion in *purdah*. You want his balls, so they keep you quiet, locked up at home, never saying I love you, and never holding hands.

I wanted to cuddle my father like Minny does Blackfoot. I didn't dare. So that the sad silence of fascist countries lived in the home; cold and polite it was, nothing more to the untrained eye. But a grave it was to emotion.

You bitch. That's what Father said in his eyes, when the truth came out, the love I felt for him. You bitch, get over there, he said in his eyes. So I fell into my Mother's arms.

Adam was waiting to hold me. I thought he'd cling to me, pick me up like a little girl and take me away from it all. His arms would be soft like a woman's. His voice would be soft like a woman's.

"Stay over there," he said, "out of the way."

So I went, into the entry of the antique barn, where the warriors stood dressed in suede and feathers, pink and turquoise, huge dolls, in a children's playroom. The way it was when I was little. I joined the dolls while Adam walked slowly to Blackfoot and faced him square, so close they could have been touching.

The air between them was hot. It flickered, the space

between them, like the land when it bakes under the burning sun. And I saw their lips touch, as if they were kissing, and I saw them suck on each other, as if sucking the essence of life in each other. They touched as if lovemaking.

You're talking about yourself, said Adam.

The fire flickered behind them, dissolving shapes, making them meet and mate and withdraw so fast, with the speed of light and the room glowed warm.

I've got balls, said Blackfoot. I'm a man, he added.

That makes me a pansy, does it? That you have balls? asked Adam, laughing gently. His eyes were soft, his mouth good-humored. He'd lost that anxious look that drives furrows into his brow, with the force of steel. He'd lost that sad look that makes him seem sometimes old as his father. I stood there, by the toys, a boy or a girl, I didn't know. Back I was into my childhood, safe with the toys, one of the boys, neutered and motionless, lying so still in bed so no one would hear, freezing my fears to silence. It's cold in here. No one comes by, but you're still, so they won't come by and turn on you. You're quiet so they won't unleash that fury under their eyes that burns bright like a fire.

Who's got the balls here? said Adam, laughing. Is that the quiz show? Who's got the balls? and he laughed and laughed wildly. One set of balls between us, Blackfoot, is that the game? I'd like to know why we both can't have balls, be men, you know, meet on equal terms? I've been trying to do this with you since we met, but you've got that chip on your shoulder, Indian-victim syndrome, I've-been-fucked-over look, and it comes out like this, all of a sudden, crazy, man. It's crazy, Blackfoot. You hearing me?

It's that bitch, said Blackfoot, pointing to me. Telling me shit, lies. She's in it to get my balls now that I won't give them to her. What ye doing, man, with some bitch that wants another guy's balls?

You cool it, said Adam. Keep it to me, your insults. Don't provoke me to lay into you, Blackfoot.

Then Blackfoot smiled, triumphant. He grabbed Adam, he took his arms, but Adam fought free. He threw himself down on Blackfoot; the two of them fell in a heap, arms and legs kicking, rolling round. Then they leapt up.

You asked for it, Adam said, and he punched Blackfoot square on the nose. Blood flowed. Blackfoot's face was dripping with it.

Poor Blackfoot, this is the worst of him now, the underside, the self that's left him wandering from Angel to Marta and searching in me for his dreams and Emma Bluegrass.

"I don't believe this is all of you, Blackfoot," I said, so soft to myself. "You'll rise from this, if it takes Adam to knock you black and blue. Let your blood flow, for a moment. It's what you want, a man to touch you like this, I see it now in your eyes, as you hate me. I am the land. I am the wound. I am the broken woman, broken in two like a dried-out branch of a dead tree, dead with *your* rage. We see eye to eye, Blackfoot. Down in the worst of me, I too have gone, hating my womanhood, all that makes me a mother, a woman, a girl. I'd sling words like yours at myself, lying in bed, alone with my hand on my flat, boyish breast, just a girl. Don't make me a woman, please, oh, Lord."

Get her away. I'll kill that bitch, screamed Blackfoot, pleading in his eyes.

Stop me, Adam, he said in his eyes.

And Adam flew like an eagle over him, covering Blackfoot from head to toe with his body. Pinioning arms and legs down like a butterfly caught and displayed like Minny down on that bed with Abe. "It's the truth what happened, Blackfoot. You can't kill me because she's fucking Abe. The truth still stands whether I'm dead and gone. Her body's no longer a virgin's," I said.

"Shut up," said Adam. "You're driving him crazy," he said. "Leave it till later, honey," he added in soft tones. "Do you want him to go for you, sweetie. The way you're talking, I'm thinking you're liking it now."

"I liked it once," I said, "I was used to it then," I added, knowing how different my life would have been had I never listened to words like these hurled at me, actions made of abuse done on my doorstep, made in my bed, words of abuse I let live in me.

And the two of them looked up into my eyes, blood-spattered faces, almost clinging together now that the violence seeped from their limbs and a sadness fell on them, needing each other to hold themselves down away from me.

Thus, they lay on the floor on the Navajo rug of orange and turquoise diamonds and black lines, as if after lovemaking, *triste post coitum*, that's how they did it; they held onto each other so as not to kill me, their mother saved, Jesus was sacrificed, men die, but you go crazy imagining women dying, Mary, the womb you came from bitten away with your lust. That drives a man down to madness. So they lay in each other's safety, bloodying like a sport each other's bodies, like in football, baseball. It was just a sport and harmless, you can see it now in their eyes. Their love is safe in each other, there's even a look of gratitude now in Blackfoot's face. He's smiling at Adam, patting him on the back, he's coming to, the best of him saved from madness.

"When something goes wrong, there isn't someone to blame, not always," said Adam. "I learned that last week," he said. "Remember, Blackfoot, what I said?"

"The stuff with your Dad?"

"The poor guy," said Adam, "had no idea what he passed down to me."

"But I've given her love," said Blackfoot. "It's Angel's fault. That bitch is always away. You'd think she'd care about her daughter, wouldn't you? But she's off stealing stuff from my shop, peddling Lord knows what else on the road."

"You're getting like me," said Adam, "soon you'll be looking like me, you'll lose those bright eyes and turn sad. You'll end up worrying, picking at things. I don't know how you'll put up with me," Adam said to me. "Sweetie, perhaps you didn't. Perhaps you left me. All these days away from me gave you time to decide."

"Someone's to blame," said Blackfoot quietly, half drunk with pain. "If it's not Angel, it's me."

"You can take on my job too," said Adam, "try the guilty and save the innocent, judge man on a daily basis, like a stern God, putting the balance of life right. You can take on my job and my

God and have my Dad too. You could enjoy it, a week or two, like a vacation from self. I'll lend you my clothes. But the silk hurts like sackcloth, Blackfoot. You know when you feel this bad, pleasure hurts. The ladder you move up is paved in glass so it breaks your feet as you climb. Doing well just hurts when you're to blame, and Dad told me he gave you Gaily's name. I saw her. She'll get you a job, on the periphery, where you'll move into the center in time. But you can be me if you want, turning blame into your currency. You know, I've got to change jobs. I chose a job that'd put me with guilty and innocent folk all day. That was my world, Blackfoot, if you want it."

Then Blackfoot cried. He let go of Minny and leant towards Adam, their hands touching. They said nothing. He was in ecstasy, in thanks to Adam. No longer tied to him as a child to save, no Indian victim child, no innocent needing Adam's charity, no longer a player in Adam's moral world where you are right or wrong, good or evil, depending on him.

"I'm not joking, I've dropped your case," said Adam.

"I'll be having to look out for myself this time round," said Blackfoot.

And I want to be part of that look in their eyes moving towards each other, that friendship with passion inside it, making it true. I want to walk into it there, and hold them, but being a woman I can't. There's something fraternal in this. You have to be of the same sex to feel it, the passion, the iron gate holding it back because you're of the same sex, you don't let go. And I turned away in fear, seeing infinity lying before me, the moment I step inside that circle, binding them, holding them at safety's distance apart because I can take my body with me into the circle that binds; as when the Badlands take the light into their greying haunches, the rainbows stretch for miles, each color of the spectrum streams out endlessly. There's no safety in me, Adam. Stay where you are in Blackfoot's arms as he cries with relief and you hold him, father and son, and son and father reconciled, like king and prince handing over the crown, the natural movement of life's achieved, as they look so straight, so clear into each other's eyes, Nature relaxes, seeing two men like this in passionate dignity; the survival of our kind is well tonight inside these two men's arms. Wars would be child's toys, played on a wooden board, with dominoes, for simple minds, if men could feel like this, close in each other's arms, all violence spent.

"Daddy, come here," said Minny, seductive. "I'm scared," but she smiled. I know how she likes her father's body, strong in the firelight, shirt torn so his chest beats in it, his heart rises and falls like a drum, eyes like a God's, those pools of blue light that have the depth of brown, and hazel. The blue in his eyes leads to infinity, downwards.

Blackfoot sat still. I've never seen him deny her commands like this, ignoring her, so that she cries. Daddy, I'm scared. But she giggles too, liking the blood on his face, but his body now in full view, the way you want to eat his flesh in its fullness, lick it like meat, devour him.

"You know," he said simply, looking at me so cold, "I don't leave my bedroom door open for her to see. Minny sleeps in her own bed."

"Then how does she know?" I asked. "She knows what to do like a woman."

"And how did you know?" asked Blackfoot, sad with the thought of revenge discarded, and just a lostness to take its place, walking the new world where his daughter's not a virgin, sadly treading this new deflowered land.

But now the violence was out of him, his eyes were cold to me, as if I'd done it, as if I'd led Minny to Abe so she could fuck, as if I was the root of evil. He looked at me, but away from Minny, stroking her with his hand, holding his eyes on me, the root of evil. And those rays of blame and hate and diverted pain from Minny and further back to other women who let him down, all were directed at me and I wanted to put my hands out, holding back the boiling heat of the vicious sun.

Not I.

What did I do? I saw her fuck, with my own eyes. I was a witness. I should have kept quiet, just as I did at home, never feeling, holding the sex down when it came out of me, blushing, taking the blame back into myself, owning it. Somewhere in me you'll find a reason to blame me. Somewhere, you can always place blame. I'd take that uneasy feeling into me, knowing I didn't commit the crime, but wanted to, took a few steps into it in my dreams, sensations I had took me towards the crime of having sex when a child.

So, I turned on him with anger. This time, he'll not silence me. And I let fly, and Adam watched in awe as I set myself free, and the blame fell, like a sterile womb on the floor, no offspring; I won't listen to his lies.

"You're blaming me," said Blackfoot, sobered down by my rushing voice, wild with the sense I had of swimming free from my childhood. But then, I was like Minny, Blackfoot, I could only drown, my life depended on home, so I swam out, like her, in small escapes, and was saved, taken back to the fold. The world was there to save me, my room was there to hide me, but both kill too, everything has two edges to it and both destroy, both whittle away at love, till it has no chance to survive except in fits because it's all been stolen from you, your birthright taken, your body feels like a stranger's when you are wet with sex, you are free to go at some point in time (with me it was years after Minny) into a man's arms, his bed, not caring what he does because you are quite safe, you left yourself behind; your body's not you. It's a wild strength you get. Adam met me like that, with that wild strength I had putting myself into a new life while I stayed in hiding.

"Minny, come here," I said. "Come here my darling."

But she stood behind Blackfoot, looking at me in fear. My words meant nothing to her. I could see I was talking about myself, telling Adam and Blackfoot my story.

You stole me, she said. Don't go saying I wanted to go. I didn't.

I'm sorry, Minny, I said. I won't talk for you, talking as if I know your mind when I don't.

You tell him you stole me, she said.

But I kept quiet, for I saw Blackfoot's eyes turn to her, and the hate went out of them. Resting on her made him soften, his eyes had tears in them. There's love in him for her, not blame, no need to justify her to him for the hate that swept over me like the winds of locusts and dust over the plains dies before Minny. Her small frame holds back storms. She'll get strength from that, not from me, neither a mother nor friend, someone who'll leave on the next plane, nothing to give to her for she's in Blackfoot's care.

And I felt so alone, with the small skeleton of my own story to hold on to. It keeps going on in the back of my head, the dread smell of the pollen, in the garden, down on the gravel path you slip so easy if you run. Mother and Father are standing in the garden like two men, dressed quite alike, the sound of the bees is dizzying, the petals mate with the bees, the honey drops down so thick. I learnt that story at school, how all the world mates, things come together to mate. It's not even happy. It's more than that. It takes you over. You can't stop once it's started; the river's like a sea once you dive in. So I ran out of the garden, down the street, away from them. And they brought me back, in silence, never saying a word, never saying I love you, nor asking why I had left them in fear, two men, in dungarees, like strangers in my garden.

A woman walked in. The candles down on the great round oak table went out with the wind. The fire crackled and spilt red wine over her face, like an Indian warrior doll. She was stiff like a puppet, the eyes drugged with a varnish so bright, her eyes could not see out, so they stared, blocked in their sockets and blinded, half drunk she seemed, for she stumbled. Adam stood up, but Blackfoot lay on the floor holding Minny, fear in his eyes, so blue, so sharp.

Blackfoot, she said, in a broken tone, hoarse, ill perhaps with a cough, or perhaps her voice rasped, dried out by drink, but her hair was beautiful, up in a pony tail, like a river of black.

I won't stay long, she said, as she walked to Blackfoot, smiling a sweet smile at Minny. I need some bread.

Mom, said Minny, you said you'd take me. You said you'd go to Tucson and get a car so we'd drive back.

I got no bread, said Angel.

Take it, said Blackfoot. It's in the till, and he handed the key to her from his right-hand pocket. Take it and go. You're drunk.

Mom, said Minny, pleading and clinging still to Blackfoot.

I got no bread, said Angel, how can I get us a car to go to Tucson. It don't make sense, Minny, she said. When I'll be back, I'll get *you* the car. We'll go together, said Angel, stealing into the shadow. The till lurched open. The bell tinkled, like cows in a meadow, moving.

Mom, said Minny don't leave me.

I ran to Minny to comfort her.

The till lurched shut. The door opened. The wind came in. The woman waved, to Minny, sweetly, said she'll be back with the car, when the weather's better they'll go riding down by Potato Creek like they did last year, when the winter's over. Tucson's warm. There's work there. You'll understand later, Angel said. Her perfect face, like a doll's, was parched and drug-thin. I could see wrinkles rivering out over the cheekbones, the painted lips, peaked at the top in two mountains, the eyes brown and slim, looking, able to focus now that the money was safe in her hands. The doll closed the door. The fire rose wildly and fell.

Minny screamed.

Come back.

Blackfoot held her. She kicked him, she lashed out at him.

I hate you, she said. I hate you.

He held her tight.

My baby, my little baby, he said.

I stood over them, not daring to walk into their circle of arms and kisses that held the world at bay.

I'm sorry, Blackfoot, I said. I didn't know.

Know what? he asked, barely listening, hushing Minny to sleep in his rocking arms, mother and father, all in one, love in his eyes, their blue was deep as the sea, and I loved him.

"I didn't know Angel," I said, but inside I said, I know the reason behind your early sex, because you'd go out desperate, looking for mummy out on the road. She promised to come back, bringing a car, a dream, some hope, but she lies. She'll never come back as a mother, warm and soft and sure, day by day, always there with the seconds ticking away, filling those infinitesimal moments in between one mood and the next when tears are about to come, but she catches them before they do, she's there, in the smallest moments that no one else could see when the toy drops on the floor, and you'll cry your soul out wanting it back, wanting Mummy to pick it up, and she's there, before the tears come. She's there in the space where day goes into sleep and you aren't scared, for her arms are around you. But Angel lies. She'll never be that. She'll come back with some quick thrill time, driving Minny up to the top of a hill to look down, she'll be half drunk or fully drunk or trying to stay off it and anxious as hell, she'll come back with a quick fix, like a quick fuck that hurts so because there's nothing around it, no love, no seconds of time that no one would notice when the shape of a soul is formed. So Blackfoot's there, taking her place, man-woman, with no breast, but he'll do it. She wants his love, and he'll give more. He'll not blame her for running out on the night town up in the sky, brushing death looking for Angel, the feel of her, the way her mind is elsewhere, like Abe's, the way, when it comes down to it, she feels like torture, her presence is only there to remind one she's gone for good, as a mother. She's gone.

So I reached for Blackfoot. I wanted to say, I understand your fury. I'm sorry it happened like this, that I thought *you* were the root of her fucking, your closeness with her, the way your bodies touch like lovers, your passion, the way you'll do anything for her, and I said, I thought the way that you're always loving her made her run out on the town looking for men, but I was wrong, Blackfoot. I said, Your love for her, showing it all the time, you'd ransom yourself for her, you would, your love for her keeps her sane, and I bent down and found myself kneeling next to father and daughter in awe, able to see for the first time their souls meet in safety, as they have always met, but I could never see it. The garden gate broke open. The door of my home has broken down. I can see out at long last down past the garden gate into the outside world. It's different here.

And Blackfoot looked up. He heard me. He looked into my eyes, as he did that night when he said, Liking isn't enough. You can't make love from some tepid emotion, and I said, Sex would cheapen us because it was cheap. I can't remember the actual words, but I lied, I used my father's lie, breaking myself in two, with the body dragging down like a weight on my soul, a penance, distorted shadow, desire broke me in two, ran wild without love, so I went out on the town, wanting redemption.

"'Make me a woman.' Always under some guise I said that, Blackfoot, Make me a woman," I said, in a trance. Don't you remember?"

And Blackfoot smiled, and he gave a little laugh, more of relief than of laughter, a sigh because he was no longer to blame in my eyes. "How can I blame you?" I asked, when blame is a worm eating into the trees in the garden, invisible worm, making the world sick. "You'd think that sex would be the key to the garden of innocence, wouldn't you? Not with my father. It broke him in two, leaving his manhood behind. Everything came under his scrutiny, saying no was the answer. No and more nos, until there's no room to breathe."

"I wish you were my father," I said, and Minny laughed.

"I told you she wanted you, Dad. She'd stand waiting for you, all over town. I saw it, and told her, lay off, I did. I told her you're mine." And I laughed with them, seeing outside the garden gate, things mate, the world is renewed in a shudder, fire slices through it, but doesn't burn, the world is in ecstasy, no one got hurt, no one was forced out into the bad land, no one returned to dust, and the sins of the fathers were not visited on the children because.

▲▲▲

Because Blackfoot won't send her cursed out of the house into her mother's arms. He could, seeing mother in daughter and daughter in mother, that long line of deceiving women betraying him, starting with Emma and ending in Minny, the final straw. He's seen in her Woman, the flesh of women now that she's eaten the apple, known orgasm too, she's walked in and out of the Garden of Eden, touching puberty like our ancestors did. Now we'd say she's only a child, but he won't send her out of his arms into Angel's night, veering car, drinking down a few more seconds of life, down on the long road south, cocaine in her eyes, white wine in the boot, down to the last fall, vision streaming out of those shrunken eyes. Better days taste of a white powder, better days, encased in death, crest of a wave falling, falling. That is the way the world works, pleasure punished, cold downs where the soul is bruised over and over again, and trembling, Angel says. She's onto the real thing, pulse of life, all there is, stealing a few more seconds of life before she veers into mud, hugging the windscreen, still grasping for life, because it is so rare, a wafting perfume, a waking dream, gold in rocks, then it's gone into dust.

One night it will happen. She can't last long, you can see in the way her eyes flit, the way she's forgotten she made a daughter; she's given up being a woman long ago.

Then Adam stoked the fire and threw in some logs, while we watched the flames, and beyond, staring into the distance at something lost which the flames had taken.

"She was like you," said Blackfoot into the flames. "She was beautiful too, like you. I felt like I did with you," he said, shuddering, turning to me and away.

"I'm killin' you every second I'm there with you, making you wanna run, but you wanted it too. You walked away like you was dyin'. I seen that look in your eyes like I seen in hers when she'd leave. She couldn't take it, then she'd drink. She'd throw up if I left for a night.

"She walked out years ago, looking for guys. Then the guys don't work. They're always no good. So she dumps them down like a load of shit and moves on to high times, things you can depend on, like a dick in your pocket, all day long, making you feel good, cocaine.

"Now, she's got her own way. She's got it safe in her pocket, steals the bread from the till, always the same style, begging, when I know she's got more bread than me in the bank. But she wants that thing I don't give her an' never did, she never was high on me."

"You're right, Dad," said Minny. "She's like Mom. She drives real wild, an' she hugs tight, an' she stole me from you. But she missed. She didn't get me."

Then Minny looked into my eyes.

"I'm alive," she said. "Aren't I? You see."

And I looked away, to Adam, wanting his sense to save me.

"Say something, Adam," I said.

But he stood there, over the flames, reddened and shadowed, flickering features, and turned away.

"I won't answer for you," he said, staring into the flames. "I'm not your keeper."

"You know me, Adam," I pleaded. "I wouldn't do that, harm a child, a precious child, my darling Minny," and I held out my hand to Minny, just like my mother did, wanting me there. I felt in my bones, and my blood and muscles, that gesture she made, time and again, wanting her baby to hold her. It sickened me after a while. I wanted to go free, fly out like a bird from her arms and love someone else, not always her, not bound to her, hand and foot, like a slave to loving her.

"I'm not like Angel," I said, but my tone was lifeless and dry, like a dead phrase of denial.

"I didn't hurt Minny," I said, searching for something true in all this, some way of seeing out of the chaos that fell in me, some way of knowing I'm not the woman who'll kill a kid, carelessly on the road, half drunk, a woman, moving from man to man, who gave up because she was wounded. Sex was a battle. The soul got bruised. After a while it's trembling over and over again thrown bodily into another's arms without love, just a collision of souls, like dead souls crowding the banks of death, waiting to find their place in the shadow world. The body melts under passion, rots with desire.

"You can't mistake me for her," I said. "I'm not on drugs."

Then I laughed, a pure laugh gushing so clean, right through me. Grace under pressure? Like hell. Under the firing squad, against the wall, I'll save myself, with a cheap alibi like an informer, get myself free by betraying the world, disown the world, point to the ones who do it with ostentation, breaking themselves in half, burning the body up, for all to see, not her, not I, never walked out on a man, sick to the pit of my stomach wanting some *thing*, some elixir, potion, yet, drug, to take his place. I have forgotten too. My childhood dreams were smashed on the road. I left them dying, wanting someone to hold me for good, no, not I, oh, not I, only the ones who go down splendidly, open books to the world, who die in a public hanging for all to see, like Angel does. You can see death in her eyes, her shrivelled womanhood, the lost stare because she's no longer searching, so sight is wrapped in a paper bag. But I see into myself, knowing the girl who ran from home into a man's arms, down to the coast. The sheets in the inn were blood red, a fishing village's gentility faded. I walked out deflowered, in pain, just a quick fix, making a wound.

"You're a woman," he said. I remember the tone of his voice, so cloying. "I've made you a woman," he said. But we did it together. My hands and his opened me up. I helped him to dig that hole deep into me so it hurt. I tried. I tried so hard to become a woman. Is that what being a woman is?

"Is that what drew you to Angel? That pain running right through her, Blackfoot?" I asked. "Like a wound that won't heal. Each time you go for a man, you open it up. Is that what we share?"

"Is it that bad?" Adam said, just smiling. "It feels that bad with a man?" And he looked into the flames as if he was trying to hide his laughter. He turned away, in a sort of disdain for my sadness, not believing I'm seeing below the surface. I'm seeing now into unbroken time, so that all floods back, and I feel like that girl for a moment, opening up. Years have gone that hid her from me. The paths I took to avoid her lead back into her eyes. She's looking at me, before I disowned her, wanting a man.

"She don't have nothing to stop her. She didn't have nothing but that, the way she'd turn on men, and the way she'd lose herself in yer arms. She don't have degrees, ideas, that sort of shit. She was just a girl, that's all. Ah, there weren't no way to go, but to keep trying to get it from guys." Said Blackfoot.

"She don' have your mind," said Blackfoot. "She don' have yer job. You don' need guys like that, for everything, you don' need 'em at all."

And Adam turned round in a flash, and he smiled at Blackfoot. "That's when I met her. The last thing she wanted was guys. She had Dad, backing her up, being her friend, she lectured worldwide, she didn't give a damn for us guys."

"That was when I disowned her," I said.

"Who?" asked Adam

"Angel," said Blackfoot. "The Angel in her."

Then he cried. A tear, would that I'd touch it, came from his right eye, staining his face with a meandering stream, and another came in silence. He didn't weep. It was relief I felt in his arms. He held me; he held her, forgiving her, then, in me. And his arms were hard like the branch of a tree, encircling me. Like a baby he was for a second, rocked in my arms. I'll comfort him. I will. Being a woman, who cares this time, if he sees in me, me or her. This time I'll let him have eternity in me, more than myself, I'll be, I'll be a force, a mother, woman in all of us, reuniting with him. More than my name and my self and my own history; my family's gone in a whiff.

All that held her at bay, bowed down like reeds to the wind.

We took the empty road to Interior, into the buttes lit white by the moon. All this is mine, form without man, beauty without man, movement without man, made of the shapes of infinity etched on mud, white in the moon. No consciousness here to hold to, no one to pull and tug at the heart. Long, long ago I found a way to live up in the night sky, innocent then of all I know of her ways. She was the world that gave birth to me, life to me.

"Let's stop the car and walk," I said.

I got out. I looked up and saw where I belong in this world. Each generation may tell a different story, but look for yourself and you'll see your destiny, how a place was made for you on this earth, as it was for me, made by my seeing. Where I looked, I was. Where I chose to turn I belonged to glorious images, lights upon lights and the cool chill. I'd walk out of the house into the garden.

"Let me kiss you," said Adam.

No one was there in the garden. Night uncovered my self. It was safe to come out and see my glorious destiny, being part of this world, my eyes creating beauty, then resting on her, letting her fill me up with herself and I lay back down on the cold grass and she filled me. Wild child, don't let them tell you to go back home to the four-walled prison. Here you are joined back to the living, no family features, no restive heritage, nothing can close your eyes to the place you hold in this world, unknown souls looking up to join you, this is no palace for kings and queens, this for all, no walls surround her, she's yours for the taking and no one can take her from you.

"Let's get out in the buttes and walk. You'll see what we're here for," I said.

"I'll hold you," said Adam.

I walked away, for no one can get you out here. You've died in a way, living in tune with a consciousness made of stone and storm and gas and the winds of millions of years etched in mud, the Badlands sing of this. I have befriended this world before man, form before thought, the restfulness of a place uninhabited. This is the place to go, where all has gone. I came here. Night after night, when they'd gone, I went down into the garden holding a red blanket onto the ink black grass, finding myself.

Just like this, I said. I didn't give in. I found better things to do than staying around at home, stifling, thinking that's all there is, a prison.

"I knew there was more to life," I said. "You were a child then," Adam said, and he laughed. "Rousseau's child." I faced him square and cold and in silence, as if disdain were in me, my face moved out of reach.

"I'm not my Dad," said Adam, "don't think I'll leave you wandering here in this deathly place at night, into these Indian graves. You know the Badlands stink of the innocent slaughter at Wounded Knee, like they're buried inside buttes in shapes and wrinkles. That's why I came, looking for Dad's mind, hopped on the plane to the nearest nation's graveyard. That's where he goes and crumbles. That's where he fails. He didn't help them. He wasn't a man. He failed in his own eyes. Families died and he ran impotent like a coward away. That's where he lives deep down. I saw him for real. I broke the chain. I'm no longer a boy," he added, his voice still sad, like a stream flowing, sure but so grey, grey mirroring grey clouds on a winter's day. It's cold in his voice, so sad.

"He was only a boy," I said. "Thirteen, or ten. How old was he when his family left Germany? How could he help?" I asked.

"When you left, I collapsed. I went to Dad. He said that's how it happens. It happened to him, this collapse, taking him back to the old days long before Mom left and he hid in his bedroom then, couldn't move. He said I grew up so quick, looked after him. I grew old too soon, taking her place. I held him together.

"Then she came back. It took him months to recover. He went back into the end of time. That's how he put it, when there is no one left on earth and an end to earth, broken in failure. You know, I thought he was talking about his work, theories of earth's demise and birth, that sort of stuff. But no, he was going back to the camps to graveyards he's never seen, back in his mind like he does. Just the words were enough to send him back into time, stories of how his Viennese sister-in-law jumped from the balcony knowing that Nazis were coming. She had visions, two years before they came.

"He lived those visions, he said, when Mom left and again. Why wait to die when you knew there's an end that comes, made in man's mind and the mind of the earth? There's nothing to live for. No kids. No generations. Hitlerian mind of the world, he said, killing the very last child of my blood.

"'Imagine, my son,' he said, and it took him back to his father who died in Rome months before the Germans came, so Grandma brought Dad here to the States alone. He saw how it happens. Day in, day out, he was there, never escaping the graveyard, he said, except in me. I saved him, he said. I held him together when Mom left. I took him out of the camps in his mind; he said I was the future. 'Don't crumble like me,' he said. 'You're a man,' he said.

"Then he held his hands over my head and blessed me. Over it fell like a cool fluid. It cleared my head. I knew I'd come to you then," said Adam.

And in fear, he came towards me, into the brittle lights of the stars, the bones of rock, the death world to him, life to me, thus, in this way we'll hold together our bodies, opposing worlds in our closed eyes.

Can't you see how I see the Badlands? I told him near as I could of infinite time locked in light, burning worlds turn cold and gas goes still into rock, the winds move all. You can see the rain here making hollows. Look over there.

It's safe with me. Take my hand.

And we walked into the night.

His hand went in my mouth he's revving up like a wild deer out of sight my blood is whiskey his arms are mine under the cold wind we defy it to taste the smell of his seed it lies on my tongue, my food, my drink, over my lips a lipstick I'll wear his seed glistens my chest the moment cleansing out I come like a babe renewed from a long sleep my head whistles with pleasure a child grows happy from this kind of mating

I said, Touch me

And he felt the seed on my hand

I said, Kiss me

His lips touched his seed on my lips and smell the smell of it, burnt and cool, sour and sweet on my lips all tastes in it changing changing a drink dreamt up from his mind and mine. Take the body and blood of man. Rock him to come taking your cunt around him, eyes closed to see inside him, gather his seed like the wine, lick his flesh like the wafer.

Open your mouth to receive him.

I'll do it again. And again.

We went down body and soul on the rocks under the sand white buttes my hearts digging a space right through me pounding away with a shovel getting rid of contentment throwing it out of my innards just like a useless lie till I'm wild for him want the world to fill me woman and man and father and son in my guts

I want the answer on death and to undo it I want the world to fall with me like she did as a child down on the red blanket under the still same sky at night.

Adam I'm ready, I said. Then he came.

He's at it again. God is smoking, covering up the sky with grey yellow smoke from a dying cigarette end.

"It's Indian smoke, a signal from tribe to tribe. It's coming back from the old days for Blackfoot's Wild West show; he's resurrected the old language, the way they'd talk in the sky."

"So much for your God talk," said Adam.

Naked, I can't see his body. The dawn is streaming in, making his body dark, and so luminous, black, made of an excess of light, he's bursting with light, it's charring him. Out of the two windows in the Chieftain Motel in Interior, bright light is cleansing the sky, but she can't. For some God is at it, stubbing a dying cigarette end, red on the horizon. It's beautiful too, I say, even the filth of it, the way he's letting the earth be eaten up by his habits. It's sick but so beautiful too, the reds smudged against grey. The pinks merging in yellow. Small suns, popping up wildly over the purple line of the sky, finding a way, with the force of bullets to make it on earth.

"Don't say this place has got to you," Adam said. He turns round. His body covers me, just to look at him moves me now that I'm tuned to him.

Somewhere, I can't let go. The old God still wanders. Worship, I will something or other; now Adam's body's here, better than death to hold to, his body can take me on, just like the gilded light, splintering down, trickling down cathedral walls of heaven. Somewhere, I'll worship, give it all up, enlightenment, and look for life inside another's deity.

"This place *has* done it," I said, removed the raw edge of fear, the kind of fear that stops you from taking risks, so you can't worship anything. You stay at low ebb, never going up where transcendence goes, way above you, blasting through you like fire. "I'm talking about you," I said, "not God. He's dead. Gone for good in his old anthropomorphic form. But the things we do to him live on, after he's dead."

And we lay down on the bed, shafts of light from those damned heavens gathering up our bodies. He licked my cunt. He licked the crease of my thighs. He licked my toes and my ears till tears came from all of me, out, like a river.

We drove down to the smoke-charred sky, to meet it. "That's where the Wild West show begins," said Adam. "I think we'll stay for the day, to wish him well, then leave via Rapid City."

But the smoke's too high. It's covering everything. Look how the hot air's angry, sparks keep flying, bits of charred paper blow by. It looks like a plague of locusts or winds of dust. The wind rushes backwards and forward not knowing which direction to go in, fighting itself. A mind of confusion. The sky is wild with the stinging feel of the smoke.

So we drove through the sun-picked wrinkles of mud, looking down on the fire-free plateaus, the fake mountains, the *papier-mâché* mountains, the Hollywood *trompe-l'oeil* of the Badlands, the pure illusion of it all, because it can crumple any minute, you'll wash it away by too much crying. But those mud-caked mountains withstood time. Millions of years, they say, in the making. "Illusion lasts," I said, "the fiber of dreams lasts, made of mud, painted over by rays of light making prisms, rainbow colors that die for a split second when a cloud passes, resurrected, again and again."

Down we drove to the little church at Wounded Knee, and the other that's red and white, blood colored, closed up, martyred and still. And down in the rolling land in the rim of the valley, to see Blackfoot's rodeo, camera-less, rolling on. So small it looked, the horses, penned in and bucking. So small the sound of the Indian drums and the feathered dancers, so small, like a child's toy, something you'd put together for fun and leave lying on the playroom floor.

So Blackfoot's Wild West show, covered in smoke, steaming over the plains, grew near. And each curl in the road took us down, down through each ring of hell, into the center, his truth, the story he wants to be told, getting closer. We dipped down, lazily, Adam humming "Monkey, Monkey, Monkey, whatcha do about the monkey? Watch the monkey ..." over and over ... "Watch the monkey get hurt."

And the car fell down into a dent in the road and we skidded down and round, lazily in slow time, dream time, the nearer we got, nothing seemed to matter, but for this slow dance down to Blackfoot's circle, the lacerated horse whining by the barbed-wire rodeo fence, the children wandering backwards and forward from taco stalls to the pow wow circle filled with Indian blankets and Navajo rugs and feathers for sale, and those suede boots with tassels for sale and rugs for sale and a tepee for sale, nothing mattered, but this. We had come to the center where time stops and what is enacted will be, again and again. We knew it. Our lips were brown and dry with unsteady breath, and we held hands like two kids, hearing Blackfoot's voice distorted over the loudspeakers, telling a story.

His voice crackled and spluttered and sank, while the horses whined, louder and louder, no buffalo came, no cameras, nothing he'd planned for months was there, in its place an arena for Indian cowboys, American heroes. And ranchers tried to become men, dead drunk down on the bleeding back of a half-starved horse, tying the fragile legs of a calf together, dragging its girlish frame through the mud. One after another, boys and men, and one girl, Calamity Jane, did their tricks on the bucking broncos and fell. One after the other the Navajo blankets went, into the auctioneer's arms, and down, on the rough grass. Sold. And again. Like a factory line, nothing was new, all was an old style, auction and rodeo, but for the broken voice of Blackfoot, telling a story of Sioux gods, gods of the plains and gods of rain, meeting and mating, stories of how we came on earth, myths of creation, all jumbled and garbled, and deities' names you could never say, names in Sioux.

"All gone," he said. "But I'll tell the stories again, just so you know where you came from. Just so you know where it all started, and what we've come to now," he said, and Minny and Marta clung to his jeans in awe.

And he droned on again, telling of Ghost Dances, Sun Dances, months made of the moon, and fish drinking up lakes quite dry and men becoming white rocks, black clouds, and the sun dripping perfume into the sea out of love, so she'd smell good for mating and nature and man were one in harmony, that kind of stuff, but it's gone, goodbye, no more, all empty, nothing left, you can't believe in it now, it's not a question of faith but truth. "This is my side of it, it might be poetry," Blackfoot said, "my offering, nothing more, I don't have more to offer."

And I cried. I heard it was over. A civilization died in his mind. He's given it up. The earth is no longer animate. Nothing is peopled with spirits. The world sinks back into shape, American shape, where it's bought and sold and you ship it.

It's safe for the moment, his Navajo rugs are safe, for here all that is sold is safe and given value and will sit in homes, like stray cats who've made good. But the spirit of things won't go easily. See how the air's burning with rage. It's not over, just like that, from one minute unto the next, that a civilization is extinguished. I see Minny taking those patterns into her head so her dreams some nights are shaped like that, the stories shaped in the form of that turquoise Navajo rug that Adam and Blackfoot lay on. She'll get it back, sooner or later. There's no junk in her eyes, just clearsightedness, stinging a bit with pain, as in me, I see her in me, how the seeing hurts but you stay there, looking while all have turned away. It took so long to see it, how life works, but now you've got it. In her eyes it's mirrored, all that you know with relief as a flock of cultures scatter over the ground, and a flight of geese from the stagnant pond below rise up at the sound of a gun shooting and shooting. There's fire coming out of the sky. Some war dreamt itself onto this Indian land. One tractor coming towards us exploding in flames. We could have been anywhere. Smoke and fire and guns smell the same in all lands, have no nationhood, nothing but what I touch in the air, the moment of death being made. Just listen. You hear silence so cruel closing the throat. The spirit has gone.

Somewhere.

And I'll look over, above and inside the pyre, to find where Abe's gone now that his body's burning, running out from the tractor, coming towards the crowd, a napalm memory sweet for America, Vietcong flying in fire, taking her back to those day-long soaps of American sons killed day-long and night-long on TV. Abe's fallen into the earth, eaten away by color, the plumage of glorious endings. The feathers a warrior might have worn, those pink and orange and scarlet feathers and flowers too, bursting from him and trickles of blood on the earth being dried so soon by the flame.

But she watched, Minny and I. She watched, the one of us, made together of one, like a mirror we were now watching the death of Abe, seeing into the moment of death with eyes open, curious too. And we watched, knowing inside ourselves he's gone, no tears in our eyes. She looked straight into the flame while the crowd turned away in horror, cries ran through like a shudder of pain, the pow wow circle; the children hid in their fathers' arms; the horses whinnied, but she walked slow to this burning grave, her father following, subservient, walking a few steps behind her, tears in his eyes, and Marta holding his hand to comfort him.

Minny came forward, that look in her eyes of knowing the world, the way it happens. Nothing had died in her eyes. No life. No joy. I could see it was all there, part of her revelled in this, the swaying crowd bending to her, the way she can turn them on, even over the dying, she'll hold the stage.

She turned to Blackfoot and said, "Them Penningtons killed him."

She smiled and laughed, seductively, turning her Daddy on, over the edge of death she stood, an acrobat, walking rope, doing a pirouette, while the world grows sick to its stomach watching, knowing the way she could fall. But she's dancing in between death and the fall. She's seen where Angel walks so free, burning the body up. Living it up on the edge of oblivion, something will seep through of this incandescence, this moment when all is burnt out of the flesh is revoked.

They move her away, pouring water over the corpse, but the crowd is on her, silent for her, in awe. Then a kid, breaking the silence, asks, "With a gun?" And a man cries, "Out with it." But she stands holding the moment in pleasure, it's too much to lose to tell just like that, so she eyes them with triumph, awhile.

"They killed him," said Minny, looking aghast, eyes up to heaven, pointing. "Tellin' him, up there's your Mom, and there's your Dad, waitin' for you. When you're a good boy, you'll go up there to Heaven. Dumb-ass listened. It got to him. That's where he went today, like mos' days, lookin' for them."

Then she turned round to Blackfoot.

"Dumb-ass thought that he'd found them up in some fake Jesus palace. Dumb lies. Don' you believe them," she said to the crowd, a prophetess, filled with strength of a woman, overflowing with power, it dripped from her. You could smell the animal force in her then, released. Then she walked away, sullen, mulling over her words, making her sad, at the worthlessness of lies, how they lead nowhere. You can be killed by lies.

So she walked away, away from Blackfoot and Marta, away from the crowd, but they followed her, all with one eye, down to the rodeo barbed fence, where the horses grazed peacefully, and her body melted into the scene, her sadness gave sap to the grass. Everything framed her, the bulbous clouds, blue sky making her red hair shine like a horse's tail in the breeze, and she stayed there, thinking, alone, that's where he'd go if he could get into the replica world made of plastic, the world that looks like this one, but there are no wars, and no bad words, and no sex, just airport hymns everlasting. That's where his skull would go if he could, taking that white-ass dream with him, killing Indians off to get there, killing himself off, Indian son, with no past, leaving behind an image, that's all, of violent dying. Where has he gone?

Where has he gone? I asked, turning away from the blackened flesh and the bones showing, as if the corpse had been rotting now for years, plunged into death's time so soon, with no transition, no way to get ready for this, only that dream the Penningtons gave him, stuffed in his eyes, of replica worlds, clean sofas, white man's dreams of a German bakery, there where you'll eat all day, and grow fat.

"He could have killed her," said Blackfoot, breaking my dream. "My baby, he could have killed her," he said in tears, and he walked away to his little girl, who kicked the fence with her golden shoes, so the grazing horse looked up and smiled. He picked her up and held her up to the sky, in some kind of thanks to someone, herself perhaps, because she's alive, because she is saved from Abe's flesh and Angel's, saved by her mind that sees further. She won't go looking for life in death. It's that simple. That's what he gave her, now as he holds her tight, and up in her arms, like the birds overhead, they feel they're flying, that's what he'll pass to her again. This is the time when time stops and souls are conceived. You feel it now in the air, it's dream time, seeing myself in Minny, seeing her sink in my soul, that girl, someone I almost was, becoming me. I'm up in his arms, flying up for the deep sheer ride into his arms where life circles breathtaking the world spins round stars come up and down night and day collide, and again we go, round in his arms, like I never did, not caring if cunts and pricks touch through the seams of my little girl's dress, not caring if breath smells sour, a man's breath raw like the feel of a winter wind. The violence I see in his eyes sometimes, sometimes I see it, but I don't care. When you do this flesh becomes light. Inside your bones is a river. You're just moving, all becomes waves and waves of light moving into the plains, moving like waves in one sea.

And I went to follow them, caught in the breath they're breathing, just like a child thinking the stage is real, I thought I could go with them, my own life would wait while I learnt more from her, took her in me and made her mine, again and again, but they're walking out, down on the lane, past the rodeo grounds into the tobacco-stained valley of Wounded Knee. I've got to stop them.

Adam's arms are around me. He holds me. The shadows of Minny and Blackfoot slip into the distance, blotted against the sky. They've left like a spirit going, nowhere to live but in me, nothing to take from me but time inside me. No one can take me now. No spirits wandering from death will own me. No one will steal me out like they did from myself so all emotion strays from my grasp, wisps of air, and thunder, all rummaging through me looking for someone to home in.

Abe's corpse may wander at night in my dreams. I'll see him again and again, the rotting flesh, the eyes gouged out by fire, the plains smoking with Abe's fire, world gone awry under God's country's grasp, America blasted again with myth, myth of its own downfall, Cassandra's image of this new land. But it won't steal me away, taking me down so I am the murderess owning the match that killed him and set the farmlands alight so crops die in a morning, charcoal winds like plagues of locusts whistle through homes saying the first-born son has been killed. I didn't do it. Just in my heart, one night, when he lay, helpless, asleep like a lamb, in Jesus' manger, I could have so carelessly left him to die, never taking a gun or noose, casually walking away, doing nothing at all to kill him, just by forgetting he's there in a derelict jail where he belonged in rotting flesh. He was already halfway there, not much to do to help him, frail like the aged, just a small push and they'll go down on the road to death a little quicker. That's where we all go, weaklings go first. The damaged crop of the world go first, like a sickness ridding myself of him, that's how I wanted it; but I know how it happened, know the dream of his corpse came from me. That is my center. No one can own me now. No one can take me. I'll stay looking at Abe a long time, looking inside myself. His bones tell my story. Now is the time to tell what he was to us before we lay him to rest, I said to the kneeling figure, bronzed in the breaking light that's sliding down through those plains clouds piled like graves one over the other, stone slabs marking God's death.

"Adam," I said, "get up."

My man was bent down by the broken flesh and the smoothing bone of Abe, searching.

"I saw a speck of light," he said, "coming out from his fist."

"Get up," I said, ready to drag him off, now that he's brushing Abe's hands with his hand, rubbing the palms so light comes out as from some tatty T-shirt, glittering gold comes out, like in some cheap movie, as in a Pennington video version of death. He rubbed Abe's palm and tinsel light scattered out from the boy's palm.

"Take it," said Adam, all eyes of the crowd on him, police making their way towards our pow wow circle, breaking the ring of awe.

Take it, said Adam. A lesson for us.

So I held the pendant. It glittered, gold in the light, the body of Christ crisscrossed over the cross, head bent to one side, girl's hair falling, those golden tresses catching the light, his body in everlasting pain, pictured in pain because he thought to take the sins of the world, he took the noose and gun, and the hand that held them. He'd take away the rage that sits like a dove inside me, taking my woman's blood out of me, leaving behind an empty shell.

What the fuck are you up to, Adam? I asked, giving the golden cross back, hearing my voice lost in the fray, police moving the crowd like cattle, this way and that, over the loudspeakers stories of crops, whole farms blown down by Abe's fire.

America ruled by chaos, parentless children ruling the land in death, just a small boy made so much chaos, only one moment of death for him. Now the aftermath's just beginning, the helicopters bouncing down, police scurrying. First time Abe's ever provided much for his world, given them all a job. Now it's beginning, cameras rolling and notebooks open. Making his own myth, he's just begun a new life, falling into the rank and file of children who kill because they had nothing, whose rage burns down America's fertile fields, her sweet farms, her cold sterility. Fire will melt it all, and eat it up, but no one will be cleansed.

Get down on the ground, quick said a guy.

A shot went up in the air. They're calling to order, quieting down the crowd, throwing panic on panic, sirens blaring, different voices taking the loudspeakers. Politicians come down, the sheriff's here, smiling. The tribal leader is here, dressed in jeans and a war bonnet, taking the mike away, speaking in oratorial tones. The boy must come with us. The Penningtons killed him.

Adam is bent in prayer down by the corpse. I see him down through the feet of the crowd.

Get him away, the voice said over the loudspeaker.

Get that guy off the body, the sheriff screamed.

White ass. The wind of the crowd sailed high, in rhythm they're out for Adam's blood. In rhythm, all of one voice, they're calling for blood, turning despair into blame.

White ass they cried, like a huge snake, winding around the body, the crowd ripples, shaking in time to itself. The snake swerves, its tail breaking its body in two and three and four pieces, fighting itself, trying to turn one eye on its prey, but it can't in chaos working against itself, never in harmony, only one voice is there, one ancient chant of blame, one voice calling for blood with the body killing itself, disintegrating. Adam looks down at Abe. He knows not to look into the snake's eye, calm in his thoughts like a mystic freed from the world, calm because he is getting to know his own love for Abe. He saw Abe's pain before it became fire, he imagined the inarticulate cry for help that never was heard, once, from the boy.

The crowd's moving with Abe's spirit, no one but Adam to stop the flow of the boy's pain into them, barely contained now that his body had gone, so the pain pours out wildly, from his open wounds, drenching them. No one will be cleansed. The stench of guilt chokes them. They can't breathe with it, stuck in their throats, so that to breathe they need more blood to wash down the pain and more blood until there will be no one left to blame, only the Badlands buttes to feel the sun, rainbow immaculate, stuck onto ancient rock. The prairie will have herself to herself just as she always wanted it.

Adam stood up and beckoned to me. I came to his side. He said, "He wasn't an Indian. He could have been my son. He was filled with the junk of the age, filled with America's sickness. He was just a white boy deep down, so literal minded like us American boys, thinking you have to perform great feats to be free, so that taking a gun's the final answer. You have to shoot the world down to be free. Nothing is left in your mind. No emotion can match an action. All that matters is that you do and you, you prove and prove in the real world and what's inside is a shell, it's just an illusion, yourself, and what's unseen is a shell unreal and your Indian world didn't matter to him. He didn't know one Indian God, one ritual, even a feeling of love for the land. All he knew was that German heaven filled with airport music hymns, just a plastic world burnt clean by his fire. You always caught our diseases virulently, worse than we did."

And Adam looked at me as he spoke, but the crowd's rage fell into awe, the boy's spirit eased out of the snake, the snake watched with new eyes, fed by Adam's sweet words of emotion. Adam is smiling now, his hand in mine, feeling his place in the crowd, being its center, giving it backbone and heart and lungs to breathe, so it eases down on the moist earth to listen just as before, making a pow wow circle.

And then they were quiet and in some kind of prayer, keeping vigil over Abe's soul, days and nights, just like Blackfoot said you do when a member of the tribe dies. Well, Adam and I left them once they were deep in thought, no longer looking out to the world but heavy-eyed with meditation, and the rain was falling slow, like a slow dance, but no one noticed. Deep into themselves, they were like the prairie wanting herself to herself. And Adam left with me in his arms, and no one noticed. I knew he left when the boy was taken back into the tribe. He's beginning a new life in their minds. Now for the first time they're taking him back to where he came from, imagining what he would be if he had had a culture, what he would be if he wasn't a kid who lived just for one moment, disconnected, cut off from all other moments, so life is a brief flash of action, one gasp of relief, a moment of orgasm over and over again with no love around it, no one to hold you when it comes over you, that's when we left, when we knew his body was being taken back into the world's mind for the very first time. The people had never done it, caught up in an hourly struggle; you don't have time to look backwards or forwards into imagination when you're caught in the moment, American scurrying, so truly American, I said.

So there we were, hanging onto each pulse of dusk, pink light over the Black Hills, like a rose squeezed out just for the hell of it, just to smell the air as it moves up and up into the chill of pure breath. It's rising up like a wave and salt-clean, smelling of earth and that crushed rose and the endless pine trees, up to Custer. Death's on the edge of us, down one side of the mountain, down as we rise, the valley falls, holding death in her palm.

Look down. Abe's there, cradled down in the black valley we've left behind. Down she goes, as we rise, holding death in her palm, holding the boy who lies in rotting flesh. He won't leave me with Adam, alone. I'm with my man, but I can't taste him yet. Each lilt, slow dance, sacred move up the mountain away from death, takes me down to the dead boy though the valley's holding him down in her rolling grave, away from the pure air here, so we won't taste the boy's fire sweeping across the prairie. All's gone from sight, from the boy's broken world, nothing soon to remind me of him, only within those shadowed hills, the creases of night are dark with him.

Adam's driving, humming a song as we rise up and up: "Why d'ya live like a refugee, refugee ... refugee.... Why d'ya have to live like a refugee...." Running away from Abe, running away from Abe, from the rotting corpse, from the fear it will all be taken away, my vision of life, all of it, body and soul, and the colors I give to trees, the way I see this dusk, the way I know the mountains hinging on death, growing from it, like corn from the rotting clods of old crops. This, my vision, the awful colors I see dripping away on the bloody horizon, so pink has turned to blood, and the wound of living is up like a neon sign, to welcome you always, all this taken away.

Adam, your man, strong like a leader, open-eyed like a boy, sadness coming from him, no triumph in him over his tranquil duel with the tribe, Adam humming this endless song, "Refugee, refugee, why d'ya have to live like a refugee?" Over and over again as if he's singing to me. And the way I hear it, now, it's a hymn, and the mountains rising up its cathedral walls, the sky is a stained-glass window. The hymn is to my man. All this to be taken away from me, not just time, and love, but the way I see the world dying and waking up again, rolling like a wild horse into a new guise now that Adam is one man. And I saw Blackfoot's spirit go into him. This is the way I see it. I helped him. I held him tight after the pow wow circle, held him tight so he'd have it for good, this Indian world. All this will be taken away.

Down in the valley, the dark creases of death's lips' touch are filling the hills. Visions of being together lifelong taken away from me. This kind of loving my man was taken away from me long ago. No time to love and no time to get, no voice of mine to be heard. There was never the kind of time you need to pass on what's you to Adam, push it safe in his soul so he's got you for good. What can you give when half of you's left behind, in fear, half of you's tugging like death's hand, pulling all of you off from the body of life?

Visions of being together lifelong taken away from me as we drive up into goldmine country, straight up and through those western towns. You can drive through one in a second, stagecoach resting spot, we could be anywhere in America, always the same neon lights selling a quick fix bottle of whiskey cigarette laugh out on the town paper lady to jerk off on redhot beach to be given love on quick, you can steal it now, all that was taken and isn't yours by right, all that feels like a lie when it fell into your arms and was yours so easily. Your first one-night stand with Adam repeats itself. Now as night covers Custer and the perilous falls to death down on the hairpin bends of the Black Hills lanes are only in memory now,

now is the time to get it back quick and own it, take it, and fill the night with it, your vision of life.

So we got out into neon lights, into America, goldmine town, swing bar doors walking down the drive-in town, with the sky punched drunk with man's graffiti, stopped outside the Settler's Shack Motel's red flashing Vacancy sign calling out with empty rooms to be fucked tonight.

▲▲▲

"No place for death to lie here long," I said. "No place for Abe."

I like it here. The pure oblivion of it. One-night stands pile up like graves in these rooms. Each room $25.99. Each plastic table in each room is the same, knows no age, no wrinkles of skin or wood, move it. The sweet, honey-sweet, poppy-sweet smell of oblivion comes from America.

That's why I came here, I said.

Kiss me, America. Lend me your mind. Give me oblivion, just for the moment, so I can have Adam. Take him and have him. Give me oblivion, the sweet smell from your shores, the candy-store smell, the clean fresh washed clean smell of the painting over the lime green bed, purple seas and a ship from long ago going nowhere inside a storm. Give me the one chance you give, to start afresh, make it new, give me the fresh cleaned spick and span sparkling white, washed-down self, with a vacancy sign ready to be filled with a new life. America, give me your lie, just in a dream, in a fuck, in a drug, in any way you can I'll take it.

I wanted to kill the boy, I said to Adam through the bathroom door; he's smiling. At it again, he says. Haven't we had enough drama in one day?

I want to forget Abe, I said. Or remember him differently, not as the boy I hated.

So, you got what you wanted, Adam said. He's dead. He didn't mean much to you, sweetie. He's wet now, all over, his body comes down on me, heavy, and smelling of him, through the water, it's him, and the feel of a man like a current you get caught up in and burnt in now he's in you.

Digging down, drilling for oil, for that open space that's waiting for a new life, give it to me.

For that endless flow of memories coming out from in me, each thrust in me he makes, I know he sees us together before, like souvenirs floating, flotsam and jetsam. Let it begin now. Give me new life. Let me just lock away like acts of crime the nights he failed me fully, ended up useless on my body, no heat and no cold in me, just a prick inside me, a piece of wood, nothing belonging to him, nothing human attached to a face, a man, even a memory, it was a piece of junk stuck inside me, night after night, like an insult. I was a garbage can out on the street. A broken beer can, bag of chips, junk, debris, desecrating, desecrating desire, love me. Up again it always rises, make me new, let me not be, again, the same, let me forget now when we make love all the times when I felt nothing in return, his prick was a dead boy dangling from a noose. Empty my mind, America, clean out my history, so it won't be me, now as he's licking my mouth, tracing outlines of love over me, so the coolness of it burns and makes the flesh rise up like dough. Leave me time, with no forgetting and no memories to live in, so that's all you do, shuttle backwards and forwards, closing and opening up your past as if it matters, as if your ancestors make your pain daily, like gods planning an earthling's despair. Take it away, America, my fear, wash me clean in my vision of life, in the wetness of my cunt, in the wetness of his prick. Wash me clean of fear, in the first love of a baby's lips sucking life inside me he's calling out I'll cradle him bringing the boy he was into me. Wash me clean of fear.

My baby, I said.

Back to the years before he was formed and his lips touched flesh and it was his life he touched.

Just then it was himself he gave me. Let me begin again, here. I want all of despair spilled out on the street like a carcass only to leave a space for the sacred to enter into me so when he comes he'll be alive inside me soul safe intact I'll cradle him won't hurt the life inside me his life and mine inside me, tell him you're new, resurrected, his prick moves you now.

So I told him. I said,

I could kill for you now.

Sweetie, he said, the boy's death's got to you. Let's take a walk and clear the air.

Down one long road into the neon light and town and all, man and nature jarring as usual. We heard one lone bird awoken calling out untimely all chaos retrieving itself in the wideness of this sky and those neon lights, fake daylight, stuck like a bandage over the night, hiding eternity,

mirroring me,

what I've done to myself, here in Indian country.

I see myself.

▲▲▲

I'm no liar now. I knew it, making love, and now it won't leave, eternity bursting inside me, death defying as if my image of death was just some dream I had as a kid in despair, making some respite from living, bandage over the wound of eternity with death, killing myself, suicidal. That was death. I invented it, day in, day out, got my daily dose, cutting life to the quick so it always hurt, suicidal, so subtly, secretly.

So no one knew.

Not even I, I said to Adam. It was my attempt at happiness. I tried in my own way.

"Like Abe," said Adam, "in his own way, he tried."

It wasn't as if I wanted to treat the body of life like mud, Badlands buttes, made of aches and dust to dust and the storms, so nothing's there really. All light and the rainbow colors you get some days are illusions beauty is transient, tramplike, gone quicker than dust in the wind. Happiness is a lie, that's how I saw it. You have to perform miracles over life just to exist to breathe when you feel her, she's there, unknown, bringing you new into yourself, wild like a dream from nowhere, bird crossing the sky at night, rising to touch the moon, and down there, they're chanting for Abe, deep down over the hills.

All this, going on, in one second, opening out.

And you, for instance, still by my side years later, after we've tried for so long just to breathe easy together.

▲▲▲

"You always knew how to live," said Adam. "I know once I can throw away America, I can get down to living. You've got to throw her away and mourn her and then what's sacred returns just like it did today with the tribe praying for real for Abe's soul. Some day we'll get it back some of the truths the Indians knew how to live."

And he took my arm and on and on he raged about America, her dead forgetfulness, blindness to seasons, revulsion at life's changes, her breeding of no emotion all repressed so sentimentality seeps out like pus from her wounds. On and on he went in an ode to America loving her more and more as he spoke of his hate for her, wild for her now with love, and I listened up to the peak of the hills he went quiet and turned his eyes onto me soft and sure.

"The boy lapped up America's junk, her fundamentalist lies, and spewed them out in death. I'm not him. I've seen beyond her lies, no reason to keep hating her now. She's not stopping us from nothing. Look how she's stretching out like nothingness, plastic and more plastic like you say can't move."

And we looked down onto Custer and he said,

"You'll stay here with me, babe, long as it takes to be together and then to the end? All that?" he asked, looking out into the night as if the night was an emptiness full threat a blow in the heart a broken heart an unknown fate some kind of death, sticky inside the moist clouds above. It's not, I said.

Each breath is ours. She's full with us. We've made her. Look how she's sacred, rising up in our hands you touch her right she's like a tree shuddering wild in the wind growing to your touch, like a prick unfolding. She is a bed we'll lie on, down on the grass we'll make her that. She'll give what you ask and the more your breath is sacred she gives the moon as yellow and you give blue cool blue breath to make green merging so as you breathe into her I see colors piling upon colors under the night. Just like her cornfields you grow with her. We'll make her into a swaying ecstasy tree of life untied from the old old garden. We'll find water in her. Down there's the glinting eye of the stream in the yellow corn moon painting with us our breath we'll do what we want with America dream her up and invent her watch her come to us shyly with some sweet offering we shall wrap her in the smell of our love, Adam.